THE DAUGHTER SHE GAVE AWAY

LISA TIMONEY

Boldwood

First published in Great Britain in 2025 by Boldwood Books Ltd.

Copyright © Lisa Timoney, 2025

Cover Design by JD Smith Design Ltd.

Cover Images: Shutterstock

The moral right of Lisa Timoney to be identified as the author of this work has been asserted in accordance with the Copyright, Designs and Patents Act 1988.

All rights reserved. No part of this book may be reproduced in any form or by any electronic or mechanical means, including information storage and retrieval systems, without written permission from the author, except for the use of brief quotations in a book review. This book is a work of fiction and, except in the case of historical fact, any resemblance to actual persons, living or dead, is purely coincidental.

Every effort has been made to obtain the necessary permissions with reference to copyright material, both illustrative and quoted. We apologise for any omissions in this respect and will be pleased to make the appropriate acknowledgements in any future edition.

A CIP catalogue record for this book is available from the British Library.

Paperback ISBN 978-1-80557-043-1

Large Print ISBN 978-1-80557-044-8

Hardback ISBN 978-1-80557-042-4

Ebook ISBN 978-1-80557-045-5

Kindle ISBN 978-1-80557-046-2

Audio CD ISBN 978-1-80557-037-0

MP3 CD ISBN 978-1-80557-038-7

Digital audio download ISBN 978-1-80557-040-0

This book is printed on certified sustainable paper. Boldwood Books is dedicated to putting sustainability at the heart of our business. For more information please visit https://www.boldwoodbooks.com/about-us/sustainability/

Boldwood Books Ltd, 23 Bowerdean Street, London, SW6 3TN

www.boldwoodbooks.com

For my dad, Kenneth, with love

PROLOGUE
SIX MONTHS AGO

Meg

Meg tapped the screen of the phone she'd attached to a tripod on the old kitchen table, switching the camera to selfie mode. She blinked, finding it hard to believe it was her own gaunt face staring back at her. She turned her head from side to side, knowing that even six months ago, she'd have killed for those razor-blade cheekbones. She only had them now as a by-product of dying. How bleakly ironic.

Suddenly, she had a memory of Grace's hands on her cheeks when she was a small girl, maybe four or five years old. Meg had been putting the rubbish out when her daughter woke from a nightmare. Frightened, her little girl came downstairs to find the house empty, her mother gone. When Meg came back inside, Grace flew at her, gripping her so tightly that Meg could still now feel her thin arms around her.

'Mummy, I thought you'd gone away,' Grace said through hiccupping sobs.

Meg kneeled down and took her in her arms. 'I wouldn't leave you, silly.'

Grace pulled back, taking Meg's face between her soft palms. She stared at her, eyes huge and wet, her bottom lip trembling. 'Promise you'll never leave me, never, ever.'

Meg smiled. 'I won't leave you, Grace, not ever.'

'Do a promise.'

Grace's tiny voice was so earnest, Meg had smiled and shaken her head. The idea of leaving her little girl was preposterous. It was the last thing she would ever do. 'I promise.' She kissed the top of her head. 'I'll never leave you, my beautiful girl. Never.' She'd meant every word.

And now she was breaking that promise, and it was shattering both their hearts.

Swallowing down tears and fixing her gaze on the screen, she opened her lips to try out the words she'd practised in her head since her diagnosis four months ago; the words she'd tried and failed to say to her daughter before she screamed at her to get out of her room. If she listened carefully, she could still hear the sound of Grace crying. Her anguish now carried down from her bedroom and soaked into Meg's spongy heart. She thought it was already full up with a heady combination of love and pain, but it seemed there was room for more.

Her parched tongue stuck to the roof of her mouth. That could be a side effect of her medication, but she knew it was more likely due to the fear gripping her stomach and squeezing it into a sickly ball. The thought of death frightened her, of course it did, but filming this confession scared her more. Grace refused to listen to her when she tried to explain, so if Meg wanted to tell the truth of what happened, she had no choice but to speak to this camera instead. Family life as they knew it had ended. The agonising knowledge that she wouldn't be around to rebuild the safe, trusting world she and her husband, Simon, had tried so very hard to create made more tears collect in her eyes.

She took a sip of water from the glass by her elbow then wiped her eyes dry. The wooden slats of the dining chair were hard against her bony back. When she shifted position, she noticed the ring light she'd placed on the table behind the tripod to soften her features highlighted her jutting clavicle, reminding her of those awful pictures of displaced, starving children she saw on the news. She leaned across the table and switched the glare off. Even that small movement made her queasy. No amount of good lighting could disguise the sunken hollows under her eyes, or the fact her eyelids were now naked, eyelash-less. She blinked, thinking how much she looked like a fish or a reptile.

She breathed in through her nose and lay her palms flat on the table, the wood scarred from stubby pencils pressed too hard on paper and cups dropped from toddler's slippery fingers. The papery skin on the back of her hands made uneven crisscross patterns over protruding green veins. They were the hands of an old person. It wasn't fair. She was only thirty-five. These hands should be applauding her beloved child at the end of school plays or catching balls on sunny afternoons in the park. Instead, they had tried to hold her daughter to her chest while her half-child, half-woman body shuddered with heaving sobs after she'd learned how she'd really come into this world.

Meg swallowed. She couldn't afford to think about all the things she was going to miss, or the fact that she and Simon should have shared the truth with their daughter from the start. Over the last fourteen years, they'd told themselves and each other that it had never been the right time. They were too happy or too sad, or Grace wasn't old enough. Then, in a heartbeat, she was going through puberty, so better to wait until the teenage hormones subsided.

How cruel, Meg thought, that her time had run out before any of them were ready. Now Grace might never forgive her for what she and Simon had done back then, and all the lies that had followed. And it was too late for her to ever make amends.

She lifted her head and waited for the nausea to subside. She had to focus. It was time to film what she needed to say. Simon had understood it might be too hard for a fourteen-year-old to absorb all the information right now, especially when she was still reeling after learning her mother only had weeks to live. This video was an attempt to explain, apologise, and beg for forgiveness and hopefully, show Grace there was a way she could find comfort, if she was brave enough. It was the only way Meg could think of to make sure Grace knew every detail of what happened and could digest it in her own time.

She adjusted her headscarf, took another sip of water, pulled her dry lips into a fixed smile, and pressed record.

1

PRESENT DAY

Cassie

The swooshing started in Cassie's abdomen, rose up to lift her lungs, halting her breath in her throat. Once, she'd believed she'd never experience that kind of joyful exhilaration again, so she stopped on the pavement to savour the moment. She wanted to catch it in a jar and store it away, so she could bring it out to marvel at when life wasn't quite so shiny.

Luke turned and squinted across the road at her. 'What are you doing?' he said. 'Come on.'

She wanted to tell him how gorgeous he looked, his strong arm reaching down to hold their seven-year-old son, Alf's hand. She wanted to say that just the sight of him and Alf in that unremarkable moment made her heart soar in a way she thought she would never feel again. After everything that had happened before, she was so, so grateful Luke and Alf were hers and that, at almost forty years old, her life was better than she had ever thought possible. It was perfect. They were perfect. Instead, she said, 'Coming,' and followed them across the road and into the pub.

After the brightness of the May sunshine, the dimly lit interior felt gloomy. The hoppy smell of spilled beer grew stronger as the door creaked closed behind them and the swooshing feeling at her centre disappeared, replaced by flat disappointment. The pictures on the pub's website had led her to believe this was the ideal venue for the party she was planning for her upcoming birthday, but the photos were clearly misleading. They'd made a wasted trip.

She was about to express her disappointment to Luke when a young man with a goatee appeared through a door behind the bar. 'Cassie?' he said, dipping out from behind and approaching her, arm outstretched. 'I'm the manager, Ross. We spoke on the phone.'

'Hi,' she said, shaking his hand. She decided she may as well let him show them around since they'd made the trip. 'This is my husband Luke, and this is Alf.' She smiled down at Alf, suppressing an amused smile when he offered his small hand to shake, mimicking his father.

'Good to meet you, young man,' said Ross, shaking Alf's hand and mirroring his serious expression. Ross turned back to Cassie. 'That's the formalities out of the way, so if you follow me upstairs, I'll show you the room you were interested in.' He marched across the scuffed wooden floor to the far side of the bar where he held open a door leading to a narrow staircase. At the sound of a phone trilling, he grimaced. 'That's the booking line. Why don't you three go up and have a look around? I'll join you in a minute.'

When the door closed behind them, Luke said, 'I like him. He's all right.'

'All right how?' Cassie reached the top of the steps and let out a relieved breath when she found herself in a square room with huge windows on three sides. The sunshine flooded in to illuminate a black and white chequered dance floor in the centre. This, at least, was exactly like the pictures on the website. Better.

'Take note, Alf,' said Luke. 'This is an important life lesson.'

Cassie smiled as Alf looked earnestly up at his father as if he were some kind of guru. Luke was always passing his wisdom on to his son. In any other man she was sure she'd find it trite, but Luke's lessons were always so thoughtful and considered that she often ended up learning something herself. That was what she got for marrying a counsellor, she supposed.

'Your mummy made the appointment with Ross, right?'

Alf nodded, his hazel eyes trained on his father's.

'And when we turned up today, Ross spoke to your mother first, using her name and shaking her hand before mine.'

'Yeah.' Alf's eyebrows met in a confused expression so cute that Cassie wanted to scoop him up and kiss his round face.

'And that was the right thing to do, but too often that's not the case.'

'Patriarchy,' said Cassie, nodding at Alf as she grasped the point Luke was making, and the swoosh of joy returned. She fought the familiar voice in her head whispering that she didn't deserve such a lovely man, or the son they both adored. She tried to silence the sound, forcing her feet to move across the dance floor, imagining music pumping from the speakers either side of the record deck set up near the far wall and the room filled with people who loved her.

'I don't get it,' said Alf.

'Even if a woman is the person in charge, often, when

another man is present, men talk to them first, because they presume they're automatically the authority figure. Ross didn't do that. He clearly understands a man isn't always in charge and that's a good thing for everyone.'

'So, Mummy's in charge?'

'Always,' said Cassie. She took Alf's hands and pulled him to the dance floor, swaying in time to imaginary music.

'Unhelpful,' said Luke, shaking his head. He shoved his hands into the pockets of his jeans and gave a theatrical sigh.

'You're right, sorry.' Cassie twisted Alf in a circle then moved him to face her, tugging him along as she pretended to waltz around the space. 'Sometimes I'm in charge, sometimes Daddy is, but mostly no one is because we are equals and work together.'

'Am I ever in charge?' asked Alf through giggles as he tried to keep up with Cassie's footwork.

'God, no,' said Cassie. 'You don't get to be in charge until you stop picking your nose and you eat your green beans. If we put someone who makes terrible decisions in charge, where would we end up?'

A polite cough sounded over Alf's laughter.

Cassie stopped dancing and turned to see Ross at the top of the stairs, his cheeks pinched as though trying to repress a smile. 'He doesn't really pick his nose,' she said, pulling Alf in front of her and resting her hands on his chest.

'I try not to,' said Alf, 'but I definitely don't eat green beans because they're gross.'

'Noted,' said Ross. 'I like a person who knows their own mind.' He looked around the light-filled space. 'What do you all think of the room?'

Cassie took in the disco lights suspended on the ceiling, the mirror ball glinting in the sunshine, the red velvet-covered seats around small tables on the periphery of the room and could easily visualise welcoming their friends to her fortieth birthday party here in three months' time. 'I love it,' she said. 'It's perfect.'

There was that word again – *perfect*. At last, everything was as it should be. The past was in the past, and nothing could spoil the life she had now.

2

PRESENT DAY

Cassie

The rattle of pens dropping into pencil cases began as soon as the bell rang to signal the end of the school week. Before the inevitable squall of thirty-two Year Tens discussing plans for the weekend hit its crescendo, Cassie raised her voice. 'And don't forget to fill in the careers questionnaire before our next lesson on Monday.'

They didn't respond, but she didn't mind. Some of her colleagues insisted the students carried on with their work until they gave permission to pack up. But even at thirty-nine, Cassie still remembered how it felt to hear the bell signalling the end of Friday's lessons when she was a teenager. Sometimes it would be a rush of excitement if there was a party or plans for a shopping trip with friends. At other times she might just feel an overwhelming exhaustion, a need to be out of the school building with all its rules and expectations and back in her own bedroom surrounded by her posters of Charlie Simpson from Busted.

From behind her desk in Room D2, Cassie watched her form gather their belongings. She was glad one of their Personal and Social Education sessions was timetabled for last thing on a Friday afternoon. It gave her the opportunity to catch up with her form. She felt like a shepherd, always trying to steer them along the right path, often running in one direction or another, trying to keep an errant student on the right track. Minel swung his rucksack at one of the girls in a ritual Cassie recognised as teenage flirting. She caught his eye and he dropped his bag, giving her his trademark impish smile. 'Sorry, Miss.'

When all books and pencil cases were deposited in overstuffed rucksacks, Cassie said, 'Have a good weekend, everyone.' She grinned at the hurried mumbles in return as they jostled their way out of the door. Her classroom in the English block always seemed eerily quiet when the students left. Even though she could hear voices from outside, there was an unnatural stillness inside the room; an absence. It was a feeling that never failed to unsettle Cassie, so she gathered her things quickly and set off for the staffroom.

Becca, the Head of English and Cassie's closest friend, was sitting at a desk facing the far wall when Cassie arrived. She turned as Cassie sank into a chair and let out a huff of air. 'Another week over, thank the lord,' Becca said. 'Anything fabulous planned for the weekend?'

Cassie wrinkled her nose. 'Just a bit of party planning for the big four-O, unless a seventh birthday party at Goals counts as fabulous?'

Becca threw her head back. 'Gahhh, absolutely not. That's the stuff of nightmares. I can't begin to express the gratitude I feel that I never, ever have to go to another kid's birthday party again.' Six years older than Cassie, Becca had had her family in her early twenties so both her daughters were at university. When the youngest moved away, Becca and her husband discovered they didn't have much in common any more and amicably parted ways. But the split had been harder than Becca had anticipated, and she spent much of that time in Cassie and Luke's spare room, because – even though she didn't want to be married, it turned out she didn't much like being alone.

Eventually, she'd come to embrace her single status, and now she was 'exploring her options'. This exploration seemed to take the form of internet dating on an industrial scale, and the stories of her antics were one of the things that made working at Stonehaven Secondary School quite as enjoyable as it was.

'Go on, tell me which hot man you're seeing this week,' said Cassie. 'Let me know what I'm missing out on.' In truth, she didn't think she was missing out on anything. She'd married her first husband too young, she could see that now. She blamed a combination of growing up with disinterested parents and meeting a charismatic charmer when she was at her most vulnerable for the way she'd fallen head over heels in love. It turned out to be a devastating mistake, and following the brutal heartbreak when that ended, she'd been determined never to put her trust in a man again.

But that was before she met Luke. He was everything her first husband hadn't been: honest, thoughtful, an open book. Luke's own father had been a compulsive liar. His family and his childhood had been ruined by dishonesty and he was determined to live his life differently. Cassie had gone into her second marriage with her eyes wide open but her heart slightly closed. She kept something of herself back, locked in a dark place that even she hardly ever dared to open.

'This week?' Becca dropped her chin onto her chest. 'The

cheek. This one isn't fresh out of the box. You could almost say we're dating.'

'Exclusively?'

'Let's not get carried away,' Becca said, laughing and flicking her bleached blonde hair over her shoulder dramatically. 'I'm still...'

'Exploring your options?' Cassie finished for her. 'Good for you. Although, I don't know where you find the energy.'

'It's not easy.' Becca pursed her lips. 'New men expect a bit more than the ones you've been training for a couple of decades. I even have to wax my bits, did I tell you that?'

'I don't want to know,' said Cassie, covering her face with her hand. 'Please don't give me the details. I've got a visual imagination and I don't need a picture of your coiffed pubic hair in my head.'

'I had it waxed into a heart shape. I've got a picture, do you want to see?' She picked her phone up and started to scroll.

'No, I bloody don't,' said Cassie, turning away.

'Spoil sport.' Becca laughed and put her phone down. 'I haven't really got a picture, you idiot. But I have got an appointment with a cauldron of hot wax at six, so I'm getting these essays out of the way now.' She tapped her pen on the pile of papers on the desk in front of her. 'I can't wait until GCSEs are over. Marking past papers is a form of torture.'

'I hear you.' Cassie dug into her cotton bag and dragged out a pile of blue A4 books. 'If I never see another essay on Lady Macbeth's role in her husband's downfall, it will be too soon. I need to get this lot out of the way before I go home. Alf's got a play date so I can probably get them done and fit in a quiet glass of wine before Luke picks him up.'

'Right, heads down,' said Becca. 'I'll race you to the finish.'

An hour later, Cassie's neck was aching from being bent over the pages of books, trying to decipher the scrawling handwriting of some of her Year Elevens. She startled at the sound of Becca's pen hitting the wall. 'I wish you wouldn't do that,' she said. 'It makes me jump every time.' She looked across at the wall above the desk Becca invariably used. It was pockmarked from the impact of hundreds of Bic biros being hurled at force.

'It's my little rebellion,' said Becca. 'You can't take away my small pleasures.'

'It's criminal damage,' said Cassie. 'You're ruining that wall. Imagine if you saw a kid in your class do that. You'd go ballistic.'

Becca stuck out her tongue. 'You're such a rule follower. I run a "Do as I say, not as I do" regime. You should know that by now.' She narrowed her blue eyes at Cassie. 'You do know that if you never do anything wrong, you'll have nothing to go over and over in your head at three o'clock in the morning when you're peri-menopausal, and then what will you do while you're wide awake? It says in the women's rule book that the hours between 3 a.m. and 4.30 a.m. are to be set aside for overthinking and self-loathing. What about that rule, eh? What are you going to do about that?' She crossed her arms and stuck out her bottom lip.

Cassie forced herself to laugh, despite the images springing like firecrackers into her brain. 'Maybe I don't have as unblemished a record as you think,' she said, closing the exercise books and shoving them into her bag to avoid looking Becca in the eye.

'Ha, whatevs,' said Becca. 'You carry on pretending you had a misspent youth, if it makes you feel better. But I know the truth.' She tapped the side of her nose. 'You can't fool me, Little Miss Good Girl.'

But Cassie could fool Becca, like she'd fooled Luke and

everyone else for more than a decade. She was still thinking about that when she opened up her school email account to make sure there was nothing she needed to deal with before the weekend. And that was when she saw the email, from a name that made her heart stall in her chest.

3

PRESENT DAY

Cassie

Cassie waved a limp hand in Becca's direction when she said goodbye and left the staffroom, but she couldn't tear her face away from the screen of her laptop. There, at the top of a list of emails, was a name she hadn't seen for almost fourteen years: Simon Gately.

The room felt suddenly hot. She put a hand to her chest, feeling her heart thundering against her ribcage. The other hand moved the mouse until the cursor pointed to the email, the blue dot by its side signifying it was unread. It could stay that way, she thought, hovering the tiny arrow over her ex-husband's name. She could click on the side bar then the little trash bin. Two taps on the mouse pad and this hideous reminder of the past she'd tried so hard to bury could disappear.

Focusing her eyes on the subject box, she took in a deep breath, trying to steady her racing pulse. 'Meg's passing' was all it said. Did that mean what she thought it did? Was the woman who had been sleeping with Cassie's husband right back when Cassie had a new life growing inside her actually dead?

In that moment, Cassie was frozen, her body in the staffroom at Stonehaven, her mind a decade and a half away, at the exact point that set the devastating events rolling. She could see it all as if it was happening in front of her now, playing out like a horror film in her head.

She was back there. Her period was four days late, so she nipped out at lunchtime and bought a pregnancy test at the local chemist. She peed on the stick in the staff toilets, at the school where she'd taught English since graduating. She thought her hand was shaking because she and Simon hadn't been trying for a baby. They were only twenty-five, and although they'd been together since their first year at university, they'd agreed to wait a few years to start a family. But when Cassie watched the second pink line on the test grow stronger and more definite second by second, she was surprised to find elation burst inside her. The nerves were anticipation, not fear. This was unexpected, but now it was real, Cassie knew she wanted this baby more than anything in this world. She was certain Simon would too. He was going to be the best father ever, nothing like her own dad, who was so engrossed in his work during the week and golf at the weekend he barely registered he had a daughter at all. She and Simon would be a team; the best parents ever.

Excitement fizzing inside her, she recapped the test and took out the Ziploc bag, which still held the remains of the sandwich she hadn't felt like eating at lunch. Now that made sense, along with the queasiness and sore boobs she'd been experiencing for a couple of weeks. Dropping the crusts and crumbs into the toilet, and the test in the empty bag, she became lightheaded when she imagined presenting it to her husband. She envisioned his face, those lines tracking from his eyes to his mouth deepening with an enormous grin.

She struggled her way through Lower School Drama Club, wishing she'd never agreed to fill in for the usual teacher who was off sick. She made all the right noises about their improvisations, reminding them they should devise a piece that only needed the number of people in their group, not the entire cast of *The Prisoner of Azkaban*. She looked at the Year Seven and Eight students in a new light. Once upon a time, these living, breathing souls had been a second pink line on a pregnancy test. She hoped their mothers had experienced the same joy as she did right now. She found herself imagining the child inside her at this age instead of concentrating on the performances at the end of the session, hoping it would have Simon's dazzling blue eyes and her own wavy dark hair. There was so, so much to look forward to.

At last, it was time to leave. Simon was a drama teacher and had rehearsals for a production of *Fiddler on the Roof* at the school he taught at. The last few had gone on for far longer than they were scheduled to, then he was playing five aside football with friends and wouldn't be home until at least nine. Unable to keep the news to herself, after standing in at Drama Club, she drove the twenty minutes to the school where he taught. She parked at the far end of the car park at the back of the drama studio, far away enough for Simon not to see her immediately when he came out. She wanted this all to be a great big memorable surprise. Since drama was his thing, she would make this monumental occasion as dramatic as she could muster.

The front portion of the car park was empty except for two cars: Simon's familiar Peugeot 207 and an old Nissan Micra, which had seen better days. Cassie was surprised. She'd expected at least a few parents to be waiting impatiently for their offspring to spill out of rehearsals. She'd been prepared to wait until Simon came out last and locked up so she could surprise him when he was on his own. Maybe they'd finished early today. At least Simon was definitely still there. She put the Ziploc bag, with the test in, into her pocket and reached for the car's handle just as the door to the drama studio opened.

She paused to take in the sight of her gorgeous husband emerging. He was smiling and his eyes were bright. He ran a hand through his hair, thick on top, and clipped short at the back and sides by Cassie last weekend. She'd done a good job, she mused. His mouth moved and he glanced over his shoulder. He must be speaking to someone behind him, probably the school caretaker. She took her fingers off the handle. The news bubbling up inside her was for his ears only. She wanted them to be alone when she shared the fact he was about to become a father for the first time.

A young woman with a bob ending in sharp points at a striking square jawline stepped onto the tarmac behind Simon. Not the caretaker, then. She looked too young to be a teacher, but too old for a pupil. Cassie assumed she must be Meg, the student teacher Simon had mentioned a couple of times. She said something which made Simon laugh and turn towards her. Cassie wished she could see his expression, because something about the way the woman gazed at him unnerved her. Her mouth was slightly pinched and her head lowered, so she was gazing up at Cassie's husband through thick eyelashes.

Maybe it was time to reveal herself. Nausea taking her by surprise, Cassie suddenly needed to be out of the hot car. She twisted her body to the door, but before she could move her eyes from the windscreen, the woman glanced around the car park, said something through smiling lips, then took a step towards Simon, closing the gap between them. Cassie froze, unable to compute what was happening when the woman's hands, silver rings on every finger, combed through her husband's hair. Instead of leaping backwards, shouting for her to back off, Simon moved closer. His hand, platinum wedding ring glinting in the light, snaked around the woman's waist, pulling her into him. Cassie watched in horror as his lips met hers, his buttocks clenched as he pushed himself against this stranger. She saw the deepness of the kiss as they stumbled back towards the door, the woman's back pressed against it as Simon pushed his groin into hers, then moved his hands over her breasts.

Without her mind processing it, Cassie's hand went to the centre of the steering wheel and pressed down hard on the car horn. The pair jumped apart. Simon turned. His gaze landed on Cassie's car. The colour drained from his face.

4

SIX MONTHS AGO

Meg

Meg took another sip of water, then lifted her face to the screen. Would she ever get used to seeing a bony skull covered in almost translucent skin staring back at her? Perhaps the ring light was a mistake. She turned it off, but when she looked back at the screen, the kitchen lights above made her sallow cheeks and hooded eyes look like she was wearing Halloween stage makeup. She switched the ring light back on and prepared a smile. 'To make you understand why we did what we did, I think I need to start with how your dad and I met.'

Her mind spun back fifteen years to when she was still a student teacher who drove a battered Nissan Micra and thought she had her whole life in front of her. If she'd known how that life would turn out – or end, to be more accurate – would she have acted the same way? Of course she would. It was inevitable; irresistible.

'Despite what you might be thinking now, most of what we've told you is true. I was a student teacher working at the school your dad taught at but, unfortunately, that wasn't the full story.' She put her hand to her lips and closed her eyes. Admitting this first lie, even if it was a lie of omission, was one of the most difficult things she'd ever done.

She swallowed and looked back at the screen. 'Before I say more, let me tell you how I felt when I met your father. I know I've told you some of it before, but now you know the... context, if you understand how it truly felt, maybe then you'll find it easier to comprehend why we acted the way we did.' She smiled weakly, her mind going back to the first time she'd laid eyes on her husband. 'I remember it so, so clearly. He had his back to me when I went into the staffroom. He was digging in his bag for something. I was with another student teacher who was attached to the PE Department, and she was beautiful; I mean, really beautiful. She was the kind of girl who makes you feel invisible when you stand next to her because everyone just gawps at her. You know what I mean? It didn't help that she was always in a skort, so her perma-tanned legs were out, yelling, *Look at my smooth skin and toned thighs!*' Meg shimmied her hands and attempted a laugh.

'Anyway, he turned around and glanced at both of us, and he didn't seem to notice her legs, or her mouth with its pink lip-gloss. He just looked at me.' Remembering the first time she and Simon locked eyes made tears collect behind her own now. Locked was the right word. It was like their vision was set from that moment onwards and it would only ever truly connect with each other's.

'I used to have this severe bob that ended about here.' Her hand went to her jaw, then touched the fabric of the headscarf at her nape, the understanding that she would never comb her fingers through her own hair again making her voice hitch. She composed herself. This wasn't the time for self-pity. This was about Grace. She dropped her hand. 'And I wore bright red lipstick, and looking back I can see it was a strong look, especially for teaching practice. I obviously wanted to stand out, but since I was about to spend the next term beside Aphrodite herself, I remember assigning myself the ugly best friend role... until your dad turned around and looked at me.'

The moment expanded in her mind. She saw Simon's sandy hair and how the top button of his shirt was undone, his tie askew in a way she would grow to love. But it was his eyes that struck her instantly. They were the brightest blue, and when he smiled, creases began at the corners and tracked down his cheeks all the way to his mouth. Wrinkles shouldn't be attractive, but since his were clearly etched by smiling, she loved every single line, which was lucky since they'd grown deeper in the years they spent together. She could read their mutual happiness in those lines.

'When he looked at me, it was like electricity passed between us. I know it sounds corny, but I swear, Grace, I've never experienced anything like it.' She paused. 'That's not true. I have. The only other time in my life I've felt that instant, uncontrollable love was when I first saw you.'

5

PRESENT DAY

Cassie

'Got no home to go to?' said a gruff voice behind Cassie.

She jumped, closed the lid of her laptop and turned to see Jack, the caretaker, standing in the doorway to the staffroom with a bucket in one hand and mop in the other.

'Sorry, yes, erm, I was just leaving.'

'Don't hurry on my account,' said Jack, flapping a blue microfibre cloth at her. 'I was pulling your leg. I'll do the loos first if you've got marking to finish.'

Cassie zipped the laptop in its case and shoved it in the bag with the books, suddenly desperate to be out in the fresh air. 'No, it's fine, thanks.' She stumbled in her hurry to leave the room, waving at a confused-looking Jack and wishing him a good weekend before rushing down the stairs, through reception and out into the grey afternoon. The day had started as an early spring day should, with bright sunshine and fluffy clouds, but the clouds had gathered during the afternoon, then darkened and now goosebumps lifted the hairs on Cassie's arms as the chill breeze cut through her thin shirt.

Oliver Simms, a boy in Year 9, was standing between her car and the one belonging to the head teacher. He was a sullen teenager, the kind who always had one eye on the teacher so they could get away with nefarious activities and never get caught. Any other day she would have asked him what he was up to, why he was still on school grounds at this time of day, but her head was full of memories and tears pushed behind her eyes, so she clicked open the car and climbed into the driver's seat.

A glint of something bright caught her eye, and she turned her head just as Oliver's hand closed around whatever it was. He scurried away towards the school field. Too lost in her own thoughts to give him any further attention, she started the engine and drove home.

Parking next to Luke's Ford Focus on the paved drive of their 1930s semi, she killed the engine and realised she had no memory of travelling home. The only thoughts in her head had been of Simon, Meg and what happened to the poor baby. She didn't feel ready to face Luke, so she sat in the car and watched light raindrops pepper the windscreen. The clouds burst then, and soon water veiled her view of her front door with a mesmerising pattern of silver and white, shifting and distorting as water thundered against the car's bonnet.

A bang on the window made her jump. She turned to see Luke's face grimacing under an umbrella. 'Come on,' he shouted.

She opened the door, the sound of the rain thudding against the umbrella and the driveway suddenly deafening. Luke held the umbrella over her and put his hand on the small of her back. How typical of Luke to see her waiting in the car for the rain to stop and find a way to help her. He stood in the small hallway now, laughing at the sudden downpour, holding the umbrella over the threshold and shaking it. 'I don't blame you for not wanting to get out of the car in that,' he said.

'Thanks,' she said, a rush of love for her thoughtful husband adding to the emotions roiling inside her. 'British springtime, eh?'

'How was your day?' Luke folded the umbrella and threw it in the corner near the door. He always asked how her day was. He always listened while she told him, and for the whole of their marriage she'd told him the truth. She told him when the man who fixed the photocopier in the staffroom asked her out, telling her he didn't mind if she was married, they could still 'have a bit of fun'. She told him when she made a mistake, forgetting to press record when her exam group did an assessment that was meant to be filmed and go off to the exam board, and they'd had to do the whole thing again and it wasn't nearly as good. The good and the bad, she told him all of it.

'Good, yeah. Nothing much to report.' The header on Simon's email seared across her mind's eye. 'Bit dull, really. What about you?'

'Quiet day,' he said. 'I think it's time to start advertising again.'

'Oh, I'm sorry to hear that.' Cassie hung her damp coat over the banister and kicked off her shoes. Most of Luke's clients came through word of mouth and he much preferred it that way. She knew he felt like having to advertise was a sign of failure. 'On the plus side, it means there are fewer people in the world who need your services, which means everyone is happier. And you've made a significant contribution to that.' She squeezed his hand and walked along the hall to the kitchen at the back of the house.

'I like your thinking.' Luke followed her as she took a cold bottle of white wine from the fridge and waved it at him. 'No thanks,' he said. 'I'll have one when I get back from picking Alf up.' He sighed. 'I feel mean saying it, but if everyone else being happy means we can't pay the bills, that makes one person less happy: me.'

Cassie took a glass from the cupboard and sloshed wine in. 'Things aren't that bad, are they?' Money was always tight since her teacher's salary didn't stretch as far as it might if they lived outside the M25, and Luke's policy of keeping the cost of his therapy sessions as low as possible meant they had to budget. But they didn't have expensive tastes and they'd never wanted for anything. She calculated how much the wine in her glass cost. Considerably less than if she'd bought it in the pub, but it was still an extravagance. She would miss it if they couldn't afford it, but it was nowhere near as important as Luke's peace of mind. She sat at the kitchen table next to the patio doors looking out over their sodden square patch of garden, then back at her husband. 'We don't have to have the birthday party if you're worried about money.'

Luke sat next to her. 'No, it's fine, I'm sure a couple of adverts will solve it. I'm sorry, I shouldn't have mentioned it. I didn't mean to worry you.'

She laid her hand over his. 'Of course you should have mentioned it. A problem shared and all that.'

'You know that's a load of bull, don't you?' Luke said. 'Research shows a problem shared just makes two people miserable instead of one.'

'Oh,' said Cassie, frowning. 'I didn't know that. I like a good complain.'

Luke lifted a finger and she smiled inwardly, knowing he was about to share some of his counsellor wisdom with her. 'But research also shows that if the sharing is used to reach a solution, then it is productive and helpful for both parties; hence my job.' He lifted his hands and grinned.

'No moaning unless it's aimed at solving a problem, then. Got it.'

'Exactly.' He leaned closer. 'But I think there's a caveat for married couples. You are allowed to complain to me about anything and everything, day or night; in fact, I'd be hurt if you didn't.' He kissed the end of her nose and she smelled tea on his breath and a hint of his citrus aftershave. God, he was lovely. She didn't deserve him.

'Good to know.' She thought about the current problem sitting in her inbox. She should share that with Luke right now. But she didn't know what the body of the email said and it could lead to questions that might be so incendiary they could blow her marriage apart. 'And next time I have a problem, you can bet your life that I will whine at you relentlessly.'

'Can't wait,' said Luke. 'Now, you put your feet up and enjoy that glass of wine while I go and collect our boy.'

She waited five excruciating minutes after she heard the car door slam and the engine start to reach into her handbag and take out her phone. Her heart pummelled her ribs when she clicked onto her school emails, scrolling with shaking fingers to the one with her ex-husband's name.

6

PRESENT DAY

Cassie

Cassie's surroundings seemed to fall away as she focused on the first contact she'd had from her ex-husband for fourteen years. The kitchen blurred, and she felt suspended in a vacuum that made it hard to breathe. She'd had all her formative experiences with this man. She'd thought he was her soulmate and, when they made their marriage vows, she'd believed with every fibre of her being they would grow old together.

Then he'd betrayed her, and when they last spoke they had promised each other solemnly that they would never make contact again. Ever. It seemed no vow was sacred to that man.

Hi Cassie

I'm sorry to email you via your school email address, but I couldn't think of another way to contact you.

I've agonised over whether to get in touch at all…

A buzzing started in Cassie's ears. She put the phone face

down on her lap and took three shuddering breaths, staring out past the rain-spattered patio doors at Alf's trampoline surrounded by tall netting. She visualised him jumping up and down, shrieking with delight as he dropped onto his bottom, then bounced back up to his feet, throwing his arms in the air with a look of triumph on his heart-shaped face. Alfie, her gorgeous boy. Her priority. Gritting her teeth, she lifted the phone and continued to read.

> ...but I thought I should tell you that Meg died of pancreatic cancer five months ago. I don't expect you to feel any sympathy for myself or Meg, but our daughter is struggling and I wondered if you might be willing to help?
>
> I know this goes against what we agreed, but I'm asking for the sake of our child, not myself.

Nausea swilled in Cassie's stomach. The woman who'd once destroyed her life was dead. She closed her eyes. That wasn't right; it wasn't all Meg's doing. It had taken two people to tear Cassie's life apart and Simon was the one who'd been married to Cassie at the time. It was *his* child she'd been carrying when she'd discovered he and Meg were sleeping together. Despite her best efforts, her brain took her back to the awful day she discovered his betrayal, then on to the following week, sitting in that clinic, waiting for her turn to have the new life growing inside her terminated. She could smell the disinfectant and see the nurses in blue scrubs calling out names from a clipboard, as one poor soul after another followed them down a corridor.

She could hear Simon begging her forgiveness as clear as if he was in the room with her now; the agony in his voice as tears poured down his face. That was when it started, she thought now; the depression she hadn't been able to truly shake until

Luke came into her life. It hadn't begun when she saw Simon and Meg together outside his school's drama department. That was pure shock. But when the shock subsided, it left a darkness that ran through her veins and coated her skin. She noticed how it had taken hold of her for the first time that day when she felt she had no choice but to terminate her pregnancy.

Even now, the black cloak she'd worked so hard to climb out from under was still there, swirling in her mind, ready to cover her again if she didn't fight it. Since meeting Luke, she'd sometimes gone months without the edges of the darkness trying to suffocate her. The worry she might not be able to avoid its pull had almost made her deny Luke the child he so desperately wanted. The fact that Simon's betrayal had not only cost her that baby, but also could have denied her the family she had now, the most precious thing in the world to her, made her stomach clench tight.

'I'm so scared the depression will come back if I get pregnant,' she'd told Luke the evening after he proposed. They were in her bed in the small flat she'd rented. The elation and adrenaline of the engagement had turned to a gnawing anxiety that she wasn't able to give this wonderful man the life he was entitled to. 'I know how much you want a child. But I don't know if I can go through that after what happened last time.'

Guilt had curdled in her gut as she recalled the first conversation they'd had about her pregnancy and the depression that followed at the start of their relationship. She'd been so distraught when she'd got to the part about the accident that had caused her baby to be born prematurely that Luke had pre-empted her, saying, 'Oh, love, I'm so sorry you lost your baby.' He'd held her to him. 'A stillbirth is such a harrowing thing to go through. I'm so sorry.' She'd stopped talking then and rested her head against his chest, listening to his heartbeat, wondering whether to tell him the truth. Her baby had lived and she'd given her away. But his hand stroking her hair was so comforting, and she didn't want to feel its inevitable pause when she said those devastating words. And that part of her life was behind her, so she decided to look forwards instead of back. She stayed quiet and let the lie become his truth.

When he'd asked her to marry him, there was nothing she wanted more than to accept and have a baby with him. But deep down, she knew she didn't deserve either of those things.

He'd pulled her tightly into him, his chin resting on top of her head. 'I know the pregnancy hormones could have exacerbated how you felt, but finding your husband was having an affair could easily have been the trigger for your depression. I completely understand how what came afterwards would prolong an episode, but it's worth considering the way you felt wasn't anything to do with the pregnancy and was entirely caused by what happened to you.'

She blinked into the dark, loving this kind, gentle man even more. She wished she'd told him the truth when they had that conversation two years ago, but now it was too late. If she was going to lose him anyway, she wasn't sure she could bear for him to know she was a monster too. 'But what if it was the pregnancy that caused it and it happens again?' The black cloak swooped nearer than it had in months.

'Then you'd be in the fortunate position to be married to a trained counsellor,' Luke had said, 'and someone who knows when it's time to get medical help.' He'd kissed the top of her head. 'But if you're that scared, then I don't want to put you through it. I still want to marry you and spend the rest of my life with you, whether we start a family or not.'

She'd cried properly then, and it was as though his words and her torrent of tears filled up the churning black well of sadness inside her, freeing her to believe it was the circumstances that had caused her depression, to go ahead and have Alfie and to start her life over afresh.

But now the email had brought the blackness back. She was still staring at her phone when she heard the voices outside. Her kitchen came back into focus when Luke's key turned in the lock.

7

PRESENT DAY

Cassie

Alf came bounding into the kitchen. 'Tye's mum let me have chocolate and strawberry sauce on my ice cream after dinner, even though I didn't eat all my peas.'

Luke trailed in behind him carrying Alf's school rucksack. 'Which might explain why he's quite so full of energy at the end of the school week despite the fact it's almost bedtime.' Luke wilted, his knees bent and his jaw comically slack.

'I'm not tired,' said Alf. 'Can I go on the trampoline?'

'Look out of the window,' said Cassie, forcing herself out of her memories and into the room. She pulled Alf towards her and squeezed his skinny frame tight. She felt the rise and fall of his bony ribs and breathed in the little boy scent of damp hair and classroom. This was what mattered. Her boy and Luke; her family.

'Oh,' said Alf, wriggling free and moving to the patio doors. His breath fogged the windows. 'It's wet.' He put his hands on the glass, and Cassie didn't tell him off, even though she'd have to wipe greasy prints off later. Instead, she marvelled at those ten small fingers she and Luke had miraculously made together. This boy was the best of them and she loved him so much it sometimes overwhelmed her.

'You all right?' She turned to see Luke looking at her, his dark brow knitted.

This was the downside of being married to an emotionally intelligent, intuitive man. 'Just tired,' she said, turning back to watch Alf trace his name into the condensation on the window, despite the fact he'd been told not to do that a hundred times. How many spouses used the 'just tired' excuse for a change in their mood every day? How many of them were trying to mask something as potentially tumultuous as her? she wondered. Not many. Or perhaps there were millions; after all, she had experienced more than one life-crushing incident in her life and Luke didn't know the half of it.

'I'll do bath time,' said Luke. 'You put your feet up.'

He kept his eyes on her and she almost argued, but in that moment she didn't have the energy to listen to the inevitable blow by blow account of Alf's day. Knowing that added to her guilt. She worked with teenagers and was fully aware that all too soon, Alf rating his school lunch out of ten and the chattering about the painting he did in art would soon be a distant memory, replaced by grunts, or monosyllables if she was lucky. She smiled weakly and said, 'Thanks, love.'

'Come on, son,' said Luke. 'Give your mum a kiss and up we go.'

Alf slumped onto Cassie's lap, mouth drooping at the edges. 'I don't want to go to bed. I'm not even a little bit tired.'

Cassie pulled him onto her knee. 'Wait until you're my age. You'll spend half your day dreaming of being under your duvet.' She planted a loud kiss on his cheek. 'I love you, you little rascal.' She tickled him under his arms and his giggles were like music. 'Sleep well.'

'Night night,' he said, sliding from her knee, leaving a cold patch on her lap. 'Love you too.' She could still feel the absence of him when Luke came downstairs forty minutes later.

'You haven't moved,' he said.

Cassie blinked, as if waking from a trance. 'God, sorry.' She looked at the clock on the oven, hardly able to believe the time that had passed. 'I meant to make the stir fry. I'll do it now.'

'Hold on.' She went to stand but Luke sat beside her and pulled her back down. 'What's going on? You were fine when I set off to get Alf, then we get back and you're somewhere else. What's changed?'

'Nothing. I'm fine. Just tired.'

Luke's eyebrows raised.

'Honestly.'

He breathed deeply. 'You know what that word means to me, Cass.'

Her insides twisted. She was painfully aware of how important openness and trust were to him. After this long together, he could read her, and if she wasn't careful he would find out her lie of omission and his trust would be shattered for good. That would be utterly devastating for all of them. 'Okay, no, I'm not all right. Sorry, I should have said straight away, but I've been trying to process it. It doesn't feel real.'

He stayed quiet, his hazel eyes with flecks of green trained on hers.

'An email arrived in my school inbox today. It was from Simon.'

Luke's eyebrows dipped in a V. 'Simon?'

Cassie almost laughed. Of course the name wouldn't immediately jump out at Luke like it did for her. They knew at least four Simons between them, and he'd never had his whole life ripped apart by one of them. 'Simon Gately. My ex-husband.'

Luke's brow lifted in understanding. 'Ah. Right.' He nodded and Cassie could imagine all the questions forming behind those gentle eyes. She knew he would be weighing up what to say next. He pointed at the empty wine glass sitting next to her phone. 'Top up?'

'Yes please.' She waited until he stood and opened the fridge to carry on. 'Meg, the woman Simon had an affair with, has died.'

Luke's hand stilled and the liquid stalled at the neck of the bottle of wine. 'Right.' He went back to pouring and brought both glasses over. 'Do you know why he felt the need to share that information with you after all these years? What did he gain from it?'

Cassie visualised the sparse text in the email. She should show it to Luke. She should ask his advice. She should never have let him believe Grace was dead. She couldn't believe she'd done it now. Sometimes, when she was awake in the dead of night, she allowed her thoughts to punish her by telling her that even one person thinking Grace had died would make it more likely she would come to harm. That thought made her twist in pain, however irrational it felt in the light of the day. 'I don't know.'

'And how has it made you feel?'

That was such a counsellor question. She had to push down a flare of annoyance. 'Unsteady. I mean, I hadn't given either of them much thought for years.' That was a lie. She thought about them, or at least the baby, every single day. 'So it was a shock to even see his name.' She lifted her hands from the table. 'And to hear Meg died, well, it's awful. She must've only been about thirty-five.' She took a drink of wine. 'But even though I know it's incredibly sad when someone dies so young, I can't force myself to feel sorry for either of them, and I think that probably makes me a terrible person.'

'It doesn't make you a terrible person. This is a deeply complex situation. You're bound to have complex feelings about it.' He had no idea. 'Give yourself time to sit with it.' He sipped his wine. 'Have you replied?'

'No, I haven't replied.' That seemed like an odd question to her.

'Perhaps you should.'

'Why?' As far as Luke was aware Simon and Meg were two people who'd betrayed her and ruined her mental health. Why on earth would he want her to engage?

'To give you some kind of closure. You must've wondered what their life was like after everything that happened, and now you know. And, as you say, it's terribly sad. It's possible he's told you this as a kind of apology.'

'Apology?' The word came out harshly.

He held up his hand. 'Hold on. Let me finish. It might be that his guilt has added to his grief and he might well believe this awful thing has happened because of what they did to you back then.'

Cassie pursed her lips, half regretting telling Luke anything. He was too reasonable and the last thing Simon Gately made her feel was reasonable. 'I doubt that very much.'

'What other reason could he have for reaching out now? Can I read the email? Maybe I could help work out what his motives were.'

Cassie stiffened. 'I deleted it.' Her fingers itched to grab her phone and actually bin the message before her lie could be exposed.

'Oh, right.'

How instantly and easily he believed her. She disgusted herself. Familiar self-loathing made her skin feel like it didn't fit. Her scalp was too tight. She scratched her head, then stood and walked to the patio doors so she didn't have to face Luke.

'Well, the only reason I can think of is that it was his way of letting you know he hadn't lived happily ever after and he believes this is his penance.' Luke's tone was calm and thoughtful, as if she was sitting across from him on his therapy couch. She didn't deserve his considerate words. She was lying to his face. 'I think if you did offer your condolences, it might help both of you.'

Cassie closed her eyes, the conflicting emotions threatening to overwhelm her. 'It's brought all those feelings back to the fore. My mind keeps replaying those horrendous weeks. I remember sitting in that abortion clinic...' Tears tumbled onto her cheeks, and she didn't know if she was crying for herself or the poor baby that she'd initially been so delighted about, then wanted expunged from her body in the space of one agonising day.

'I truly think that if you replied to Simon, you might both find some peace.' Luke stood and she felt his warmth behind her. He placed his hands on her shoulders.

'I can't,' she said, shaking his hand away. His sympathy made her guilt worse. 'Please, don't ask me to. I can't think about this anymore, it's too much.'

Tears pouring down her face, she turned towards the door, needing to escape Luke's kindness and be on her own with her guilt. Alf stood in the doorway, chin puckered as though trying not to cry himself.

'Mummy?' Alf's small voice tore through her sobs. 'Why did Daddy make you sad?'

8

SIX MONTHS AGO

Meg

Meg dabbed at her face with a tissue. 'I'm sorry, I promised myself I wouldn't cry, but...' She wiped another tear away then took a deep breath. 'Parents are meant to keep promises, aren't they?' She looked intently into the screen. 'The first time I held you in my arms, I promised you I would do everything in my power to make your life happy. You were so tiny. Just a little dot. I remember lifting you from your Moses basket and being astonished at how light you were, hardly there at all, even though you were already everything to me and your dad. Everything. And that's never changed, Grace. I absolutely promise you that.'

She sipped from the glass of water. 'But I've failed in my promise to make you happy, and I'm so, so sorry. In my defence' – she lifted her palms – 'if I could do anything about this awful disease, I would. I would give literally anything to see you grow into the extraordinary woman I know you're going to be. But there's nothing I can do to change what's about to happen to me, so instead, I'm going to do my very best to change the course of your future by telling you more about our past.'

The back of her mouth tickled and she drank, then cleared her throat. 'So, I've told you how I felt when I first met your dad, and you'll be able to ask him how he felt when he first saw me, but that's where it gets complicated. We should have told you before tonight, but it was never the right time, and, if I'm honest, I was always worried it would stain your view of me.' That was true. No mother wants their child to know they are capable of shameful behaviour. But even now she was hiding her ugliest reasons for keeping Grace in the dark about her background.

'I'm not proud of what I did. It's against the girl code and I'm ashamed to admit it even now, but as you know after our conversation earlier, back when I met him, your dad was married to a woman called Cassie.'

The image of Cassie's face when she'd caught her and Simon together in the school car park flashed into her mind, and her stomach flipped like it always did when she remembered that day. It had been all she could do not to throw up onto the tarmac, although she still didn't know if that was through the shock of being caught or the thought of losing Simon.

'I knew he was married from the start. He wore a wedding ring.' She looked down and shook her head. 'I'm not going to pretend otherwise, because I'm making these videos so you know the truth. All of it; not just the parts that show us in a good light. I know I should have suppressed my feelings for him, but that's the problem with feelings; they refuse to be controlled. I did try.' She raised her eyes to the screen. 'Honestly. But I think there's more animal instinct involved in human relationships than we realise. It was chemical, tangible. It was only when...'

She pulled the green silk headscarf with the black pattern

further down her forehead. She was tempted to tug it down to cover her whole face because of the shame of what she was about to say. 'When we found out Cassie was pregnant, we stopped our affair.'

The hollowness she'd felt back then returned to her gut. 'The day Cassie caught us kissing, she was coming to tell Simon she was expecting his baby. Obviously, she was distraught to find out about your dad and me... It was awful. I wouldn't wish that on anyone. I keep imagining how I'd feel if your dad cheated on me, and it makes me feel sick to my stomach.'

She put her hand to her concave abdomen. 'Understandably, Cassie threw your dad out, and then she told him she was going to terminate the pregnancy.' Her bottom lip quivered. 'He was broken by that. He loathed himself for what he'd done to her. We talked and agreed that, however hard it was, we could never see each other again. My teaching practice was almost over, so I went off sick for the last week, and he begged Cassie to take him back.'

Meg closed her eyes and rolled her shoulders. 'I didn't hear from your dad again until a week later when he messaged to say he'd managed to persuade Cassie out of the termination at the last minute, and she'd agreed to have the baby and let him try to make it up to her. We made a pact to block each other's numbers and never see each other again.' She stared into the screen. 'It was the hardest thing I ever had to do, but it was the right thing too. I had to walk away so you could live.'

9

PRESENT DAY

Cassie

Cassie rushed to the kitchen doorway where Alf was standing, a distressed and confused expression on his face. She folded him into her arms. 'Oh, sweetheart, Daddy didn't upset me. I read something sad, that's all, and we were talking about it.'

Alf pulled his head back and looked at the tears on Cassie's cheeks. 'What did you read?'

'Just something on the news.'

She heard Luke's footsteps approach and wished she'd said something else. When Alf was born, true to form, Luke had said he'd like them both to tell him the truth as much as possible. Luke didn't believe children should be shielded from the realities of life and death. He thought careful use of language and always keeping dialogue open was more productive. And she'd just shown him how easily she could lie.

'I'll take you back up,' said Luke. 'Come on.'

He held his arms open, but Cassie kept Alf close. 'It's okay, I'll take him up.' She could sense Luke's disapproval but wanted

Alf's arms to stay around her neck, to keep his unconditional love close. He was heavy and she had to release her hold on him on the bottom step of the stairs. She glanced back at Luke, who was leaning on the door jamb to the kitchen, eyes narrowed, and knew he had questions.

To avoid those questions, after settling Alf, she went into their small ensuite and ran the taps to fill the corner bath. She was soaking in too-hot water and lemon-scented bubbles when there was a knock on the door. 'I'm just in the bath,' she called, hoping he'd get the message she didn't want to be disturbed.

'Okay if I come in?'

She closed her eyes. 'Course.' She sank lower in the water, glad the bubbles frothed over most of her body. Nakedness never usually bothered her, but after today she felt raw and exposed.

'What was that about?' He closed the toilet lid and sat down.

'What?' Cassie knew what but was buying time to think about how she could justify lying to their son. The water was too hot. Sweat rolled from her forehead into her eyes.

'That rubbish about the news?'

She took clouds of bubbles in her hands and squeezed them through her fingers. How did they stay perky in water this hot? She was being broiled. 'You think it would be better to tell him I was upset because my ex-husband emailed and it reminded me of the time he was shagging someone else?'

'Don't be facetious, Cass. I'm trying to understand.'

'There's nothing deeper, Luke, honestly.' Why did she keep saying that? 'I just said the first thing that came into my head because I didn't want our sensitive little boy to think it was you who'd upset me. That's all.' She let her hands fall under the water, leaving dark gaps in the white froth.

'I think maybe we should talk about what we tell Alf in future.' He spoke softly.

Cassie turned to face him. 'What do you mean?' His questioning look had been replaced by sympathy. She couldn't bear to see the kindness in his eyes so turned back to the bubbles.

'He will need to know, one day. Not now, obviously, but when he's old enough to understand.' His voice seemed amplified by the tiles.

She had the urge to slide under the water so her head would submerge and his words would distort then disappear. 'I don't agree.'

'Your past is part of you, Cass. You're his mum, but you're also—'

'I'm his mum, and that's it. That's all he needs to know.'

He let out a long sigh. 'I see a lot of people who have never been able to assimilate their view of their parents with them as individuals. That leads to a disconnect.'

'You're not my therapist, Luke.' Sometimes she wished he worked in a shoe shop, or anywhere that meant he didn't analyse everything that came out of her mouth, or her aura come to that. She moved her legs back and forth, concentrating on the push and pull of the water against her skin. 'He doesn't need to know what I went through. Who wants to know about their parents' dark past, especially when it's ancient history?'

'I wouldn't exactly call it a dark past. More a past that has dark experiences in it.' Cassie wondered if he would say the same if he knew the truth. She never wanted to find out. 'And I think it will help him to see you more fully. It might also help him to see that, no matter how bad things get, there's always a future. He could see what you overcame to get to this point in your life. And you know I think mental health should be discussed more openly.'

'You think he'd benefit from knowing about the abortion clinic?' She was being intentionally difficult and she knew it.

'You always come back to that.' Luke came over and knelt next to the bath. He reached into the water and took her hand. 'The guilt of almost terminating that pregnancy has been eating you up for fifteen years. It's had such an impact on your mental health, and it kills me that you're still carrying it with you.'

Cassie's throat tightened. She watched the bubbles attached to the hairs on Luke's wrist pop. She remembered Simon on his knees, like Luke was now, imploring her to give him a second chance and keep their child. She could feel the sense of darkness already falling over her as she made the decision to stand and allow him to lead her out of the clinic and into his car.

'I wish I could make you see you focus on that because of an irrational need to blame yourself for what happened afterwards. The truth is, none of it was your fault.'

How she wished it was as simple as that. If it was true that all of her guilt came from almost terminating that pregnancy, then she would have therapy and she would try to move on.

Luke held her hand tighter. 'Cassie, it's not your fault your baby died.'

She clamped her mouth closed to stop the truth from gushing out, but the words still screamed inside her head. *Grace lived and I gave her away. She is suffering and it's killing me, but I can't help her without destroying my family. I am a terrible person and you don't really know me. I am a liar, a liar, a liar.*

10

PRESENT DAY

Cassie

Cassie glanced at Alf through the car's rear-view mirror. His rosebud lips were downturned. 'You okay, buddy?' He nodded, still staring forlornly out of the window. Cassie's shoulders tensed. She'd tried incredibly hard to act normally over the weekend but clearly hadn't done a good enough job because she'd caught both Luke and Alf eying her suspiciously when she didn't laugh at a joke, or missed something they'd said because she was in a world of her own. She didn't want to be somewhere else. She wanted to be present for her son and her husband. She certainly didn't want to be back at the edge of the black vortex in her head. She couldn't fall in there again, especially when she could see it was affecting her son.

After dropping Alf off and watching him slope into the school grounds with a heavy stone in her stomach, she made her way to school, glad to see Becca's white Fiat following her into the staff car park. 'How was your weekend?' said Cassie, slamming the car door and falling into step with her friend. The weather had turned warm at last, but even the cloudless sky didn't lift her mood.

'Rampant,' said Becca, grinning. She tugged at a blue silk scarf tied around her neck in a pussycat bow that was a far more fussy look than her usual shirt and smart trousers. 'Look.' She moved closer to Cassie, pointing to a dark red bruise on her neck in the shape of a mouth.

'A hickey? At your age?' Cassie widened her eyes. 'You're as bad as Year Nine.' It seemed to her the minute kids turned thirteen they joined a race to burst as many blood vessels in as obvious a place as possible to prove they were prematurely sexually active. 'Also, we're politically opposed to love bites because they're proprietorial, aren't we? Isn't it basically boys marking their territory like spraying cats?'

'Nah,' said Becca, rearranging her scarf to hide the mark. 'I tried telling my girls love bites were anti-feminist a few years ago and got shot down in flames. They reckoned that as long as you give and receive equally and with full consent, it's all good. Like oral sex. To prove the point, next time I saw my youngest's boyfriend, he looked like a walking blood blister.'

'Not a conversation I expected to be having before my second coffee this morning,' said Cassie, unable to imagine a time when her precious little boy would arrive home with ugly red marks on his perfect skin. She nodded at Becca's neck. 'So you consented to that?'

'I didn't really notice he was doing it, if I'm honest. We were in the throes, if you know what I mean.' They headed towards the entrance. Becca stopped when she noticed a streak of silver along the passenger door of the head teacher's electric-blue Tesla. 'Someone's keyed old Finnegan's pride and joy.' She pulled her teeth back in a grimace. 'There'll be hell to pay for that.'

A vague memory of someone with a piece of bright metal in their hand right next to the car on Friday came into Cassie's head. She tried harder to focus on it, then remembered. 'I saw Oliver Simms hanging around here when I was leaving on Friday. I did wonder why he was in the staff car park at that time.'

'Year Nine? The tall one who's always scowling?'

'Yes, that's the one.'

Cassie keyed in the code for the building, and at the buzz of the door unlocking, she pushed it open. The drop in temperature inside made her feel like she was walking into a cloud.

Becca curled her lip. 'Nasty piece of work, that one. You should tell Finnegan.'

'Tell Finnegan what?' The head teacher's voice made both the women jump. He was standing just inside the door, chin raised. His sallow cheeks, dark moustache and clipped manner always reminded Cassie of John Cleese, which made it hard for her to take him seriously, even though he was in charge of this enormous comprehensive and had been her boss for over a decade.

'Sorry, Keith, I was just...' Becca waved vaguely out at the car park, the skin above her scarf turning bright pink. 'We saw the scratch on your car.'

'And is there something you want to tell Finnegan about that?' He raised an eyebrow at Cassie, who felt like a new Year Seven who'd been caught vaping in the toilets.

'You do have a fantastic surname, Keith,' she said. 'You can't blame us for using it.'

'Hmm. Follow me, if you would.' He turned and made for the office and Cassie half expected him to do a silly walk. When they were out of earshot of any students, he peered down at them. 'So, what do you know about the damage to my car?'

'Nothing for certain,' said Cassie. 'I was just telling Becca I saw Oliver Simms in the car park at around six-ish on Friday and I wondered why he was there.'

'Did you ask him?'

'No, I was...' She couldn't say she was preoccupied with an email from her ex-husband. 'I was on the phone, so...' When had she started lying all the time? 'And he scurried off when he saw me.'

'Hmm,' Finnegan said again. 'I had a budget meeting at the council in the afternoon, and didn't get back until close of play on Friday, and I'm sure there was no mark on the car when I arrived back here. I noticed it when I left at six-thirty, so the timing would be about right. Did you see anything else incriminating?'

Cassie bit her bottom lip. 'I vaguely remember something glinting in his hand, but I couldn't swear to it. As I said, I was preoccupied.' Was it even fair of her to offer that information? 'Did the CCTV show anything?'

'It only covers the school entrance, not the car park,' said Finnegan. 'I'll have a word with the lad and see what he has to say.'

'I didn't actually see him do anything,' Cassie said, feeling suddenly nervous about being drawn into an accusation.

'I'll investigate,' said Finnegan. 'He's holding a grudge against me since I said he couldn't be in the football team until his punctuality improves, so—'

He was cut off by the bell for registration sounding and Cassie sagged at the knowledge she wouldn't have time to grab a coffee in the staffroom before form time.

'See you at break,' said Becca, walking towards reception, where students were already moving in all directions like swarming insects. 'You can tell me about your weekend then,' she said over her shoulder.

'Nothing to tell,' called Cassie after her, but her words were swallowed by the voices of a hundred teenagers heading to registration. She left the office and steered herself towards her classroom. Just before she reached the corridor, she saw Oliver Simms walking towards her.

'Simms.' Finnegan's voice boomed from behind her. 'I want a word with you. Follow me.'

The boy looked up towards where the headmaster had begun to ascend the stairs to his office. He huffed and his shoulders dropped. He took a couple of steps forwards and then paused when he noticed Cassie standing still while students manoeuvred around her. His bottom jaw jutted forward and his eyes narrowed to dark slits. He barged the shoulder of a small girl who was passing in the opposite direction as he set off towards the headmaster. Cassie opened her mouth to reprimand him, but the girl wandered on her way unharmed, and something in the malevolence of his stare made Cassie think again. She'd been teaching for the best part of twenty years, and she'd learned there were some students you had to pick your battles with. She also knew there were some who decided to go into battle with you.

11

PRESENT DAY

Cassie

Cassie's temples thrummed with a headache and she was desperate for a coffee by the end of first period. Thankfully the lesson was quiet reading with an unusually compliant bunch of Year Sevens, so she'd had time to think about what to do about the email from Simon. She decided she would reply, and that would be the end of it. After that, the darkness in her head would lift again and she could get back on with her life. The end of this situation couldn't come soon enough.

Nitim, a bearded Physics teacher, was in the staffroom kitchen when she walked in. 'Cassie, hello.'

'Morning.' Cassie checked the inside of the mugs for the least stained. She found one that looked like it had at least been washed in the last week, then flicked on the kettle, hoping Nitim wouldn't try to start a conversation.

'I see you've chosen the Bromley FC mug. Are you a fan?' Nitim's voice was monotone. It was a wonder his students weren't lulled into sleep. Perhaps they were.

Cassie checked the exterior of the mug and saw the red and black shield. 'Not especially. It's just the cleanest.'

'They were founder members of the Southern League, you know.'

Cassie scooped two spoonfuls of instant coffee into her cup. 'Is that right?'

'Of course, they only reached the English Football League in the last couple of years.'

Cassie smiled and nodded, wishing she'd chosen the mug with *Sexy Beast* written on the side in pink, despite the lipstick mark on the rim. She wondered what factoids Nitim would have to hand about that. Maybe he'd tell her the history of Ann Summers without a single change of cadence?

'Anyway, better get off. Best not to leave the sixth form alone in a room full of Bunsen burners for any longer than necessary.' He raised his mug to her and shuffled away, leaving her wondering whether it was ever necessary to leave a group of students with potential fire hazards. Did anyone need caffeine that much?

Coffee in hand, Cassie went through the staffroom and was relieved to find it empty. She opened her laptop and clicked onto her school email account. Scrolling past the few messages about safeguarding policy and enrichment courses that had come in since Friday, she moved the cursor to the email from Simon and clicked on the mouse pad to open it. She reread it, her heart rate increasing with every word. She clicked on the reply button.

Dear Simon

She sat back, trying to grasp the right words. All the plans she'd made about what to write had evaporated. She wiped her slippery palms on her trousers and hovered her fingers over the keys.

'Coffee?' Becca's voice made her jump. She closed her laptop.

Becca raised an eyebrow. 'Someone's got something to hide.' She tucked in her chin. 'What have I told you about looking at porn during school hours?' She wagged her finger and smirked.

'I wasn't—' Heat rushed to Cassie's cheeks.

'I'm joking,' said Becca. 'Obviously.' She peered at Cassie. 'Although you've got a guilty look about you, so now I'm wondering...'

Cassie shook her head. 'You made me jump, that's all. I thought you had Year Thirteen this period?'

'I have,' said Becca, 'but they're doing group work, so I popped up for a cuppa.'

'Am I the only one who stays with their sixth form classes for the whole period?' said Cassie. 'Nitim left his with a room full of Bunsen burners and flammable chemicals.'

Becca shrugged. 'Risky. But half of mine are old enough to legally marry without parental consent, so I think they can manage an analysis of *Not Waving but Drowning* while I get a caffeine fix.' She turned. 'Was that a no to coffee?'

Cassie raised her mug. 'Got one, thanks.'

'Okay, enjoy your porn. See ya later.'

Cassie waved, then thought of the Stevie Smith poem and shivered. Dark waters had been creeping up on her since she'd seen the email. She had to stop the tide. When she was sure Becca wasn't coming back, she opened the laptop again.

I'm sorry for your loss.

Was she? She still hadn't processed the fact that Meg was

actually dead. Every time she thought about it, her brain catapulted her back to that time, and the emotions were so violent there was no space for this new, bleak information in her swirling brain. She was sorry for Simon and Meg's daughter, though. She was innocent and just the thought of what she would be going through brought tears to Cassie's eyes. But she couldn't afford to allow that to become her problem. If she did, she knew the black cloak would come for her and if that happened, Luke, and more importantly Alf, would suffer. The downward spiral had already started this weekend, and it was her job to shield them from that, and worse. She took a deep breath and carried on.

> I am sorry you and your family are suffering, but I don't think it was fair of you to ask me for help. Everything that happened back then was your doing. Yours and Meg's. You know what happened to me in response to your actions. It took me years to recover and get my life back on track and now that it is, I can't afford to risk my mental health again. I have a husband and a seven-year-old son now, and I need to do what I think is best for my own family.
>
> I am sorry your daughter has lost her mother, but please don't contact me again.

She sipped her coffee, which now tasted bitter, agonising over whether to type 'best wishes' or 'kind regards' or some other banal platitude. It wouldn't be 'love from', she knew that much. She had loved Simon so very much, once upon a time. He had been her first real love. They'd been in the same tutor group at university and had got together in the first weeks of the first term. Her mother had been concerned the two of them were too insular. 'You're meant to meet hundreds of new friends at university,' she'd said. 'Not pair up and settle down like a middle-aged couple.'

Perhaps she'd been right, but Cassie imagined if she'd been out partying every night, her mum would have been critical of that too. Cassie had never once managed to gain her mother's approval, or her father's attention, and so when Simon seemed to not only love her, but admire her too, his validation became enough. It became everything.

She looked back on her eighteen-year-old self now with pity. Talking to Luke had helped her see that a hyper-critical mother and distant father had made her crave affirmation. She'd become a people pleaser at an early age and fallen so hard partly because Simon listened to her intently and filled the gaping hole her emotionally neglectful parents had left. How ironic that the gap Simon left behind was even bigger.

He didn't deserve her best wishes or her kind regards. She signed off the email with just her name.

12

PRESENT DAY

Cassie

Cassie expected to feel lighter after she sent the email to Simon. She hoped she was closing the door on her past again, but she hadn't slept well and by the following morning an uneasy feeling had infiltrated her body, making her super aware of her heavy limbs and eyelids. Her mood seemed to have transferred to Alf too, because he hadn't regained his usual bounce. Another thing to feel guilty about.

'Everything all right?' she asked when he put his coat on without complaining he was too hot and didn't need it. If he let her zip it up, she would really start to worry. Thankfully he tugged it away when she tried to fasten the ends of the zip together.

'I can do my own coat.' His voice was sullen. Perhaps this was the start of it. She'd heard plenty of parents complain the tween years started way too early. But he'd only turned seven last month. Surely that was too young for hormones to kick in?

In truth, she suspected his mood was because of the atmosphere in the house, and guilt pierced her again.

'What's up with you, fella?' She kept her tone light. 'You're Mr Grumpy Pants this morning.'

'I'm fine,' he said, picking his rucksack off the floor and hooking it over one shoulder.

There it was: the 'I'm fine' that meant he was anything but. 'You can talk to me if something's bothering you, you know that, don't you?' He made a noncommittal sound and followed her to the car, and they drove to his school in silence.

When she arrived at work, grey clouds hung low in the sky and the first spots of rain spattered her face as she tapped in the code to open the door. Didn't May used to be the start of glorious summers, or was that nostalgia kicking in for a time before her life imploded? She was almost forty; officially middle-aged. Perhaps she would start to look backwards more than forwards now like many older people she knew. The thought was horrifying.

Finnegan was marching from the office when she stepped inside. He came to an abrupt halt. 'Ah, Cassie.'

'Morning.'

'Could you pop to my office for a minute?'

Nothing good ever followed that question. Her stomach dropped further as she followed Finnegan's long strides up the stairs to his office on the second floor. 'Take a seat.'

Cassie sat in front of his ancient desk with the green leather inlay as he folded his long limbs into the chair behind it. 'I feel like I'm going to get a telling off.' She'd worked under Finnegan long enough to call him Keith, or choose not to, and to speak plainly.

'Not at all,' he said. 'Just giving you fair warning.'

She stiffened. 'Of what?'

'Young Simms' parents have taken umbrage to the suggestion he might be the perpetrator behind the criminal damage to my car.'

'But I didn't say he was. I only said I'd seen him in the car park.'

Finnegan took his glasses off and cleaned them with the bottom of his tie. 'That's what I told his father. I knew better than to accuse the boy outright, but it seems my gentle probing was taken as an accusation and I got a rather shouty email from Mr Simms Senior.'

'Shouty?'

'Entirely in capital letters.'

'Christ.' If teaching had taught Cassie anything, it was that if a pupil was belligerent, entitled or rude, there was every chance at least one of their parents would arrive on parents' evening, chest puffed out like an indignant pigeon, ready to tell you exactly how you were failing their child. 'What did it say?'

'That their son was at home with them from 5 p.m. onwards last Friday.'

'Oh,' said Cassie. She began to question herself. She thought back to walking into the car park after getting the email from Simon. Yes, she was distracted, but she had seen Oliver Simms, she was sure of it. That wasn't a face you could mistake. 'I disagree. I saw him after six.'

Finnegan shrugged. 'I'd love to have the evidence to corroborate that, believe me. But instead I have a pugnacious parent who is accusing you and me of holding a grudge against their sweet, innocent child.'

'Marvellous,' said Cassie.

'Indeed,' said Finnegan. 'I'm sorry I mentioned your name. It was remiss. He's not in any of your classes, is he?'

'No, thank goodness.' Cassie wished he hadn't disclosed her

name either. Oliver might not be in her classes now, but he could well be in the coming years, and parents didn't forget when someone slighted their child – even if they hadn't.

'Right, well, I don't think there's anything further we can do without proof. Very frustrating, since the child is clearly the one with the grudge, as my damaged paintwork would attest.' He put his glasses back on and raised his eyes to the ceiling. 'Bring back the days when a teacher's word meant something and deceitful children didn't rule the roost.'

'Back when Moses was a boy?' Cassie smiled. 'I blame the parents.'

Finnegan smiled back at the well-worn cliché. 'Indeed,' he said again. The bell for registration rang out and once again Cassie would have to start the day with a caffeine deficit. 'Anything else?'

'No, thanks, Cassie. Just continue to be the valued and reliable member of staff you are.'

'No good buttering me up now,' she said, smiling at the praise nevertheless. She stood and made for the door. 'See you later.'

'Have a good day,' said Finnegan. 'Don't let the blighters get you down.'

* * *

The blighters did get her down. It was what she and Luke called a 'snag your cardigan sleeve day' where every single thing you try to do goes wrong, and even attempting to enter a room leads to you catching your sleeve on the door handle, ripping your clothes and bruising your wrist. She acknowledged it was probably her state of mind that had led to her despair when the photocopier jammed at lunchtime as she copied the poem for her afternoon class to annotate. She almost cried as she tried and failed to tug the stuck paper from the mechanical innards. She missed most of the time she could have spent relaxing and still didn't have the copies she needed for her planned lesson.

By the time she got home and cooked, she was exhausted and overwrought, so when Luke came into the front room after dinner and sat next to her with an earnest expression on his face, she wanted to scream into a pillow. 'Could we have a chat?'

The last thing she wanted was a heart to heart. 'I'm a bit tired. Can it wait?'

'It's about Alf.'

She shuffled more upright. If it was about Alf, then she would never be too tired to talk. 'What's up?'

'He's been quiet this week, don't you think?' He rubbed a finger back and forth on the sofa arm.

Cassie nodded, pulling a cushion onto her lap. 'Yeah. Have you tried to speak to him about it? He says he's fine when I ask.'

'That's what he said to me, but we all know what that means.'

Cassie thought back to last Friday, and her insides shrivelled. 'What do you think's up?' She tensed. She knew what Luke was about to say.

'I'm not sure, but... don't bite my head off... it started when he thought I'd made you cry last week. He wasn't himself all weekend. He was quiet at Harry's party at Goals, and that's not like him. He even left voluntarily without his usual strop about wanting ten more minutes to play.'

She couldn't argue. Ordinarily there was nothing Alf liked better than playing football with his friends. Throw in a beige buffet and cake and it was his idea of heaven. Was it any surprise he never wanted to leave and usually complained and sulked when it was time to go home? 'I told him it wasn't anything to do with you.'

'You have been distant since, though, Cassie. If I've felt it, he will have too. He's an intuitive boy.'

The temptation to cover her face with the cushion and wail into it was strong. Instead, she gripped the underside and squeezed. 'I'm sorry. The email threw me. I'll get over it, but I need a bit of time. I've told you what happened back then, and being reminded of it all...' Tears threatened, and she grabbed the velvet fabric tighter.

'That's why I think you need to address it, Cass. I don't think you've worked through it.'

'With all due respect—'

'Ooof.' Luke frowned. His hand stopped moving on the chair arm. 'We're not doing that, are we? "With all due respect" usually means with no respect at all. You might not want to give what happened any more thought, but at least hear me out.'

She slumped back, lips clamped.

'Giving birth to a stillborn child is one of the most traumatic things a woman can go through.'

'Thank you for mansplaining that to me. I might not have realised otherwise.' Cassie knew she was being cruel, but every word he said caused her pain and she felt the need to fling some of it back at him.

She wanted him to stand and walk out, but he didn't. Of course he didn't. He was Luke, and he was no stranger to absorbing anger from people who were suffering and lashing out. 'The fact you'd considered terminating that pregnancy added an extra layer of guilt onto what I imagine you already felt because, like many women the world over, you probably blamed yourself for not being able to keep your baby safe.'

Cassie covered her face with her hand. 'Please stop.'

'I can't bear to see you in this much pain.' He put a hand on her leg and the warmth was more of a burn than a comfort.

'Then let me deal with it in my own way.'

'But you're not dealing with it. You've shoved it so far down that you think you're over it, but it only took an email to bring it back to the surface.'

'Just leave me to do this my way.' Why wouldn't he listen? She couldn't bear this. Tears soaked into the velvet.

'Avoiding issues doesn't solve them, and I'm sorry, Cass, but it's impacting Alf, so I can't just leave it.'

Her chest heaved in heavy sobs. 'I can't talk about this now.'

'All right, all right.' Luke squeezed her knee. 'But I want to say one more thing before I go up and say goodnight to Alf. I truly believe holding on to the anger you felt for Simon and Meg has stopped you being able to fully grieve for your baby.'

He had no idea. She grieved for her daughter every day of her life.

He continued. 'Don't bite my head off, but I think maybe Simon reached out to you as part of his grieving process too.'

That's not true, Cassie thought. *You don't know*. But then whose fault was that? Hers. It was all her fault. She wanted to pull the cushion over her ears so she couldn't hear his words, but he carried on. 'And if you could just find the strength to reply to him, I think—'

'No!' She threw the cushion down on the floor. 'I don't want anything to do with that man. I want to forget he ever existed. Why can't you just let me...'

She stopped shouting at the sound of footsteps thundering down the stairs. The door flew open and Alf stood, his little face red and tear stained – again.

13

PRESENT DAY

Cassie

The following Friday, Becca came into the staffroom at the end of the day and sat at her usual desk. Cassie could feel her eyes on her. She turned to face her. She didn't need the scrutiny she saw on Becca's face. She knew her eyes were red-rimmed and puffy without having it pointed out to her. She hadn't slept well since their failed attempt to placate Alf earlier that week, and the effort of trying to appear normal was killing her. 'Stop staring at me. It's unnerving. Do some work and throw a pen at the wall, like normal.'

'I'm just wondering what's up with you.' Becca pulled at the collar of her shirt, which was turned up and looked odd and dated.

'Nothing,' said Cassie. 'I'm tickety-boo.' She forced a smile and nodded to Becca's shirt. 'Why are you suddenly channelling Princess Diana circa 1995?' She tugged her own collar up and dipped her head, looking across at Becca through fluttering lashes. She had to at least attempt banter. She knew

Becca wouldn't get off her case unless she acted like her usual self.

'This bloody thing is still hanging around.' Becca turned down the collar to reveal the purple speckled remains of the love bite. 'The scarves were playing havoc with my menopausal internal thermometer.' She laughed. 'Try saying that after a drink.' She lifted the collar again. 'Anyway, I think I look quite demure.' She pinched her lips and lifted her chin, raising her eyes to the polystyrene tiles on the ceiling.

'Keep telling yourself that,' said Cassie.

'So, come on, spill. Why are you acting weird?'

Cassie huffed. 'I'm not acting weird.'

'Keep telling yourself that.'

Cassie pulled a face at Becca. 'I'm not sleeping well, that's all. I'm tired. You've forgotten what it's like having to look after anyone but yourself. We don't all go home to a soak in the bath before languorous sex with a younger man, you know.'

'I don't do languorous,' said Becca. 'I do—'

'Nope.' Cassie held her palm towards Becca. 'I am too knackered to even listen to your sexploits.'

Becca laughed. 'I know a cure for tiredness: let's get some rocket fuel in our systems.' Rocket fuel was what Becca called alcohol. She'd been almost teetotal when she was married and bringing up her girls, but since the divorce, she'd discovered alcohol gave her more confidence, and she was experimenting with that as avidly as she was her newfound sexual energy.

'It doesn't have the same effect on me. You know that,' said Cassie. 'Your rocket fuel is my sedative. If I had a glass of wine now, I think I'd fall asleep.'

Becca bounced in her seat. 'Oh, come on. It's Friday and it's ages since we went for a drink. Just a quick one. It's been too long.' She drew out the last word, reminding Cassie of how Alf spoke when he wanted extra ice cream or another bedtime story.

She couldn't deny it had been a while since the two of them spent any time together outside school. 'I don't know. I've got a pile of marking to do.'

'All work and no play makes Cassie dull AF,' said Becca. 'Hasn't Alf got one of those endless clubs kids go to after school? I bet he has. Let's start the weekend with a quick catch up over a nice chilled glass of white wine. It's not a lot to ask, is it?' Becca pouted.

Alf did have a football match and he was being dropped off home by another mum afterwards. And if she was honest with herself, Cassie was in no hurry to be home alone with Luke at the moment. She closed the book she'd been marking. 'All right then, I'll message Luke and tell him I'll be a bit late. But don't blame me if I fall asleep mid-sip.'

'With this sparkling company?' Becca stood and twirled, holding on to her collar, head back and blonde hair flowing, like a middle-aged Marilyn Monroe. 'Not a chance.'

* * *

The pub closest to school, The Black Horse, was stuck in the last century, with a sticky carpet and scruffy tables with peeling beermats. At least none of the sixth form would be seen dead in there, so it served its purpose. When Cassie and Becca stepped out onto the pavement after an admittedly welcome glass of substandard Pinot Grigio, Cassie blinked at the bright light. 'I always think it should be dark when I come out of there,' she said. 'It seems wrong that it's still only five-thirty.' The gloomy decor of the pub wasn't the only thing making her feel like it was bedtime. The wine had the predicted soporific effect, making her eyelids heavy. She yawned. 'I feel quite tipsy.' She should have stuck to her guns when she'd asked for a small glass, instead of letting Becca order them both a medium. At least she'd managed to fend off any awkward questions by asking for stories of Becca's dating life. It had been just the distraction she needed.

'Lightweight,' said Becca. 'Want a lift back to your car?'

'No, you're all right. I probably need the walk to wake up before I drive.' She gave her friend a hug. 'Thanks for that. Have a great weekend. Can't wait to hear all about it on Monday.' She paused. 'Almost all of it, anyway. There are some parts I'd prefer you kept to yourself.'

'Sharing is caring,' Becca sing-songed, before getting into her car.

Still smiling, Cassie strolled up the road towards the school car park. The air was warm on her cheeks and the wine had allowed her shoulders to relax. The headache she'd had for the last week was fading. Simon hadn't replied to her email. It was over. She could get on with her life.

A group of kids was gathered at the entrance to the school grounds. There was a shout and suddenly the group closed in. Cassie knew the signs. More shouts rang out, deep voices swearing mixed with the higher pitch of unbroken voices. 'Oh, for God's sake.' Cassie quickened her pace.

The huddle had moved onto the school driveway, blocking the entrance to the car park. There were at least eight boys crowded around a pair who were dragging at each other's clothes and snarling. 'Boys, stop it.' Cassie's voice was lost in the roar from the group. 'Lads,' she yelled again.

One of the boys fighting was taller and broader than the other. He threw a punch at the other's face. Blood spattered and Cassie's heart began to pound. 'Stop it, right now.'

They didn't acknowledge her and after more punching and struggling, the two boys were on the floor, fists and legs flailing as they pounded at each other, the crowd around them jeering and shouting. The unmistakable sound of skull on concrete rang in Cassie's ears. The smaller boy's face was covered in blood. It flowed with the snot from his nose and she could see he was crying.

Instinct kicked in and Cassie tore into the fray, dragging the onlookers aside. She pulled at one boy's blazer and he flung his elbow back to shake her off. The sharp bone connected with Cassie's lip and pain made her shout out, 'You little fucker.' The group heard that. Even the boys on the floor stopped struggling. They all stared at her as she raised her hand to her face and touched the sticky wetness where her lip had burst open from the blow.

14

PRESENT DAY

Cassie

'What the hell happened to you?' Luke's dark eyebrows knitted as he rushed down the hallway towards the door to take a closer look at Cassie's lip.

It was really throbbing now. She'd been horrified when she inspected it in the mirror in the car's visor as she sat on the drive. Her lower lip was twice the size it should be and the split reopened every time she moved her mouth. 'I broke up a fight.'

'At The Black Horse?' He lifted his hand to touch her face.

She ducked out of the way, the concern in his eyes too much. 'No, some stupid kids.'

'What kids?' Luke took her bag from her and hung it over the banister, then turned back to her.

'I was going back to school to get my car and came across a group of lads from Year Nine, I think.' Her voice sounded strange as she tried not to move her mouth. 'You know what they're like at that age, full of testosterone and entitlement, always trying to prove themselves. They were circled around two boys who were really going at each other. One boy was a lot bigger than the other, so when I could see the smaller one was going to get properly hurt, I went in to stop them.'

'And one of them hit you?' His voice was an octave higher than usual. 'That's ABH. Was it one of your students? What did Finnegan say? Christ, Cassie. We need to go to the police.'

'That's not... No one hit me.' Cassie could feel the blood seeping onto her chin again. She took a bloodied tissue from her pocket, hating how it must look to Luke. 'I was caught by an elbow when I tried to get to the pair who were smashing seven bells out of each other.'

'That's still—'

His face was still crumpled and she needed to make him see it wasn't that big a deal, otherwise she'd have to do something about it, and she didn't have it in her. She knew she should have filled out an incident report immediately, but she'd been shaken, and all the boys had run off so quickly that she didn't see there was anything useful she could have done, so she got in her car and drove home. She also knew that if it hadn't been Oliver Simms who'd struck out, she probably would have reported the incident right away, and she wasn't proud of her cowardly decision to let it pass.

'It was a stupid accident, that's all. No one attacked me. One lad gave the other a bloody nose, but I don't think he was seriously hurt. I see at least three fights like this a week.' That wasn't strictly true, but she heard about them from other members of staff. She'd certainly never got caught up in one before, and now the adrenaline was leaving her body she was shaky and weak. She put a reassuring hand on Luke's arm then followed a delicious cooking smell through to the kitchen and ran herself a glass of water. A pot of chilli was bubbling on the stove. Her mouth watered.

She wondered if she should tell Luke about her swearing at Oliver Simms. She couldn't believe it when the owner of the sharp elbow turned around and she saw that unmistakable scowl. She was sure if she'd just split a teacher's lip, she'd have been contrite to say the least, even if they had called her 'a little fucker'. Instead, Oliver had rubbed his elbow, stuck out his bottom lip and said, 'You can't say that to me.'

Cassie had ignored him and pulled the smaller boy to his feet, Finnegan's words of warning about Oliver replaying in her head. She calculated that the boy hadn't meant to hit her, and she had dragged at his clothes, which was probably violating some code or other, not to mention swearing directly at him. The bloodied boy was wearing the dark blue uniform of the rival school up the road, and the fight suddenly made sense. When she turned around, most of the group had disappeared. The boy wiped his nose on his sleeve and sloped away, despite her offer of help.

'What a week.' She dabbed at her lip and was pleased to see the bleeding had slowed.

There was a scraping sound as Luke dragged out the top drawer of the freezer. He pushed ice cubes from the tray onto a tea towel then twisted it to make a ball. 'Hold that against your lip. Hopefully the swelling will go down before Alf gets back.'

'Thanks.' She took the bundle and held it against her face. The thought of her little boy seeing her injured hurt more than the cold cotton against her pulsing lip.

'You sure you don't need to report this? Surely school needs to be told?'

Cassie knew she should have at least made an incident report. 'The boy who was losing the fight wasn't from our school, and it all happened so quickly I didn't see the faces of the others clearly.' She omitted that Oliver Simms was the only one she could confidently report, and she'd sworn at him, so she decided it was better not to make a fuss. 'It wasn't on school grounds, so there's nothing school could do.' Another lie. They were becoming second nature. 'That chilli smells good.' She spooned in a steaming mouthful, wincing at the sting, which made her eyes water when the hot, spicy sauce touched her lip.

When Alf was dropped off after football half an hour later, she stayed in the kitchen and waited for him to come through, quickly checking on her phone camera that the concealer and nude lipstick she'd applied was still in place.

'What's wrong with your mouth?' Alf said as soon as he saw her. His scrunched face was a smaller version of Luke's earlier, and she hated herself for worrying the two most important people in her life.

'I just banged my lip. Nothing to worry about.' She smiled, but felt the cut open. She dabbed it with the clean tissue she held in her hand.

'On what?' His voice was small and unsure.

She opened her arms. 'Don't look so worried. I left the cupboard door open and forgot when I turned around and bashed my face. Just a silly accident.' He climbed onto her knee and she wrapped her arms around him. She rested her chin on the top of his head and breathed in. He smelled of mud, grass and little boy.

'Does it hurt?' Alf said as Luke walked into the kitchen and went to spoon some chilli into bowls for the three of them.

'Being smacked in the face does generally hurt,' said Luke. 'Let that be a lesson to you, son. No one comes out of a fight unscathed.'

Cassie closed her eyes. Why hadn't she just told Alf the truth? Lying had been a mistake and now Luke would find out.

'Fight?' Alf turned in her lap, and she felt his gaze on her.

His body shifted and she imagined his wide innocent eyes looking at her. 'You said you banged it on a cupboard door.'

She kept her lids closed, hearing Luke breathe in through his nose. 'A fight with a cupboard door is still a fight,' he said, his voice tight.

She opened her eyes, hoping to give him a look of gratitude over their son's head, but he didn't look her way. He avoided her gaze all the time they ate, and for the first time ever her family didn't say a word to each other during a meal.

Scraping the last morsels from his bowl, Alf pointed at a cardboard envelope on the worktop. 'What's that?'

Luke followed his gaze. 'Something I ordered for your mum's party.'

Cassie looked up. With everything that had happened in the last week, she hadn't given the party a single thought.

'Can I see?' Alf stood and collected the envelope.

'Go ahead,' said Luke.

The sound of ripping cardboard filled the silence. Alf took a plastic bag from the package. The contents were slim and brightly coloured. 'What is it?'

'Bunting,' said Luke. 'To decorate the room for the party.'

Bunting. Cassie froze. Alf pulled the multi-coloured mass from the plastic wrapper. At the sight of those celebratory triangles, her mouth filled with saliva. Bile rushed up her throat and she ran to the bathroom to be sick.

15

SIX MONTHS AGO

Meg

The stand had begun to droop with the weight of the phone, so Meg repositioned it, straightened her back against the hard chair and continued to film. 'After we agreed to stop all contact, I didn't think I'd ever see your dad again. And I didn't want to. Truly.' She focused intently on the screen, desperate for future Grace to see she was telling the truth. 'Walking away from him was the hardest thing I've ever had to do.' She gave a small hiccupping laugh. 'Until now, obvs.' She wobbled her head, then wondered if she should re-record that part because this was no time for even pretend levity. She decided against it because it needed to be off the cuff so Grace could see this wasn't in any way rehearsed.

'The placement at your dad's school was my last teaching practice, then I qualified and moved across the river and took a job in Essex to put some distance between us. That's how serious I was about not seeing him again – I moved away from my life and tried to begin a new one in another county.'

Her mind went back to that agonising summer when she'd packed up her things in her student digs in Bromley and relocated to Woodford Green. She didn't know a soul there and all the friends she'd trained with thought she was mad for moving away. She *was* mad, she supposed. Mad with grief. As soon as the thought occurred to her, guilt made sweat prickle in her armpits. She shouldn't equate what she'd experienced with Simon back then with what Grace was coming to terms with now. She'd only known Simon for four months. Grace was losing her mother. It had felt like grief though. She couldn't think of another word for it.

'It was a complete accident that we met again. It was just before Christmas and I was a newly qualified teacher, so I got sent on lots of courses. It never occurred to me your dad might be at one of the workshops. He was already a head of department, so I thought he would be past all that, but I discovered later that he liked to keep up with the training, learn new teaching methods and that kind of thing. He still does. I think he likes a day off classes and a free lunch.' She smiled and shrugged. 'The course was in a hotel in central London. It was at a place I'd been to before, an imposing old building that would have been grand back in the day, but was pretty shabby with huge windows and sagging, stained curtains. There was this off-white Christmas tree outside that looked like it had been brought out every year since the hotel was built, getting grubbier year on year.'

She shook her head. 'I don't know why I'm telling you about the decor. Maybe it's because it's all still so clear to me; as if it were yesterday.' In her mind's eye she travelled past the tree, up the hotel's steps to the huge revolving door, and into the vast reception with its ornate decorative plasterwork and dusty chandelier. She recalled turning right and standing in front of the double doors to what would once have been the hotel's ballroom, pushing them open, then her heart faltering in her chest when she saw Simon sitting in a chair at the far side of the room.

'I didn't know what to do when I saw your dad sitting in that room. I almost turned and walked straight back out, but then he smiled, and it was like a magnet. I do know how corny that sounds.' She raised an eyebrow, then paused, taken aback by the movement of pale naked skin where her eyebrow should have been. She recovered herself and continued. 'I went to sit next to him and...' She paused, remembering the warmth of Simon's body next to hers. That was how it felt back then, as if the heat from his body pulled her in '...and that was it. I was all in again from the second he smiled at me. I couldn't have done anything about it if I tried. Perhaps I should have tried. I should probably have walked away when I had the instinct to... but then I wouldn't have had you, and I don't regret a single second of my life with both of you.'

She cleared her dry throat. 'It was as if me and your dad were pinned together from the minute we saw each other again. We left the course at lunchtime and went to a café nearby. We talked about how awful the last few months had been and your dad told me he'd felt the pull instantly when he saw me, just like I did. We'd both worked so hard to stay apart, but meeting again like that seemed like a sign, you know?' She peered into the screen, willing her daughter to understand. 'We talked for hours, about everything... Well, almost everything.'

Meg dropped her gaze. When she looked up, tears pooled on her lower lids. 'I can't remember why, but your dad went to get something out of his rucksack and this clear plastic bag fell out onto the floor. I picked it up and when I looked at it, I saw it was bunting. It was all primary colours and the label on the front said *Welcome to the world, baby girl!*'

16

PRESENT DAY

Cassie

Vomiting caused the gash in Cassie's lip to open, and it stung as she splashed cold water over it. She looked in the mirror above the sink at the blood, diluted pink as it trickled down her chin.

There was a quiet knock on the bathroom door. 'You all right?'

She held a wad of toilet roll against her lip and opened the door. 'Yeah, sorry.'

'About what? Lying to Alf, or throwing up at the mention of your party?' His head was on one side, and he didn't look angry or disappointed. He looked confused.

Cassie wilted. 'It wasn't about the party.'

Luke held his hands up. 'What is it about, then? You've been acting weird for too long to brush it off.' He rubbed his forehead. 'What really happened to your lip?'

'Exactly what I said.' Cassie took his hand, horrified he thought she might be hiding some kind of attack. 'Honestly.'

'You say "honestly" as if it's a throwaway comment, but it

isn't. You're hiding things and it's making me... well, it's making me wonder what the hell is really going on.' He shoved his hands into the pockets of his jeans, looking defeated.

'I'm not...' She was about to say 'honestly' again but stopped herself in time. She had to give him something to explain her behaviour. It was the least he deserved. 'It was the bunting that triggered this.' She gestured to the toilet bowl. A kidney bean floated on top of the water. She flushed it again.

'You were triggered by bunting?' His lip curled and she could understand his disbelief. It sounded ridiculous when he said it back to her like that.

'Where's Alf?'

'Watching TV.'

'I'll explain. Come with me.' She left the bathroom and walked along the landing to their bedroom. She sat on the bed and tapped the mattress for Luke to do the same.

He pushed the door closed, then sat next to her and leaned against the headboard. 'What's going on in that brain of yours?'

She wanted to climb under the duvet and pull it over her head. Instead, she took a lungful of air and started to speak. 'I've told you my baby was born prematurely—'

'Yes.' Luke put his hand on her leg. 'That's why—'

'And you know I find it hard to talk about what happened around that time, but since I got the email from Simon, I've realised you're right. I haven't dealt with... with what happened, and when he got in touch, it brought a lot of things back to the surface. A lot of very painful things.' If only she'd shared the truth with him back then. She could tell him now. She took in a breath, then let it go when the words wouldn't come. The stakes were just too high.

She sensed Luke nodding his head. She couldn't look at him. She kept her eyes on the fitted wardrobes along the bedroom wall, focusing on the shiny brass handles she'd never liked but had never got around to replacing. 'You know I got very low after I saw Simon with Meg, and that I almost ended the pregnancy?'

'Yes.'

'And you know I discovered they'd started to see each other again just before I gave birth?'

'Yes.' She could feel the warmth of his hand on her thigh.

'Well, that's where the bunting comes in.'

Her mind left the bedroom she shared with Luke and spun back a decade and a half to the sitting room in a different house. She could feel the heaviness of her pregnant belly and the weight of her guilt at still not wanting the life growing inside her. She was sitting in a floral armchair they'd inherited from Simon's grandma with her feet up on a pine coffee table they'd bought at Greenwich Market. It was approaching Christmas and she couldn't wait for the end of term. Pretending to be excited about the baby was even more exhausting than teaching. She hadn't told anyone at work about Simon's infidelity, and as far as everyone she knew was concerned, she was about to start the next, magical phase of her life.

She slapped on a smile and let all the mothers on the staff tell her their birth stories, watching their eyes gleam even as they described episiotomies and mastitis. The love they felt for their progeny glowed out of them, adding a new layer of self-hatred for her unnatural response to the baby nestled inside her.

Worse still, she sometimes wished her own life was over. Not in an actively thinking of taking her own life kind of way – she didn't even have the energy to think seriously about that – more of a disappointed at still being alive when she opened her eyes each morning kind of way. What sort of mother-to-be would prefer to no longer exist? What kind of mother would she be to a child she had only wanted for the first two hours she'd known of its existence? Her self-loathing sat in her stomach along with the baby. She imagined it seeping up the umbilical cord and poisoning the poor, innocent child.

When she heard Simon's key in the lock that day, she made the effort to smile. He'd tried so hard since she'd agreed to keep the baby, doing most things around the house and preparing for the baby's arrival. But she knew he was pretending too. The connection between them had been severed and she couldn't see a way to repair it. They were two bad actors caught in an eternal, terrible play.

'Hiya,' he said. 'How was your day?' He bent to kiss her. His lips were dry and barely skimmed hers. He smelled of coffee. He didn't usually drink coffee in the afternoon.

'All right. How was the course?'

He looked away. 'Fine. You know what those things are like.'

'You're later than I expected.' She hated herself for the sharpness in her tone. She couldn't stop herself from needling him, to show him she was always vigilant, that she hadn't forgotten what he was capable of. They used to speak to each other with such gentleness and warmth. She missed that. She missed adoring him. She missed feeling loved.

He reached into his rucksack and pulled out a plastic wrapper with something multi-coloured inside. 'I did a detour to pick this up.' He handed her a bag with *Welcome to the world, baby girl!* printed on a label.

The baby kicked. She put her hand on her stomach and felt the hard shape of a foot or an elbow under her taut skin. They'd found out the baby's sex at the twenty-week scan, but Cassie had never really thought of the baby as a girl. She avoided thinking about it at all. Now, suddenly, with the sight of this bunting welcoming this new, perfect little human into this imperfect world, along with the very real sensation of her wriggling inside her, a shard of hope seared through the bleakness that had swamped Cassie for months.

She smiled at Simon, the unusual feeling of her lips curving upwards in pleasure instead of an impression of it bringing tears to her eyes. Simon's eyes were wet too, but when she looked closer, there was pain etched in the deep lines of his face. 'What's wrong?'

He shook his head and tears spilled onto his cheeks. 'I'm so sorry, Cass.' He sat heavily on the sofa.

Fear knotted her insides and her uterus tightened in a Braxton Hicks contraction so strong it made her gasp. 'Why? What's wrong?' She put her hand on her abdomen. It was rock hard.

'I'm sorry.' He covered his face with his hand. His shoulders rose and fell in great heaving sobs.

'What's happened?' Adrenaline coursed through Cassie's veins. 'Simon?'

He curled his arms around his head. 'I didn't plan to see her again. It just happened.'

'Who?' But Cassie knew. She stood. Her head spun. 'Who, Simon? Is it her?'

He didn't reply, just rocked back and forth, cradling his head in his hands.

Cassie needed to hear him say it. She moved towards him, ready to grab his hair and make him face her, but her foot caught on the coffee table and she tripped, lurching forwards. A ripping pain scorched across the bottom of her stomach and she cried out in agony as she fell.

17

PRESENT DAY

Cassie

Luke's eyes were full of tears when she turned to him. 'And that's why the sight of the bunting made me react like that,' she said. 'After everything being brought to the fore last week, it was the proverbial straw that broke me.' She patted down the pillow behind her head so she could see him clearly. The compassion on his face made her love him even more. It was herself she couldn't bear.

'I'm so sorry you went through that, Cassie.'

Cassie imagined him in his therapy room, talking to one of his clients. He would ensure they knew they were safe and being listened to. He was a good counsellor and a good husband. He deserved the truth. But it was too late to tell him everything, she knew that in her bones. Even an emotionally intelligent man like Luke couldn't forgive the unforgivable. Perhaps if she told him a little more about how she felt afterwards, he might be able to help her to heal a little. Then she might be able to climb out of the dark hole she was falling down which was affecting all of them. 'You know I had to have an emergency Caesarean because I tore the placenta when I fell?'

Luke nodded. 'The placenta tore. You didn't tear it. It was a tragic accident.'

Cassie gave him a weak smile for his kindness and turned her eyes back to the brass handles on the wardrobe doors. 'When I was discharged from hospital, I was in a lot of pain, physically and emotionally. I couldn't bear to have Simon in the house after I knew he was back with her, and as you know, my parents weren't exactly going to scoop me up in a loving embrace and make everything better.'

Luke put an arm around her shoulder and pulled her in. She shuffled down the bed and rested her head on his chest. His heartbeat pulsed under her ear, its regular pattern soothing. She could smell the sandalwood scent he always sprayed in the patch of dark hair under his clavicle before putting on his top. 'I can see now that I'd been depressed since the day I discovered the affair. I never really recovered from the shock. I don't know if it was because I was already in a highly emotional state after finding out I was pregnant, but it seemed like my brain chemistry changed that day, and from then onwards everything seemed pointless. I had no energy. It was a struggle to keep my eyes open.'

'Even if you'd been on good form, a Caesarean is major surgery, and it takes weeks to get over a general anaesthetic, even before you factor in—'

'It was more than that.' She searched for the right words to try to make him understand quite how bleak she'd felt. 'It was like everything was glued down, my eyelids, my feet... Everything was heavy, too heavy to move. And I didn't want to move. I didn't feel like I could. I was so, so tired. I'd put the exhaustion down to the pregnancy before, but afterwards it was even worse. I didn't want to do anything but sleep. Being awake hurt. Everything was so raw and painful.'

'I can't even imagine what you went through. I hate to think of you suffering like that.' His breath warmed the top of her head.

Her tears soaked into Luke's T-shirt. His arm tightened around her shoulder. She continued. 'And I couldn't shake the weight of it. I stopped brushing my teeth, washing my hair. I didn't open the curtains. Everywhere I went in the house, I'd see something of Simon's, like his favourite mug or a pair of socks, but it wasn't even that. He was living with Meg in Essex by then and I knew I didn't want him back. I hadn't even wanted him when we decided to keep the baby, but I wanted to at least try, for the baby's sake. After I left hospital I didn't ever want to see him again, but he kept checking up on me.'

In her head she heard his knock on the door. He would knock and knock and when she didn't reply, he'd use his key and let himself in. She wanted to change the lock, but making the phone call to arrange it was too hard. 'He'd open the curtains and the windows and go around the house clearing up, telling me I had to get help.'

'Did you?'

'I didn't go to the doctor, if that's what you mean. I was convinced he was the problem. His affair caused the depression in the first place. The baby came early because I fell after his confession, and so I blamed him for that too. I was convinced that if he was out of my life for good, I could start to get better.' She wiped her hand across her eyes, then her wet hand on the duvet cover. 'And so, in the end, he agreed. He left me to get on with my life and we made a pact that neither he nor Meg would ever contact me again. And now he's broken that promise and those dark, heavy feelings I thought were gone for good are back, and I hate him for making me feel like this again.' She hated herself too, but she couldn't tell Luke why, so she swallowed down the guilt and self-loathing.

Luke's ribcage rose and fell with steady breaths. His body was warm against her cheek and his arm rested over her, telling her she was secure with him. That was all she wanted, to be safe in her small family. She had to protect that at all costs. Luke shifted and she knew he was going to speak, so she quickly added, 'That's why I can't engage with Simon. I was right, back then. It took a long time, but I recovered. I can't allow him to threaten my mental health like this. I can't have anything to do with that man, so please don't ask me to.'

Luke let out a breath and she knew she'd cut him off in time. 'I love you,' she said. 'And I love our family. We have a good life, don't we?'

She looked up at him, and her heart swelled when she saw the love in his eyes as he returned her gaze. 'We do have a good life. I love you too.' He bent his head to kiss the uninjured side of her mouth softly, then he drew back. 'I won't ask you to have any more contact with Simon, but I do have one request.'

Cassie tensed, sure he was going to ask her to go for therapy. She didn't want to do that. She couldn't open the box she'd locked away in her head. She wouldn't survive it.

'You know what it was like for me, never knowing whether I could believe what my dad said, so I need you to be upfront with me, Cass. Your problems are my problems, and while I understand we need to protect Alf from some things, I want us to be open and honest with him too, as far as we possibly can.'

She pulled him into her, the cut on her lip throbbing against his chest. 'I will,' she said. 'I promise.' Bile rose in her throat at the lie.

18

PRESENT DAY

Cassie

Cassie thought clearing the air with Luke would make things easier, but the feeling of dread didn't lift. Added to that, the pain in her lip woke her every time she turned onto the side where it was cut, and her spiralling thoughts made it difficult to get back to sleep. The memories she'd managed to suppress, or at least ignore for years, were coming back in vivid technicolour. By the time Monday morning arrived, her exhaustion caused her brain to feel slow and foggy.

'Up and at 'em,' she said, pulling Alf's curtains wide and blinking against the bright sunshine. With the fabric still in her hands, she wondered how long it would be until he was too old for the curtains and matching duvet, patterned with red, orange and blue dinosaurs. The thought made her want to cry. She wanted to preserve him in aspic, keep him small, at an age where she could protect him. That defensive urge added to her resolve to keep her past where it was, so it couldn't tear her little boy's world in two.

She turned to her son, who was curled in the foetal position, gripping his covers in tight fists. 'Come on, you.' She crossed to his bed, pushed his feet aside and sat down. 'Rise and shine, lovely boy.' He didn't move. This wasn't like him. He usually jumped out of bed, ready to embrace the day.

'I've got a tummy ache.' His voice was muffled against his pillow.

'Say again.'

He turned his head and half opened his eyes. 'I'm not well. My tummy hurts.'

Cassie touched his forehead. It was warm, but not unusually so. 'How does it hurt? Is it a sharp pain or an ache?' She put her hand on his back, the feel of his ribs through his cotton pyjamas making her wish he ate more. Would she always have a million tiny little worries about her boy? Right now she was calculating whether he had food poisoning, appendicitis, or what her mum used to call lazyitis whenever Cassie herself asked for a day off school.

'It just hurts.'

That wasn't going to make the diagnosis process any easier. She checked her watch. Mornings were minutely timed and they were already a few minutes behind schedule. 'Some breakfast will help. Come on, up you get.'

Alf groaned, then rolled out of bed and flopped onto the floor.

'Stop messing about, Alf. I haven't got time for this.'

Luke stopped in the doorway. 'What's up?'

'He says he's got a tummy ache.'

'I *have* got a tummy ache,' Alf moaned, lying on his back on the carpet and rubbing his tummy like a caricature of someone with an aching gut.

'Okay. Sorry to hear that, son. Let me have a quick word

with Mummy,' said Luke. He nodded for Cassie to follow him into their bedroom. When they were inside, he spoke quietly. 'That's a classic school avoidance tummy ache if ever I saw one.'

'Why would he want to avoid school? He loves school.'

Luke rubbed his hand over his face. 'It might not be about school. It could be that he's felt the tensions here and—'

'I'm doing my best,' Cassie whispered. 'I've been smiling like a loon for most of the weekend.' She really had tried. Luke had no idea how hard.

He put a hand on her shoulder. 'I'm not blaming you. I'm just saying he might be feeling destabilised and hyper-vigilant because the atmosphere around here has been different to usual. He might be worried about what happened to your lip. I know you want to protect him, but sometimes children want to protect their parents too, especially their mothers. He might want to keep you in his sights. He could be having a lot of complicated feelings right now.'

Cassie slumped against the wall. Counsellor Luke could be equally perceptive and annoying. More guilt settled on the layers already calcified inside her. 'What do we do?'

Luke pulled his lips back in an apologetic grimace. 'I've got my supervisor session this morning... Can you...?'

'I can't just take the day off.'

'I know, it's not ideal. But you're not feeling great yourself, are you?' He let his head fall to the side. 'And it would only be one day. It would probably do both of you the world of good.'

He could say that again, and it wasn't like him to suggest something as unethical as taking a sick day when she was capable of working, so he must have really meant it.

They turned at the sound of Alf's feet on the carpet. His chin puckered when he looked at them. 'I'm not pretending. It hurts here.' He lifted his pyjama top and Cassie melted at the sight of his tender pink flesh. He pointed at his belly button and Cassie remembered the exact moment the stub of his umbilical cord came away; the thing that had connected him to her, allowed her to nourish and care for him, even before she held him in her arms. She recalled how frightened she'd been that the placenta might rupture like last time. More than that, she worried she wouldn't be able to love him. All the time they were trying for a baby, that fear paralysed her. But she had. From the very second she'd known she was pregnant she had loved him with a fierceness she didn't know existed in her. He had shown her she was capable of loving her child, and that had been healing beyond measure.

'I'll stay home with you,' she said. 'Let me call both schools, then we'll snuggle up in here, shall we?' She peeled back the duvet on the king-sized bed, smiling as Alf bounced into the bed and snuggled down, already seeming to have fully recovered.

She didn't regret staying home for a second, not even when he squirmed and wanted to get up ten minutes later. Not when he ate two bowls of cereal, or wanted to go on the trampoline before lunch. If she could spend every day cocooned away from the world with her son, worn out from bouncing, next to her on the sofa under a blanket watching the Disney Channel while she snoozed, she would.

Wonderful as it was to have a duvet day with Alf, it was clear Luke had been right; this was about avoiding school. While she gazed at his gorgeous face, laughing at the cartoon on the TV, she wondered what was going on in his head – and how much of it was down to her.

* * *

'Have you got a thick lip? Is that why you were off yesterday?' said Becca when Cassie slumped into a chair in the staffroom at first break the following day. She put on her red-framed reading glasses and examined Cassie's face. 'It wasn't Luke, was it? It's always the ones you least expect.' She winked.

Cassie shook her head, quietly pleased that it was so unlikely Luke would hit a woman that Becca could take the piss. Her lip was healing at an astonishing speed, so she was disappointed Becca had even noticed it. 'You shouldn't joke about that.'

'Okay. Sorry. What happened? And don't tell me you walked into a door.'

Shame of having used the same cliché as many genuine victims of domestic violence when she spoke to her child washed through Cassie. 'If I tell you, you've got to keep it to yourself.'

'Shit.' Becca's face grew serious. 'I was kidding about Luke. He didn't—'

'Of course he didn't. For God's sake, Becca, you know him better than that.'

Becca lifted her hands. 'Okay, sorry. I'll zip it and listen for once.'

Cassie moved forwards on the seat and gestured for Becca to do the same. 'When I went to get my car after the pub on Friday, a group of boys were fighting outside school.' She told Becca the rest, including the part about swearing at Oliver Simms.

'And you didn't come in and report that straight away because...?' Becca lifted her top lip over her teeth.

'Because Oliver Simms' parents already think I've accused him of something he didn't do. Even though he did.' The unfairness of that still stung, even though she was in no position to judge someone for lying.

'But he did elbow you in the gob.'

'Yes.'

'In front of witnesses.'

Cassie rolled her eyes. 'Oh, come on. As if any of his cronies are going to tell the truth.' She huffed. 'And I did drag his clothes and call him a little fucker.'

'He is a little fucker.' Becca crossed her arms and pursed her lips.

'Oh, well, that's all right, then. When the Chair of the governors and the kid's parents ask why I swore at their darling boy, I have a cast iron case, which I'm sure they'll all agree on.'

Becca nodded decisively. 'Exactly. But it won't come to that. He's hardly going to have complained, is he?'

Out of the corner of her eye, Cassie saw Keith Finnegan march into the staffroom. When she turned, he was staring at her, grim-faced, and she understood how wrong Becca was.

19

PRESENT DAY

Cassie

The atmosphere in Finnegan's office was distinctly cooler than it had been last time she sat across the desk from him. His moustache drooped at the corners and his eyes were narrow slits behind his glasses. Cassie made fists in her lap and dug her nails into her palms as tears collected in her eyes. She was mortified. She was a grown woman, a professional; why on earth was she on the verge of crying before anything had even been said?

'I'm sure you realise I've called you in here because of an allegation made against you.'

'Allegation?' She tried to keep her voice level.

Finnegan sighed. 'Oliver Simms' father says you physically and verbally assaulted his son on Friday evening.'

'Assaulted?' She blinked, the cut on her lip tingled. 'I tried to pull him away from a fight,' she said. Surely Finnegan knew her better than this?

Finnegan seemed to notice her lip for the first time. He

leaned forwards and peered closely, then sat back. 'I need to know the whole story, Cassie. I should have been made aware of this immediately after the altercation happened.'

'The altercation, as you call it, didn't happen between me and Oliver Simms. It was a boy from North Hill High who was being kicked senseless. What should I have done? Left them to it?' She touched her lip then checked her finger for blood. It was dry, thank goodness. 'I was just trying to stop him being battered. It was instinct.'

'I don't doubt you had the best intentions, but... this happened on school grounds?'

'Well, yes.' She shifted in the chair. There was no use pretending because he clearly already knew.

His eyelids fluttered as if he was trying to hold back his emotions. 'As you are aware, anything that happens within the school's parameter should be reported. Why didn't you fill in a report? Jack is always on the premises.'

'It was outside school hours, so...' That was not a valid excuse and, by the disappointed look on Finnegan's face, he knew it too.

'And what happened to your lip?' He sat forwards and inspected her face. His eyes appeared to grow behind his lenses.

She dropped her gaze to her lap, knowing this weakened her reasoning for not telling anyone about what happened. 'Oliver Simms elbowed me in the mouth when I was trying to stop the two boys from smashing each other's faces in.'

'He attacked *you*?'

Cassie shook her head. 'It wasn't an attack. I'm pretty sure it was unintentional.'

Finnegan took his glasses off and rubbed at them furiously with the bottom of his tie. 'He says he was defending himself.'

'What?' Cassie's mouth fell open. 'Self-defence? So he's

saying I attacked him? That's ludicrous.' She stared at her boss. 'Surely you can see how absurd that is?' He knew her. They'd been colleagues for more than ten years. Surely he couldn't be taking this seriously? She waited for him to raise his eyes to the ceiling and say it was the most stupid thing he'd ever heard.

Instead, he carefully re-positioned his glasses on his nose and looked at her with a serious expression before examining a printed piece of paper in front of him. 'His father alleges you dragged at his clothes and called Oliver' – he paused – 'a little fucker.' He glanced over the frame of his glasses, then continued. 'He apparently said you smelled of alcohol and he had to shake you off, which is when his elbow slipped and made contact with your mouth.'

'That's not what happened.'

'Please avail me of what did.'

It was Cassie's turn to pause. 'Well, that is what happened, but not in that order. I only swore at him after he split my lip.'

'So you did drag at his clothes and swear at him?'

'Well... yes.'

'A fourteen-year-old boy?'

'He was...'

'Go on.' His head cocked to the side.

She tried to find the right words. 'He was part of a baying mob.'

'Was he physically involved in the fight?'

She closed her eyes. 'No, but—'

'Had you drunk alcohol before this unfortunate incident?'

Her scalp tightened. 'Yes, but only one glass. I was driving. This is all being blown out of proportion. I only didn't report it because it didn't seem worth the bother. The boys involved didn't seem hurt, and the group dissipated as soon as...'

'As soon as they saw a teacher who smelled of alcohol bleeding from the mouth and swearing at a student?'

When he put it like that it did sound pretty bad. 'I'm sorry, Keith. It was a lapse of judgement, I admit that, but I didn't' – she waved her hand at the paper – 'attack him or whatever it says on there.'

Finnegan leaned his elbows on the green leather of the desk and knitted his long fingers in front of him. 'Simms' father has alleged you have a vendetta against his son, as demonstrated by accusing him of criminal damage, followed by the events of Friday evening.'

She pulled her chin back. 'A vendetta? Are they part of the Mob? That's preposterous.'

'I take part of the blame for mentioning your name in the car incident, and I suspect this allegation is a pre-emptive strike because the boy was frightened you'd report what happened and he'd be seriously reprimanded.'

Cassie saw a chink of light in this hopeless situation. 'So you might be able to tell his parents I don't plan to take any action and this could all go away?'

'I'm sorry, Cassie, that's not within my power. They've made an official complaint against you, which will have to be fully investigated.' He rested his palms flat on the table. 'It gives me no pleasure to do this, Cassie, but because this is an alleged physical and verbal assault on a student, I have no choice but to suspend you until further notice.'

Cassie's vision blurred. 'Suspend me?' Surely she couldn't have heard that right. 'I broke up a fight, that's all. I was trying to do the right thing.'

'And had you reported it, we'd be able to defend your position, but as it stands, it looks like you were trying to cover up wrongdoing.' He stood. 'I'm sorry, but I have to ask you to leave the school grounds. Please attend a meeting with myself and the governors at midday tomorrow. At this stage the police are not involved—'

'The police?' Cassie's head swam. This couldn't be happening. After leaving Finnegan's office, time seemed to warp, and the next time Cassie became fully aware of what was going on around her, she was sitting in her car on her drive and her phone was ringing so loudly it snapped her from her trance.

20

PRESENT DAY

Cassie

Cassie took the phone from her bag. The screen told her it was a call from Alf's school. She still hadn't absorbed the fact she'd been suspended from work and now she had to speak to the teachers in charge of her son. She accepted the call with shaking fingers. 'Hello.'

'Hello. Is that Mrs Monroe?'

'Speaking.' Cassie's hand trembled so hard she had to hold the phone tightly against her ear.

'It's Mrs Miah from Hillside Primary here. Alf is okay, but there has been an incident with another child. I was hoping you'd be able to come in and speak to me about it and collect Alf.'

'What kind of incident?' That word again. 'Is Alf all right?' Teachers didn't ask you to collect your child without good reason.

'As I said, he's not badly hurt—'

Cassie's blood chilled. 'So, he is hurt?'

'Please don't panic, Mrs Monroe, Alf is beside me now, quite safe. If you could make your way to school as soon as possible, I'll fill you in on the details.'

'I'll come now.' Cassie turned the key in the ignition. 'Please tell him I'm on my way.'

Her mind racing, she almost collided with a parked car on the road leading to the school's entrance and when she pulled into a visitor spot in the car park, she had to gulp in air to stop herself from crying. She couldn't let Alf see her in this state. She imagined how she'd respond if a parent of one of her form turned up in the emotional condition she was in now. She might raise it as a safeguarding issue. That was the last thing she needed, so she carefully wiped the mascara stains from under her eyes and took deep breaths in through her nose and out through her mouth to try to regulate her central nervous system.

When she thought she could stand without her knees buckling, she left the car and walked to the school's reception. She pressed the intercom. 'Hello, it's Alf Monroe's mum. Mrs Miah asked me to come in.'

The door clicked open. She stepped inside. It was almost lunchtime and the smell of various recipes cooking at once permeated the reception area, making Cassie's stomach churn. She approached the small woman behind a glass screen. She recognised her face but couldn't come up with a name. She knew from working in a school herself how important it was to acknowledge the office staff; they were the ones who truly ran a school.

She was about to speak when a voice called her name from behind her. 'Mrs Monroe.' Mrs Miah stood with her hands clasped in front of her floral dress. She was a round-faced woman in her fifties who was naturally smiley, exactly the kind of teacher Cassie would have chosen for Alf, but today her face was stern, and for once her marionette lines appeared far deeper than her laughter lines. 'Please sign in, then follow me.'

Cassie nodded, then signed her name in the book on the desk in front of the screen with wavering handwriting. She took the proffered lanyard with 'Visitor' in bold type and then followed Mrs Miah through a door at the far end into a small room with only one small window high on the back wall. 'Please take a seat.' Mrs Miah gestured to one of four grey school chairs which sat in front of shelves filled with copier paper and stacks of different coloured workbooks. How typical of a state school to have to hold meetings with parents in a stockroom.

Mrs Miah left to collect Alf and it was all Cassie could do to stay seated. The room felt like a cage, and her son was about to be thrown in with her. When the door opened, Alf rushed towards her and buried his head in her neck. She pulled him back to examine his face. A large flesh-coloured plaster was stuck above his left eyebrow. 'What happened?'

He started to cry.

'It's all right, sweetheart.' She kissed his cheeks and wiped the tears from under his eyes. 'I'm here now, it's okay.'

'Please take a seat, Alf.' Mrs Miah's tone was stern and Cassie looked up, surprised. Surely she should be comforting him too? He was clearly injured. Alf drew away from Cassie and sat, his eyes on the blue linoleum flooring. Cassie couldn't bear the distress on his beautiful face. She wanted to pull him onto her knee.

'What's going on? What happened to your head?'

Alf snivelled. Cassie reached out for his hand, but he didn't take hers. He tucked his fingers under his thighs.

'I'm sorry to have to tell you, but I'm afraid Alf attacked

another boy during morning break.' Mrs Miah spoke over the sound of Alf's sobs.

'Attacked?' Cassie couldn't believe her ears. 'What do you mean attacked?' The information couldn't permeate her brain. It was too outrageous. Alf was a kind, gentle boy. He didn't even like her to kill wasps with the spray she kept under the sink at home.

'He lashed out at a boy in Year Five. Unfortunately that boy is considerably bigger than Alf, and when the child retaliated with a push to the chest, Alf fell and scraped his head. A first aider has had a good look at it and we are reassured it's a minor graze, not anything more—'

'I'm sorry,' Cassie interrupted. 'You're saying Alf hit an older boy, a bigger boy?'

'Yes.'

'Not the other way around?' None of this made sense.

'We have several witnesses who corroborate the other boy's version of events. Of course, he's being reprimanded for retaliating, but there is no question Alf started the altercation.'

Cassie had never heard the words 'incident' and 'altercation' so many times in one day. She certainly never expected to hear them in relation to her little boy. She turned to him and spoke gently. 'What on earth happened, Alf?'

He shook his head, sending a cascade of tears onto his grey school trousers.

'He wouldn't tell us what started the disagreement,' said Mrs Miah. 'I was hoping he might tell you.'

'Please, Alf. Look at me.' She touched his elfin chin to try to draw his eyes to hers, but he resisted. 'Alf, come on. Just tell us what happened. This isn't like you. You don't go around hitting people for no reason.'

He shook his head again.

'Despite this being somewhat out of character, we have to treat it in accordance with school policy.'

Cassie nodded, trying to take it all in. 'Is the other child hurt?'

Mrs Miah shook her head. 'It's more the intention than the consequences we need to discuss.' She turned her attention to Alf. 'It would help all of us, yourself included, if you told us why you wanted to hurt the other boy.' Her voice softened. 'Alf, I know this isn't like you. You must've had a reason to lash out.'

He shook his head again.

'Unless we know why you did what you did, we can't help you,' said Cassie. 'I know something bad must've happened, or you wouldn't ever want to hurt someone else.' She glanced up at Mrs Miah, slightly ashamed her son wouldn't even look at her.

Mrs Miah sighed then stood. 'All right, Alf, I'm going to take you to sit in the office for a minute whilst I talk to your mum.'

Alf stood, tears still rolling down his cheeks, and Cassie had to stop herself from grabbing his hand and marching him from the building. The world was on its head. This wasn't fair. The wrong people were in trouble and there seemed to be nothing she could do about it. She watched, feeling impotent and distraught, as her little boy was led from the room.

When Mrs Miah returned, her expression was softer. 'I'm sorry I had to call you in. We would usually deal with something like this in-house and then talk to you at the end of the school day, but since Alf was so het up, and he wouldn't give us any reason for lashing out, I thought having you here might help.'

'What did the other boy say?'

Mrs Miah shrugged. 'Just that Alf hit him for no reason and he just pushed him away.'

'I'm a teacher too, Mrs Miah.' Cassie leaned forwards. 'And I know as well as you do that these things rarely happen in a vacuum. What do you think really happened?'

Mrs Miah's throat bobbed as she swallowed. 'There were enough witnesses to corroborate that Alf threw a punch. I'm afraid what I think is irrelevant.'

'Not if Alf's being bullied,' said Cassie, fire building in her centre. 'You know Alf, he would never attack anyone unless he was seriously provoked.'

'That may well be the case, but from what I can gather, he's never come across this other child until today, and his recent behaviour has been...' She tucked a finger into the top of her dress and pulled it away from her skin as if to let in some air. 'He hasn't been himself for over a week.'

Cassie thought of yesterday morning's stomach ache, which had miraculously disappeared the minute he was told he didn't have to come into school. 'I honestly think he's being bullied.' It was obvious, and whatever happened today confirmed it.

Mrs Miah scratched her nose. 'I'm not so sure. I noticed a difference in him early last week, so I've been keeping an eye on him.'

Not so close an eye that Alf hadn't ended up injured, Cassie thought, ignoring the fact that she knew Alf had been unsettled because of her.

Mrs Miah spoke again. 'I was actually wondering if everything was okay at home?'

Cassie stiffened. 'What do you mean?' She knew full well what Mrs Miah meant. She'd wondered the same about many of her charges over the years when they'd behaved differently to usual.

'Alf is generally such a cheerful boy, but he's been withdrawn over the last week, as if his mind is elsewhere. I was wondering if he needed support because of changes at home.'

Cassie bristled. 'Thank you, but everything is fine. He's a sensitive boy. If he is being bullied, then that would obviously preoccupy him.' She had to cling on to that, otherwise the guilt would overwhelm her.

'As I said, I've been watching him, and his friendship group is the same, and until today he hasn't had any unusual interactions with other children.'

'Until today,' Cassie repeated, 'and, as a teacher myself, I am aware of how hard it is to keep an eye on one student when so many others need your attention at the same time.'

Mrs Miah nodded. 'True.' She flattened out a crease in the fabric of her dress, as if trying to create order.

'So what are the repercussions for today?' Cassie wanted to get out of there. The cupboard was stifling.

'We'll keep Alf in internal exclusion for the rest of the day, then the head teacher will decide what his punishment will be.'

Cassie stood. 'Since Alf was off sick yesterday, and he's in exclusion anyway, I'll take him home now.'

'I'm not sure—'

'I shouldn't have brought him in. He's clearly unwell. That could be behind his strange behaviour today.'

Her tone clearly told Mrs Miah that she was going to take her son home with or without her permission, so the older woman nodded and went to get Cassie's little boy.

21

PRESENT DAY

Cassie

'Harsh as it sounds, I think he needs to learn to face the consequences of his actions,' Luke said when Cassie told him she was keeping Alf off school the following day. 'I still can't get my head around him hitting another kid, but he did, so we can't reward him for it. What will he learn from that?' He chewed his toast miserably.

'I'm not rewarding him,' said Cassie, handing him a steaming mug of coffee and sitting beside him at the table. The morning sun shone in through the patio door. It was going to be a hot day and the light painted Luke in a soft glow. It suited him. Cassie thought it must be nice to attract light, instead of always carrying darkness around like her. 'I think he's too fragile to go in today. He's barely stopped crying. Don't you think he's punishing himself enough? There's no point us adding to whatever action school decides to take. We need to be his safe place.'

'Yeah, of course.' Luke blew on top of the coffee and took a sip. 'But he needs to learn to share what's going on in his head.

This refusal to tell us why he did what he did is deeply unhealthy. You know that. And he can't go around doing shit like this and think he can just get away with it.'

That was true, but Cassie knew the feeling of being ashamed by her own thoughts and actions well enough to understand what Alf was going through, even if he wouldn't tell her why. 'He's seven.'

'He knows right from wrong, Cass, and he needs to learn to talk about things. Bottling emotions up is like carrying poison around inside you.'

How right he was. She could feel the poison buried inside her seeping through her veins again, affecting every decision she made. 'I'll try to coax it out of him today.'

'Don't you need to be in work?' He put his mug on the kitchen counter and checked his watch.

Cassie had weighed up whether to tell Luke about her suspension, but since she'd decided to keep Alf at home anyway, she thought she'd delay it until after the meeting with the board of governors. No point worrying him unnecessarily, especially with both of them being concerned about Alf. She hoped the governors would take note of her exemplary record and see sense. Then she'd be completely vindicated and back in work as normal the following day. She told herself she wasn't lying, she was just saving Luke from any undue stress. 'I have an exam class I can't miss last period, that's all. I'll ask Marie next door to sit with him. She's always offering. I won't be more than an hour and a half.'

He paused, lips tight, then sighed loudly. 'Okay, let me know if Marie can't do it and I'll try to re-jig my schedule.' He took a slug of coffee, then wiped his mouth with his hand. 'He needs to be back in school tomorrow, okay? I shouldn't have suggested he had the day off yesterday. It shouldn't become a pattern. I can't say I'm happy about any of this.'

Cassie took his hand. 'He will. I promise.'

'And I'm going to have a long talk with him tonight about telling the truth and learning how to regulate his emotions.'

She squeezed his fingers hard then let go. 'I would expect nothing less.' She stood and took their plates to the dishwasher. 'Now, off you go. You don't want to be late.'

Luke wasn't at risk of being late. Cassie just couldn't bear to be around his goodness when she felt sick with shame.

* * *

The meeting with the governors was torturous. Cassie was truthful about her lapse of judgement and admitted that the previous complaint from Oliver Simms' parents, and the fact she'd sworn at the boy had played a part in her poor decision making. She argued that having had one glass of wine at the end of the week was not relevant and it had in no way impacted her behaviour. The memory of having told Becca she felt tipsy burned in her head as she said goodbye to the four portly, middle-aged men who constituted the main part of the governing body of the school. Back out in the heat of the day, she made her way to her car, looking forward to turning the air-conditioning on.

Sweat made her shirt stick to her back, and her brain fizzed with the stress of not knowing how the meeting had gone. Finnegan had ended the proceedings with the promise she'd receive an email 'in due course'. What did that even mean? She was glad the bell hadn't yet sounded for the end of the school day, so she was alone in the car park and didn't have to answer any awkward questions from her colleagues.

She dug in her handbag for her car keys, finding them at the bottom along with some used tissues and a couple of extra strong mints. When she looked up, a girl of around fourteen was standing by Finnegan's Tesla, looking directly at her. She didn't recognise her face so continued towards her car, but when she glanced around, the girl had turned to watch her. The blueness of her eyes was striking, even from a distance, and there was something unnerving about her stillness and the intensity of her gaze.

When Cassie unlocked her car and opened the door, the girl strode over, as if propelled by something urgent. 'Cassie?'

Cassie stopped. The girl wore jeans and a cream sweatshirt, not a uniform, so she wasn't from Stonehaven. 'Yes? Can I help you?' The girl's cheeks were flushed pink, and Cassie was struck by how perfectly symmetrical her features were. Added to the freckles across the bridge of her nose, she looked like a cartoon image of a pretty teenager.

She came to a halt a metre away from Cassie. She swallowed hard, her cheeks turning vivid red. 'Cassie Monroe?'

'That's right.' Ice crept through Cassie's veins when it dawned on her where she'd seen those beautiful blue eyes before.

'I'm...' The girl swallowed again. 'I'm Grace.'

22

FOURTEEN YEARS AGO

Cassie

Cassie's vision blurred when she opened her eyes. Hazy white and blue shapes moved around her. She swallowed. Her dry throat scratched. There were voices, but they were muffled and indistinct. She closed her eyes again and faded into sleep.

A sharp stabbing in her abdomen made her gasp. She opened her eyes and tried to focus. A woman wearing a blue hairnet leaned over her. 'Hello, Cassie. You're in the recovery room now, my lovely.'

Cassie opened her mouth to speak, but the pain in her gut stole her words. Tears rolled from her eyes. A sharp sting made her turn her head. The woman was sticking a needle into her arm.

'That should help with the pain.'

Cassie closed her eyes again. The light in the room was too bright. She wanted to go back into the dark, away from the hurt in her abdomen and in her head. But now the fug was lifting and thoughts of what happened pounded into her brain.

Images of Simon's stricken face as she writhed on the floor in agony swirled behind her eyes, then the sound of an ambulance's wailing siren. Tears were collecting in her ears. She lifted her hand to wipe them dry but something tugged at the skin on the back so she let it drop.

It was over, at least. The unbearable darkness that had descended when she'd first seen Simon with Meg had finally come to this awful, tragic conclusion. How fitting it had happened on the day when he'd admitted seeing Meg again. It was inevitable, somehow, that it should end like this. When she'd first felt the blood between her legs after she fell, losing the baby felt like no more than any of them deserved; them for their betrayal, her for wishing she wasn't carrying his child.

She hoped the baby hadn't suffered. She hoped she had never sensed she was unwanted, unloved. Cassie had tried so hard to visualise a life where she and Simon were loving parents to a thriving little girl, but her mind wouldn't conjure the picture. She could admit now that she'd almost expected things to end this way, almost willed it.

Another pain seared through her when she finally admitted to herself that part of her had actually hoped for this. How many times had she wished the baby didn't exist? In her darkest moments, she'd imagined a life where she had gone through with the termination, she and Simon had split up and she was starting a new life on her own. When she imagined that life, she felt lighter, hopeful, even. Whenever that vision disappeared and she came back to her senses, her heavy stomach reminded her she was stuck in an existence that felt unbearable and she had no way out. This was her way out, and she deserved to suffer for wanting it.

More tears tumbled from her eyes. She was still crying when a nurse lifted the metal sides of the bed and a porter rolled her out of the recovery room and into the corridor, then into a lift to another floor. The lift shuddered to a halt and the doors swooshed open, the air chilling the water on Cassie's cheeks.

'Nearly there, pet,' said the nurse who was walking alongside her. They pushed her through double doors into a blue painted room and arranged the bed against the wall next to a bedside unit. The nurse unhooked the drip bag from where it hung above the bed and attached it to a tall metal stand. She took a tissue from the box on top of the unit. 'It's all right. It's all right, sweetheart. You'll see your baby soon.'

The horror of that hit Cassie like a train. She'd read about parents being allowed to spend time with their stillborn babies and she wouldn't be able to bear it. It was too much. She wanted to say no, to tell this nurse with the kind eyes that she truly couldn't bear to hold the baby she had let down before she'd been able to take a breath.

The gentleness of the nurse made Cassie cry harder. It was too much. She had wanted her baby gone and now she was dead. It was like a nightmare. She couldn't cradle her dead baby. She was too much of a monster to be allowed near her.

'I'll be back in a little while.' The nurse smiled gently and put a button on the end of a cord next to Cassie's hand. 'But you can always press this if you need me.'

She left and Cassie could hear her speaking to someone in low tones in the corridor. She turned her head towards the sound and her stomach lurched when she saw Simon standing in the doorway. 'Get out,' she rasped. 'Get out.' She tried to sit but the pain in her middle made her fall back.

'Cassie.' Simon's tone was urgent.

'No, get out. I don't want you here.' She closed her eyes tight, turning her head away from the man who had destroyed everything. She wasn't the only one to blame for their innocent child's death. It was him too and that woman. How dare he show his face after what he'd done to her and their baby?

'Cassie,' he said again. 'Look. She's beautiful.'

Cassie turned, nausea rising. He held a white blanket in his arms. A tiny pink face was just visible under a too-large hat. Cassie gasped for air, tried to struggle back, away from them, but the canula tethered her to the bed. 'No,' she said. 'How could you bring her here?'

Simon's face twisted. 'She's our daughter, Cassie. Look at her. She's perfect.'

What was wrong with him? How could he be looking down at the body of his dead child with a smile on his face? He was even worse than her. He was completely twisted.

Then she heard a noise, like the mewling of a cat, and a tiny hand appeared from the white fold of the blanket and flexed wrinkled, pink fingers.

Cassie gasped. The baby wasn't dead. She was alive and she was here… and that was even worse. Cassie realised Simon wasn't the twisted one. She was devastated her baby had survived. The only monster here was her.

23

SIX MONTHS AGO

Meg

Meg came into the kitchen with a cushion for her back. Her eyes were heavy and she was finding it hard to concentrate, but she needed to finish what she'd started. It was the least her girl deserved. She patted the cushion into place, settled back in the chair and pressed record.

'When we talked after the workshop where we saw each other again, your dad and I knew we couldn't carry on pretending we could live without each other. I know that must sound dramatic.' She shimmied her shoulders. 'Dramatic, me?' She smiled, trying not to notice how pronounced her cheekbones became when the edges of her mouth lifted. She looked like an animated skull. 'It's true, though. We were like Rose and Jack in *Titanic*.' Her smile disappeared. She was Jack, she supposed, stealing someone from their spouse, then paying with her life.

'That evening we agreed your dad would talk to his wife. She's called Cassie.' She made her voice gentle. 'You remember,

I told you that?' The memory of Grace's dumbstruck face when Meg told her the truth about who her natural mother was just half an hour ago made her breath hiccup. 'Unfortunately, that evening, Cassie had a fall, and the placenta that was feeding you ruptured. She was rushed to hospital and had to have an emergency Caesarean section under general anaesthetic.'

Meg had tried to tell Grace this, but her poor, poor girl had been so distraught, she was in no state to listen. She'd thought about leaving this explanation until a time when they were all calmer, but the last time she'd been for treatment, the woman she usually talked to in the waiting room was no longer there, and her sudden death had brought home how quickly her own condition could deteriorate. Meg couldn't leave anything until later, especially not something as important as this.

'Your dad was the first person to hold you.' Meg looked away from the screen, afraid her shame at wishing she'd been there too would show. 'He did the skin-on-skin stuff; kangaroo care, I think it's called. You were so tiny, Grace. Just a little dot.' She remembered the first time she'd seen the girl who would grow to call her Mummy, and keened to turn back time so she could experience it all again. 'Even though you were almost a month early, you were already strong and feisty.' She paused. 'Sorry, I know you don't like being called feisty.' She smiled inwardly at the memory of Grace telling her she was assertive, not feisty. 'You wouldn't call a boy feisty, would you?' Grace had said, and she was right. Meg had learned so much from her incredible child.

'You've always been spirited. Is that okay?' The cushion at her back slid down. She rearranged it and carried on. 'Obviously, Cassie was quite sore after the operation, and she couldn't do too much for you. They wanted to keep you in for a couple of nights to make sure you were breathing properly, so your dad gave you all your bottles, changed your nappy and gave you your first bath. He loved it, Grace. He loved you from the very first time he saw you.'

She let out a long breath. 'It was clear from the beginning Cassie was struggling.' Meg had thought hard about how to explain what happened next to Grace. She wanted to protect her from the worst of it and didn't want her to feel like she'd been rejected. Meg also had complicated feelings about Cassie. Guilt coated her memories of that time. What she and Simon had done was wrong, and she would never try to pretend otherwise, but it had led to her having the thing that meant more to her than anything else in the world – her small family – and for that she would always be grateful to the woman who'd made it possible.

'I knew she was depressed.' She'd agreed with Simon they would never tell Grace about how Cassie almost terminated the pregnancy. No good could come of that. 'And that got much worse after...' It seemed too cruel to say, like she was suggesting that Grace being born was to blame. 'But your dad thought she'd start to feel better when she was discharged from hospital. Unfortunately, she only seemed to get worse.'

She took a sip of water. 'By then, Cassie had asked your dad to leave and he'd moved in with me. Understandably, she didn't want him around, and so it was tricky for him to see you. He persevered, as you can imagine. He was determined to be a good dad. You can ask him about this yourself, when you're ready. I wasn't there in the first few days, but from what he said, Cassie wasn't even able to care for herself properly, which meant he was worried about you all of the time.

'One day, about a week and a half after you were born, your dad went around, and Cassie seemed really unwell. He insisted she went to the doctor's with him, and it turned out her stitches were infected, and she had a fever and was so tired she could hardly keep her eyes open. Your dad offered to stay but she wouldn't let him. He suggested taking you for the night and she agreed.'

Meg's eyes were glassy in her reflection on the screen as she recalled that day. 'And that's the first time I met you.' She stood and took a tissue from the box on the windowsill, then sat back down. 'I fell in love with you the first time I saw your gorgeous little face, and I have loved you beyond anything else in this world ever since, my beautiful girl.' She recalled the astonishing lightness when Simon placed his daughter carefully in her arms, as if she was hardly there at all. How did something so tiny illicit such enormous emotions? In her mind's eye, she could clearly see her tiny fingers with their paper-thin nails, and the tiny white milk spots on her perfect button nose.

'You stayed with us that night and I hardly slept for staring at you. Even when I looked away, I could hear your breathing and the little thuds as you lifted your legs and banged them down on the mattress of the Moses basket. I was bereft when Simon took you back the following day. I honestly felt like I was missing a part of my heart. That's how quickly it happened, how quickly I felt like we belonged together.'

She tugged at the tissue between her fingers, looking down as she tore off a thin strip. 'If it sounds like I was hatching some kind of plan to kidnap you, that's not the case. I would have been happy to have you in my life in whatever capacity Cassie allowed. We did try for a baby, later on, but it never happened.' She glanced back at the screen. 'I can imagine you gagging when you hear that.' She leaned in. 'You've just been a little bit sick in your mouth, haven't you?' It felt natural to banter, imagining Grace watching this back and being horrified at the thought of her parents trying for a baby.

But Grace wouldn't be pretending to stick her fingers down her throat and make gagging noises, would she? She would be distressed at seeing the woman she thought was her mother confessing she'd been lying to her for her whole life. She'd be grief-stricken because Meg was dead, and she'd be struggling because her parents had exploded her entire sense of self.

Meg covered her mouth with her hand to stifle the cry bubbling up. 'I'm so sorry, Grace. I'm so, so sorry.' She pressed the button to stop the recording and silently sobbed into her hand.

24

PRESENT DAY

Cassie

'Grace.' Cassie stared at the girl she hadn't seen since she was three months old. She had thick, wavy brown hair, like her. Like Alf. The thought of Alf was like a slap to the cheek. Alf didn't know Grace existed; neither did Luke. Luke thought the girl standing in front of her had died at birth, because that was what Cassie had led him to believe. She'd always been careful not to say 'stillborn' herself; she used words like lost, and gone, but she also never corrected him when he used the term. The shame of denying Grace's existence when she was here, living, breathing and oh so unbearably beautiful made the contents of her stomach curdle.

She wanted to reach out for her, to touch her and check she really wasn't an apparition, this girl who had lived in her dreams for fourteen years. Her pulse pounded in her ears. 'How did you find me?' The question sounded stupid when it came out of her mouth, like she was a fugitive and this poor girl was a bounty hunter, not a grieving child.

'Dad's email account is easy to get into. I saw your school address.'

Cassie gulped in air. This was too much. She was already struggling to contain her emotions following the governor's meeting and now here was the girl she'd resigned herself to never seeing again. She'd accepted it years ago. It had been hard, but it was the right thing for both of them at the time, and now the family she'd worked so hard to build would shatter if she reached out to this girl in the way her body screamed to do. Her brain buzzed with static. The muffled sound of the bell signalling the end of the school day made her jump and when she looked at the building, she saw students already swarming towards the doors. She opened her car door wider. 'Can we talk in here?' Grace looked unsure. 'Please?'

Grace stepped forwards and a second later they were sitting beside each other, and a sweet smell like the perfume her students doused themselves in filled Cassie's nostrils. 'I'm just going to drive around the corner, okay?' She glanced at the stranger sitting next to her, appalled to see fear in her eyes. 'It's going to get very busy here, so...' She started the engine, not knowing where she was heading. 'How did you get here?' Simon and Meg lived in Essex last time she was in contact with them. How had a fourteen-year-old made her way across the river to Kent?

'I got the train to London and back out here.'

'Does your dad know you're here?'

She sensed Grace shake her head as she looked the other way to check for traffic then pulled out onto the road. She knew where she was going now. It was the only thing she could think of to stop her world from collapsing. 'He'll be worried.'

'I don't care. He's lied to me enough times.'

There was nothing Cassie could say to that. She wasn't about to defend the man who had lied to her too. 'I'm sorry.'

'For which bit? Handing me over, or refusing to see me after my mum... after Meg died?' Her voice faltered and Cassie couldn't bear to hear it.

'All of it. I'm sorry you've been hurt and lied to.' Cassie indicated left and steered the car into the station car park. 'I'm sorry you lost your mum and that...' She pulled to a stop and dragged on the handbrake. She gripped the steering wheel, unable to look at the girl who smelled so sweet. She couldn't bring herself to look into the beautiful eyes, so like those of the man she'd once loved, or at the hair she saw in the mirror each day and that she rubbed shampoo into when she bathed her son. He had to be her priority now. She had already walked away from Grace once and she had survived. They both had. 'And I'm sorry I can't offer you anything now. I gave up any rights to you fourteen years ago and your parents agreed never to contact me again. Meg adopted you and brought you up. She was your mother. Not me.'

'What, so you're just going to dump me here?' Grace sounded incredulous.

Forcing her voice to remain steady, Cassie said, 'I think you should go home to your family. Do you have enough money for the train?' Cassie reached into the footwell for her bag and pulled out her purse, hoping Grace wouldn't see her hands were trembling. When she turned to Grace, a twenty-pound note in her hand, the hatred in her tear-filled eyes turned her blood to ice.

Grace shook her head, opened the car door and stepped out, slamming it behind her. She marched towards the station entrance, her narrow shoulders drawn back, as if she had to show she could still stand tall. Cassie watched her go, frozen, until she disappeared from view. Then she threw her arms over the steering wheel and collapsed onto them, her entire body convulsing with grief-stricken sobs.

25

SIX MONTHS AGO

Meg

Meg held an ice pack wrapped in a tea towel against her eyes. It reminded her of the cold cap she'd worn at the start of her treatment in an attempt to stop her hair from falling out. It hadn't worked. It still came out in terrifying clumps every time she showered. She gave up in the end. What was the point in trying to save her hair when the doctors had confirmed she was going to lose her life? She took the ice pack away and inspected her reflection in the phone's screen. Her eyes were still red, but slightly less puffy. She pressed record once more.

'It's important you understand that your dad and I did everything we could to help Cassie. Your dad made doctors' appointments for her, but after the time with the stitches, she refused to go. She was adamant she just needed to rest, so your dad brought you over to us a lot in the first couple of weeks when he was on parental leave, then, thankfully, it was the Christmas holidays.' She smiled. 'Spending that first Christmas with you was magical. Putting you back in the car seat on

Boxing Day felt like handing over my heart. You stayed with us for New Year too, and Cassie called the next day to ask if you could stay for a couple more days. She said she was feeling better for the rest, so we agreed. I was delighted, of course. You were such an easy baby. We'd take you out for a walk all bundled up in this padded romper suit.' She warmed at the memory. 'You'd stare at the leaves on the trees, your wide eyes looking comically massive in your tiny head. We'd follow your gaze and imagine what it would be like to see things for the very first time. It made us look at things afresh, you know, like you opened up the wonder of the world to us just by being in it.

'At first, I couldn't get my head around Cassie not being able to enjoy your exquisiteness like we did. But when your dad had to go back to work and Cassie had healed enough to drive again, she started to come over to drop you off at the weekend, and I saw how ill she looked.'

Meg saw herself in the screen and recognised the irony of her words. 'I mean, not as rough as I look now, obviously.' She wiggled her non-existent eyebrows. Why did she keep trying to make light of this? It was hardly as if Grace would be laughing along. 'I only saw her briefly through the crack in the door, but Cassie was incredibly thin for someone who'd just had a baby, and her skin was pale and kind of waxy. She looked like she hadn't slept in months. I didn't understand it because you were so calm and peaceful with us, but Cassie told your dad you cried so much when you were with her. She said she didn't know how to soothe you. He told me she was really distressed when she said that. She wanted to be a good mum. She felt like she was letting you down. She tried, Grace, she really tried. It's so important you know she was ill. What happened has nothing to do with her feelings for you.'

Meg picked at a brittle fingernail, dry and ridged since

chemo, wondering if that was entirely true. It didn't matter if it wasn't. It was what Grace needed to hear. She curled her fingers into her palms and looked back at the screen. 'I always made myself scarce when Cassie dropped you off. I'd hide in our bedroom. It didn't seem fair to be there, even though it was torture missing even a minute with you. That's why it seemed strange when she asked to see both your dad and me together when you were three months old.'

Her mind went back to how nervous she'd been, waiting for Cassie to arrive that day. It was a Sunday afternoon, and Grace had been with them since Friday. Meg took Grace into the communal garden at the back of the flat she rented, to show her the daffodils in the border that had bloomed in the early spring sunshine.

'I was outside with you when she arrived. I remember looking up and seeing her face at the window. She was just staring at me with you in my arms, with this unreadable expression on her face. That's the day everything changed.'

26

PRESENT DAY

Cassie

Cassie sat in the station car park for the next hour, unable to leave. At first, she'd considered running after Grace, grabbing her to her chest and begging her forgiveness; but every time her fingers moved towards the door handle, she pictured Luke and Alf, disbelief at her betrayal on both their faces. She imagined a for sale sign in front of the home she loved and Alf having to split his childhood between two broken parents. She'd tried that once and couldn't bear the thought of ruining another child's life.

So, she didn't open the car door. Instead, she wound down the window, letting in the stifling heat. She listened for the rumble of a train approaching, then the squeal of brakes and the swoosh of doors. She imagined that slight, beautiful girl, her elfin chin raised as she fought back tears, stepping aboard and making her way back to her father, where she belonged. Turning her away had been Cassie's only option. Grace would survive. She could thrive. Cassie knew only too well what a person could recover from when they had no other choice.

* * *

'Where were you?' Luke marched into the hallway as soon as she opened the door. 'Marie was messaging. You told her you'd only be an hour and a half.' He looked at his watch. 'You've been almost double that.'

'Sorry.' She slid off her shoes. The soles of her feet were wet with sweat.

'And why were you at the station?'

She froze. 'What?'

'When you didn't answer your phone, I checked Find My Phone and it said you were at the station.'

Her brain clicked into gear. 'Yeah, right. That's why I was late. A kid missed the train home after a school trip. He had to get on the next one, so I said I'd wait for him to make sure he got back okay.'

Luke's dark eyebrows met in a frown. 'Why did they ask you? You weren't on the trip.'

Cassie passed him and made her way into the kitchen. 'I know. I should have said no, but Finnegan was in a flap because the parents were freaking out, so I said all right without thinking.' She opened the patio doors to get some air to her face, but it was hot and still outside.

'Why didn't you answer your phone?'

'Jesus, what is this, twenty questions?' She didn't have any answers for him so had no choice but to go on the defensive. 'It was on silent, all right? It's always on silent when I'm at school and I forgot to turn the ringer back on.' She took a breath. 'I'm sorry I worried you. I shouldn't have agreed to wait at the station, and I should have remembered to take my phone off silent. I'm sorry.' She scanned the kitchen. 'Where's Alf?'

'Marie had a parcel coming, so she took him next door with her. She said she told you she had to get back for the delivery.'

Cassie had a vague memory of that and added their kind neighbour to the list of people she was letting down. 'I've said I'm sorry.'

He ran his hand over his face. 'I don't know what's going on in your head at the moment.'

'Nothing is going on in my head.'

'I don't even know if I believe the story about why you were at the station.'

'What do you mean?' She creased her brow and tucked in her chin. The action felt false, so it probably looked unconvincing to Luke, who was more attuned to honest displays of emotions than most. Her life had become a shitty game of charades.

He looked at her for a long moment, then shook his head. 'Who doesn't look at their phone when they're just waiting? And you've been acting so strangely recently. You know what I thought when I saw your car was parked at the station for all that time?'

She didn't answer. The memory of Grace walking away from her took the breath from her lungs.

'I can't believe I'm actually saying this, but I don't think you have any idea how different you've been recently. A couple of weeks ago we were party planning... and now...' He shrugged, looking more defeated than Cassie had ever seen him. 'It actually crossed my mind that you'd left us. I thought maybe you'd left your phone in your car and got on a train somewhere and just gone.'

Cassie gasped. Every last thing she had done, every lie she

told, was to protect her family; to keep them together. 'I wouldn't do that. I don't even want to do that. The only thing I want is for you, me and Alf to get back to normal.'

'Then why are you acting all distant and... weird? What's really going on?' Luke flung his arms wide.

She couldn't let him dig further. She had no choice but to go on the attack. 'I'm not the only one acting strangely. You're the one stalking me.' She knew that was unfair, but she had to switch the focus away from her.

'Doing what?' His voice was high pitched. He blinked. 'I couldn't get hold of you, so I checked where you were. That's hardly stalking.' He scratched the back of his head. 'Do you know what? The Cassie I know would never say that. The woman I'm married to knows I've treated people who have been stalked. I've seen how insidious it is and the damage it can do to a person.'

Cassie felt sick. He was right. He'd been worried about her, that was all. She'd have acted in exactly the same way if he went awol and left Alf with a neighbour. She opened her mouth to apologise but was interrupted by the urgent ringing of the doorbell.

Luke strode into the hall. Cassie followed, concern rising as the bell rang again. Luke opened the door and Cassie's stomach pitched when she saw Marie standing on the doorstep, Alf crying at her side.

'We were in the garden,' said Marie, her voice tight, 'and we heard you talking.'

Shame flooded Cassie's veins.

'Alf is quite upset.'

Cassie moved towards him, but Luke got there before her and crouched down to his son's height. He put his hands on

Alf's shoulders. 'I'm sorry you heard us arguing, Alf. That must've been very upsetting for you.'

Alf shook Luke's hands away and stepped into the hall, swerving past Cassie, avoiding the arms she held out for him. 'I don't like it when you argue,' he said through hiccupping tears. 'You pretend you don't, and you act like everything's all right, like I don't understand, or I'm a baby, or deaf or stupid or something. Well, I'm not.' He stamped through to the kitchen, leaving his parents standing on the doorstep with Marie, whose stormy expression suggested she was no more impressed with them than Alf was.

27

PRESENT DAY

Cassie

Cassie stayed downstairs in the sitting room listening to the quiet voices of her husband and son talking in Alf's bedroom. It was mostly Luke's low rumble, but every so often she could hear her son's childish pitch and pictured his earnest, tear-stained face as his father tried to make him understand that sometimes people argue and, unpleasant as it was, it was a normal part of all relationships. She'd offered to go up with Luke to talk to Alf, but he'd asked her if it was okay for him to speak to Alf alone. Typical of Luke to phrase it as a question rather than yelling, *You caused this, at least let me try to minimise the fallout without your interference.*

She could imagine Luke's sympathetic expression as he explained conflict was a natural part of life and as long as it was resolved, it could actually be a healthy thing. Cassie had heard this talk from him herself after they'd had their first argument almost ten years ago. Even though she knew in her bones that he was the right man for her, she'd been ready to walk away at the first sign of trouble. 'I can't do this,' she'd said, terrified of the pain from her split with Simon returning. 'I'm better off on my own.'

'Humans are pack animals,' Luke had told her. 'They need to live alongside each other, but that doesn't mean they have to agree on everything. There will be conflict in every relationship, whether it's parents and children, friends or partners. It's how you negotiate your way through conflict that matters. Successful relationships are about communication and a certain amount of compromise.'

'That's what you'd say to a client,' she'd told him. 'I'm not a client.'

'Okay.' He'd rolled his eyes. 'Would it be better if I said everyone rows, you need to suck it up and get over it?'

Cassie had ended up laughing. She wasn't sure she'd ever experienced a healthy relationship before. In her childhood home, no conflict was allowed. If she stepped out of line, she was met with silence and a withdrawal of the meagre affection or approval that might have otherwise come her way. No one talked about things. Members of her family rarely talked at all. She and Simon had discussed things but they'd been so young when they met, and she'd adored him in a way she could now see was deeply unhealthy. He had deity status in her eyes, and before she'd found out about Meg, any conflict was usually resolved by her giving in. She hoped Luke was having more luck with Alf. God knows she wanted her son to have more success with open communication than her.

She stretched out on the sofa, grabbing the green blanket from where it was folded over the arm and arranging it over her. Even though the evening was still warm, she needed the comfort of it. The events of the day had left her sapped and it was an effort to scroll through her phone to check if an email had come in from Finnegan and the governors.

A burst of adrenaline seared through her veins when she saw it had. She tapped on the email and scanned what was written. She'd been given a written warning, but no formal suspension. She threw her head back on the cushions. Thank heavens for that. She tapped out a quick text to Becca letting her know the good news, then allowed her heavy eyelids to close.

* * *

'Mate!' Cassie woke at the sound of her friend's voice. She opened her eyes and saw Becca standing in the doorway to her sitting room, dressed in a leopard-print jumpsuit and denim jacket. Her face was bright, and she held a dark green bottle in her raised hand. 'I've dropped by to celebrate the good news.' She turned the bottle and squinted at the label. 'This is only Prosecco, mind. I'm saving the champagne for if you get let off something more serious, like embezzling the English Department budget, or...' She lifted her heavily mascaraed eyes to the ceiling, then scrunched up her nose. 'What else? Leaking an exam paper?'

Cassie shuffled up to sitting, not yet fully conscious. The blanket slithered onto the floor, leaving her legs cold.

Becca carried on musing. 'Not that you'd ever do that, obvs.'

Cassie's insides flipped when she heard Luke's footsteps in the hall. She raised her hand to stop Becca saying anything about the governors' meeting, but she was too late; Luke was already standing by Becca's side. Luke looked older than Becca, despite being five years her junior, and it wasn't just that Becca was wearing drag-queen level makeup. Luke's jowls seemed to sag, and his eyes looked dim next to Becca's. Cassie had done that to him, and the prickling under her skin told her it was about to get a whole lot worse, and there wasn't a thing she could do to stop it.

'Sorry about that, Becca.' Luke gave her a hug and a kiss on the cheek. 'Very rude of me to rush off after letting you in, but the rice was about to boil over. You staying for dinner?'

'I'd love to, but I've got a date.' She laid a hand on Luke's forearm. 'Cassie's probably told you, I'm seeing someone now. Actually seeing *him*, not just his interesting bits.' She laughed and gripped Luke's arm. 'He's called Graham and he's delicious.'

'She didn't, actually,' said Luke, his face unreadable. 'My wife has been keeping a lot to herself recently.'

Becca clearly missed the metal in his voice because she bit her top lip with her lower teeth, then said, 'Thank God for that. You might not let me past the front step if you heard half the tales I inflict on her.' She pinched his cheek. 'And you're far too sweet and innocent to know the ins and outs of a menopausal woman's sex life. Ins and outs, ha! What am I like?' She waved the bottle. 'Anyway, enough about what I get up to in my spare time, I wanted to drop this off to celebrate the governors' meeting going well.' She turned to Cassie, who was wishing the sofa cushions would part and swallow her down.

'That's very kind,' said Cassie, aware of Luke's eyes on her.

'Personally, I think you should be given an award for calling Oliver Simms a little fucker, quite frankly, never mind be dragged in front of the board. At least you didn't get suspended, and have you even had a colourful teaching career if you haven't had at least one written warning?' She flung the hand not holding the bottle wide.

'Indeed,' said Luke. His eyes bored into Cassie.

There was a silence, and Becca blinked, as if registering the atmosphere wasn't celebratory. 'Anyway, I'll, er, I'll leave this with you.' She scurried forwards and handed the bottle to Cassie, giving her a quick hug then retreating to the door.

'Thank you,' said Cassie, her voice croaky.

'I'll get off then,' said Becca, looking from Cassie to Luke with panic in her eyes. 'See you, Cass.'

'I'll walk you out,' said Luke.

Cassie raised her hand and attempted a smile, but Becca was already heading for the door, followed by Luke. She waited, stomach a burning tight ball, for Luke to come back in and ask her what the hell all that was about, but when the front door clicked shut, his footsteps went past the sitting room and straight through to the kitchen. He wasn't going to ask her about it, and that was even worse.

28

PRESENT DAY

Cassie

Luke rolled away from her when he got into bed that night, and his side of the mattress was empty when she woke up to the sound of her alarm beeping. She hadn't managed to fall asleep until at least 3 a.m. and even when she did finally drop off, Grace's sad face plagued her nightmares. She should have checked with Simon that she'd got home safely. Images of the vulnerable girl being dragged off the train by faceless men had swarmed in Cassie's subconscious. Sometimes her face would morph into Alf's and then both of them would scream for help as Cassie was dragged backwards, further away, by an invisible, malevolent force. She'd been left with a hollowed-out feeling, tears threatening whenever the pictures of her suffering children seeped back into her head.

She could hear Luke talking to Alf downstairs, so she had a quick shower. All the time she washed and dressed she wondered whether she should email Simon to tell him Grace had been to see her, and to make sure he was taking extra good care of her. She sat on the end of the bed to pull on her socks, trying to compose a message in her head. Everything she thought of sounded wrong. How could she ask him to take extra care of a child he'd been parenting for fourteen years? It wasn't her place to. And what if Grace still hadn't disclosed she'd visited Cassie? She might be getting her in trouble on top of breaking her heart.

Even that thought seemed presumptuous. Grace probably wasn't broken hearted. She was more likely to be deeply disappointed or annoyed. She might have simply been curious. Just because Cassie had thought about the daughter she gave away every single day, it didn't follow that Grace keened for her. She hadn't even known she existed until six months ago. And hopefully, now Grace had seen her, she would be able to move on with her life in the knowledge she wasn't missing out on a mother. She'd seen Cassie as she really was: pathetic, deficient, a terrible excuse for a mother. It was for the best. If Grace could move past this, then it might allow Cassie to do the same and get on with trying to repair her relationships with Alf and Luke. Maybe she could start to look forward instead of back.

She disconnected her phone from the charger by her bed and clicked onto the email Simon had sent to her at the start of all this.

Hi Cassie

I'm sorry to email you via your school email address, but I couldn't think of another way to contact you.

I've agonised over whether to get in touch at all, but I thought I should tell you Meg died of pancreatic cancer five months ago. I don't expect you to feel any sympathy for me or Meg, but our daughter is struggling and I wondered if you might be willing to help?

I know this goes against what we agreed, but I'm asking for the sake of our child, not myself. Up until Meg's terminal diagnosis, Grace thought she was her natural, not adoptive, mother. Meg always felt immense guilt about what happened back then and about lying to Grace. She wanted to leave this world knowing she'd been honest and given Grace the opportunity to still have a mother if she needed one.

We knew it would be difficult for Grace to hear, especially since the only mother she had ever known was dying, but it seemed like the right thing to do. Unfortunately, Grace has taken both Meg's death, and being lied to, even harder than we anticipated.

I wondered if you could find it in your heart to talk to her, maybe let her know you're open to having some kind of relationship with her?

I know I have no right to ask, but I'd do anything to make life easier for Grace.

Please let me know if this is a possibility.

All the best

Simon

She reread the part about Grace struggling and felt a new wash of shame. She'd emailed Simon back saying she wouldn't be part of their lives without thinking hard enough about what Grace was going through. Until yesterday, her daughter was still a nebulous concept in her head. When she thought about her, which she did every day, it was as that little baby with the big blue eyes, who never truly settled in Cassie's arms. She'd forced herself to recall the crying and the wriggling, as if Grace wanted to escape from Cassie and be somewhere else. She remembered Simon saying what a peaceful baby she was with him and Meg, and it had allowed Cassie to find some kind of acceptance in the belief she had done the right thing in giving her up.

Of course, intellectually she knew Grace had grown up. She'd even imagined her at every stage of her life, but in an abstract way, certainly not as the living, breathing, sentient person she'd presented as yesterday. And certainly not as a suffering child.

She heard light footsteps on the stairs. She clicked the phone to sleep and stood, running her hand through her damp hair. 'You ready for school, Alf?'

'I'm not going.' His door slammed.

Cassie rushed onto the landing. The three letters of his name were stuck on the outside of his bedroom door along with the face of a sword-wielding pirate, complete with eye-patch and red bandanna. *Keep out!* was emblazoned on the shaft of the sword. When Cassie had hung the name plate and pirate on her son's door when he was a sweet, cuddly toddler, she had never envisaged that one day he truly would want her to keep out of his room. She went to the door and knocked. 'Alf.' She didn't wait for a reply. She pushed open the door. Alf was face down on his bed.

'Want to tell me what's wrong?' *Other than the fact your home feels like a battle ground at the moment*, she thought.

'No.'

She checked her watch. She had fifteen minutes to have breakfast and put her makeup on before it was time to leave. 'Come on, buddy. Talk to me. You're not still upset about Mummy and Daddy arguing last night, are you? Daddy explained that everyone disagrees now and again.'

'I don't care.'

Cassie knew that was code for 'I care very much'. So she lay beside him on the bed and wrapped her arms around him.

'Come on, lovely boy. Let's have a big cuddle, then it's time to get ready for school.'

He stiffened. 'I'm not going to school.'

Cassie closed her eyes and counted to ten. She couldn't afford to not turn up at work today after being given a written warning. She drew away from Alf and stood by the side of the bed. 'You *are* going to school, and if you're not downstairs in five minutes, there will be consequences.'

She left the room, trying to work out what consequences she could impose. In truth, she completely understood where Alf was coming from. She didn't want to go to school either. She started down the stairs just in time to hear the front door close. She checked her watch again. Luke didn't usually leave until around the same time as her and Alf. It was the first time in their marriage that he had left without saying goodbye. Even in the school holidays when she was having a lie in, he would tiptoe upstairs and kiss her on the cheek before leaving for work. This was a very clear message. He was angrier than he'd ever been with her. And he didn't even know the full story. What the hell would he do if he found out about Grace?

'Alf!' She shouted upstairs when he hadn't emerged five minutes later. She swallowed the mouthful of toast she was furiously chewing and poked at her eyelashes with her mascara wand while looking in the hallway mirror. 'Get down here now.' She never usually shouted at Alf, but she'd usually had more than three hours' sleep, and he was usually a fairly compliant little boy.

He slunk downstairs, dark head hanging to his chest.

'Thank you. Have you brushed your teeth?' He nodded. She didn't believe him, and he clearly hadn't run a brush through his hair because it was fuzzy at the back. She sighed. She didn't have the time or energy to worry about whether he was suitably coiffed. 'Good, now grab your bag and let's get in the car.'

They arrived at Hillside Primary as the last trickle of students hurried in. The toast and jam she'd shoved in his hands to eat on the way sat beside him on the seat untouched. She hated the thought of him being hungry but, as Luke had said, maybe it was time he understood both actions and inactions had consequences. She closed her mind to her own hypocrisy. 'Off you go. Have a good day.' He didn't move. 'Alf, I haven't got time for this. I'm already late.'

'I told you, I don't want to go to school.' He crossed his arms.

'Neither do I,' she said, then instantly regretted it. What would Luke do in this situation? She made her voice soft. 'Want me to walk you to the door?' She usually saw he was safely inside the gate and in view of the staff, then went back to the car.

He nodded, so she unclipped her seatbelt and tried not to imagine how late she would be when she eventually got to work. When they were both on the pavement, she took his hand and they walked together through the school gate and up to the entrance. When they got there, his grip on her hand got stronger. Her pulse increased. When he wouldn't let go of her fingers, she sat on her haunches and faced him. 'You have to let go, Alf.'

He shook his head and gripped her hand even more tightly.

She stood and tugged him towards the door. He resisted and she ended up almost dragging him into reception. Tears trickled from his eyes and Cassie wondered how she had become a woman who dragged her crying child where they didn't want to go. She was a terrible mother. She always had been.

'Hello, Alf.'

Cassie turned and almost doubled over in relief when she

saw Mrs Miah. 'Mrs Miah, hi.' She dipped to look into Alf's face. 'Mrs Miah is here, look. You'll be okay with her, won't you?'

Alf shook his head, released her hand, and wrapped both arms around her middle. 'I want to go home.' Cassie was torn. She wanted to hold him and cover his face with kisses. She also wanted to pull his hands away from where they were squeezing the air from her and run back to the car.

'How about you come with me, and we'll find Charlie?' said Mrs Miah. 'You'd like to see Charlie, wouldn't you?'

Alf sat next to Charlie in class and they got along well. Cassie forced herself to smile, despite feeling like a timer was clicking down in her head. 'Yes, you like Charlie, don't you? Why don't you go with Mrs Miah and see Charlie, then when I pick you up later, we can go and get ice cream at Kaspa's?' Cassie tugged at Alf's arm, ashamed at having stooped to bribery in front of his teacher, but he didn't loosen his grip. She felt a thump as he buried his head in her middle.

Mrs Miah's head fell to one side. She looked at Cassie with sympathy. 'This is because of that incident with Perry Simms, isn't it?'

Cassie's head snapped up. 'Perry Simms?'

'The boy Alf had the altercation with.' Mrs Miah bent down beside Alf and spoke to him in soothing tones. 'Come on, sweetheart. I know you had a bad day last week, but we can move past that, can't we? You're always very helpful to me and kind to the other boys and girls in your class, so we don't need to think about what happened before. It's in the past. Now we're in the present, and we live in the now, don't we?'

Alf's arms loosened, which was fortunate, because Cassie was suddenly white hot with rage. 'Do you happen to know if Perry has an older brother called Oliver?' she said, taking care to keep her voice calm.

Mrs Miah glanced up, a nervous expression in her dark eyes. 'Yes, he came here too, five or so years ago. Do you know the family? It's just that... I shouldn't really have told you who the other child involved was.'

'I don't know the parents. Oliver is at the school where I teach, that's all.'

'Oh, righto,' said Mrs Miah, taking Alf's hand. 'Shall we say goodbye to Mum and go and find Charlie?'

Alf took a step away. He looked up at Cassie with watery eyes. She bent to kiss his wet cheeks. She loved this little boy so much it made her heart hurt.

But she hated Oliver Simms.

29

PRESENT DAY

Cassie

Cassie pressed her foot down hard on the accelerator, blood thundering in her ears. When the driver in front was slow to move away at the lights, she screamed until her throat was raw, but the catharsis she expected from swearing at people who would never hear didn't come. A moment of clarity told her she wasn't being rational. Fear she was losing all sense of proportion passed across her consciousness, but it was followed by more fury at the fact this was happening to the people she loved. It wasn't fair and it wasn't right. It wasn't back then, and it wasn't now. The world was full of injustice, and innocent people got hurt through no fault of their own. Was it any surprise she was struggling to hold it together when other people's actions had such devastating impacts? The rage was still bubbling inside her when she marched into school fifteen minutes into form time.

Her classroom was in disarray when she flung open the door, students sitting on desks with their feet on chairs, their phones in hand. They were making enough noise to indicate no teacher was present, but when the first of them noticed her, a ripple of 'shhhs' went around and the others eventually fell quiet. She was usually a relaxed form tutor but must've been giving off 'don't mess with me' vibes, because even Minel stopped swinging his bag at other students' heads and settled quietly into his seat.

'Sorry I'm late,' Cassie said when they were all appropriately seated and looking in her direction. She thanked the universe for this morning's events coinciding with a day when she had form period straight after registration.

'After-school detention for you,' said Minel, shaking his head and laughing.

'Do you want to stay behind with me?' asked Cassie, raising an eyebrow.

'No, Miss,' said Minel. 'You're all right.'

'Get out your careers folders,' said Cassie, 'and discuss in pairs what would be the best route to your ideal job. And by ideal, I mean realistically attainable, not winning the lottery, marrying a royal or getting huge on TikTok.'

'You ain't heard me rap, Miss,' said Minel. 'I'm gonna be a star.' A few of them jeered as Minel preened, waving his hand and dismissing the dissenters.

'Then you'll probably want to study music or music technology,' said Cassie. Ordinarily she enjoyed bantering with her classes, but today wasn't an ordinary day. 'You need to think whether sixth form and university, or college, or apprenticeship, or a combination would be best. Think about the subjects and skills you'll need. You've got fifteen minutes, then we'll have a class discussion,' she said, addressing the group. She hadn't planned today's lesson, but one benefit of having been at the school as long as she had was that she'd taught this module before, so at least she could wing it.

While the students pretended to get on with the task, Cassie took the register and hoped no one would ask why it appeared on the system late. She then tried to concentrate on planning her lessons for the rest of the day. Her mind hadn't been on the job lately and the guilt about that was adding to the layers already calcified inside her. She reminded herself she would be deeply unhappy if Mrs Miah's commitment to Alf's education was compromised by what was going on in her personal life and tried again to focus. It was impossible. She could still feel Alf's arms around her middle. The name Simms kept replaying in her head, her anger growing in intensity with every repetition.

The name was seared into her brain at the end of the period. She could imagine it branded into her grey matter like a number on a sheep's haunch. The fact that she had a good idea why Oliver Simms' younger brother had picked a fight with her sweet, innocent son made her stomach acid fizz. When she glanced out of her classroom as her form made their way out to their next class and saw Oliver's distinctive dark head, she jumped from her seat. She barged past Minel, who was halfway through the door, and marched along the corridor, following the boy who was causing her family such distress.

'Oliver Simms,' she said, pushing her way through the crowds of students. He didn't turn. 'Oliver Simms,' she shouted. He stopped then, and turned, his frown deeper than ever.

'What?' He stuck out his bottom lip and Cassie wanted to smack the indignant expression from his face.

'What did you say to your brother?' She reached him and it was all she could do not to push him against the wall. His smell of Lynx body spray and sweat made her nostrils flare.

'What?' His lip rose in a sneer.

'You know exactly what I'm talking about.' The other students had stopped to watch and the corridor had gone quiet, but Cassie didn't notice because of the sound of her pulse in her ears.

Oliver shook his head and smirked. He started to move away. Hot bile rose up Cassie's throat. 'Don't you dare walk away from me,' she snarled.

He turned his back, and Cassie was blinded by white-hot rage. She grabbed his shoulder and spun him towards her, only coming to her senses when she heard a deep voice shout, 'Mrs Monroe. A word, please. Now.'

* * *

'What the hell were you thinking?' Finnegan paced his office.

'He got his brother to target my child!' The rage was still burning in Cassie's gut.

'Target? What do you mean, target?' Finnegan stopped and peered down at her.

'I don't know, exactly, bu—'

'You don't know.' He let out a sharp breath. 'You don't know exactly what you're accusing him of, but you took it upon yourself to physically challenge a Year Nine pupil?'

Cassie closed her eyes. 'I hardly touched him. And he's the one who's made this personal.'

'He's fourteen. You are a teacher with almost two decades of experience and a recent written warning.' Finnegan sat heavily in his chair at the other side of the desk, the cushion giving out a hiss of air. 'I don't know what to say, Cassie. It was hard enough to persuade the governors not to suspend you yesterday. One of the points in your favour was the only witnesses were biased towards Simms and no student from North Hill is admitting to being involved. This time, half the bloody school saw you lay your hands on the boy.'

'What would you do?' said Cassie, bleakness creeping through her veins. 'If your child was hurt because of someone like Oliver Simms.'

'I'd go through the proper channels. I'd present evidence and make a strong case. What I wouldn't do is swear at them and challenge them like some kind of... wild thing.' He lifted off his glasses and rubbed at the bridge of his nose. 'Honestly, Cassie, I have no idea what's got into you lately. I hardly recognise you. And don't think no one noticed how late you were this morning.'

'I'm sorry. Alf wouldn't go into school because Oliver Simms' brother—'

Finnegan held up his hand. 'I think you should save this for your written statement. You might want to contact your union representative too. I anticipate Mr and Mrs Simms will have plenty to say when they hear about this.' He sighed. 'Once again, I'm forced to ask you to leave the premises. I'll be in touch about next steps, but I can't pretend this isn't worrying me, Cassie. You've made it very hard for me to advocate for you.'

The bleakness pushed at her temples. A black vortex inside her skull spun, pulling her down. 'I'm sorry,' she said, unable to form anything more complex. There were no words left inside her head, just dark, brooding feelings.

'Me too, Cassie. Me too.'

30

PRESENT DAY

Cassie

Cassie fell onto the sofa in her sitting room and sobbed. The fury had burned out and now she couldn't believe she'd acted so rashly. She must've looked like a wild woman, pushing kids out of the way to get to Oliver Simms. She wasn't fit to be in charge of young people. She deserved to be suspended. She deserved to be sacked. A new fear gripped her. If she lost her job, then she probably wouldn't be able to get another teaching position. They couldn't afford the mortgage on Luke's income alone, added to which, teaching was all she'd ever done. She wasn't qualified for anything else. There wasn't anything else she wanted to do.

How the hell would she explain her actions to Luke? She pulled a cushion to her middle and cried hot, angry tears. She was furious at herself. Now her impulsive behaviour could have a devastating impact on all of their lives, just as they were already on the brink of falling apart.

Half an hour later, rubbing her swollen eyes, she sat, limply allowing the sadness to consume her. She blew her nose then checked her phone, half expecting to see an email asking her to pick Alf up from school. There was nothing. That was a relief at least, although once Oliver Simms told his brother what had happened, it might be even worse for Alf. That thought pierced her heart. She was trying to protect her family, and instead, she'd made everything worse. What a fool she was. What a terrible mother.

Muscle memory made her tap onto her school email account after closing her personal one. Electricity jolted through her when she saw an email from Simon. Her imagination sparked into action, the nightmare of Grace being kidnapped replaying in her mind's eye. Sweat broke out on Cassie's skin as she imagined her daughter found dead at the side of the rail track.

She clicked onto the email with a shaking finger.

Cassie
   It was a mistake to come and find you yesterday.

The email was from Grace, not Simon. Relief made Cassie weak.

I won't make the same mistake twice, so I wanted you to know you can forget yesterday ever happened. Seeing you helped me to remember how brilliant my mum was. She was kind and funny and she always, always put me first. She loved me and she was a brilliant mother.
   I hope you don't have kids.

Cassie gasped. She read on.

If you do, I feel sorry for them because every child deserves a mum who is kind and who loves them. I'm glad you gave me away. You are nothing like my mum. She would never have rejected me. People would probably call you my 'real' mum, but you're not and you never were. I miss my mum so much. She thought I should know about you, so I still had a mother after she died, but she clearly didn't know how cold and selfish you are.

I'm going to pretend she never told me about you.

You should pretend I never existed. You probably already do.

Grace.

The anger and bitterness seeped from the words and covered Cassie in another layer of self-loathing. She could see Grace's beautiful face crumpled and tearful as she wrote this, lashing out because she wasn't yet old enough to deal with the complex feelings she was experiencing. That poor child.

The sickening memory of waking up after the Caesarean and hoping her baby had been lost assailed her. She bent double with the guilt, the reality of wishing that gorgeous girl no longer existed reminding her what a loathsome individual she was. Grace was right, she didn't deserve to have a child. What kind of mother wishes her own newborn baby dead?

Another email pinged onto the chain from the same email address. Cassie opened it, steeling herself for another tirade.

Hi Cassie

I've just seen the email Grace sent to you. The settings mean it comes to my phone when it's sent from another device. What the hell is she talking about? Did she come to see you?

Simon

Cassie lay her head back on the sofa cushion. This was a living nightmare. She breathed deep into her lungs, then typed out a reply.

Grace turned up at my school yesterday. We spoke briefly then I drove her to the station.

She had the urge to ask him why he wasn't more aware of what his fourteen-year-old daughter was up to, but resisted. She was hardly in a position to judge.

I'm sorry she feels rejected. I didn't want to hurt her. I didn't want any of this. I hope she's all right.

She wanted to write about how beautiful Grace was. She wanted to say how much her eyes were like Simon's and that she could see a resemblance to her own darling boy. The urge to ask him to tell Grace she was sorry and she truly had thought about her every single day of her life was strong. How could she explain that the only thing stopping her from reaching out to hold her was the fear of losing the family she'd worked so hard to build after the devastation Cassie and Simon had wreaked on her life?

And that was the point, wasn't it? She'd only given Grace up because of the depression she'd experienced following Simon's betrayal. She'd lied to Luke when she first met him because talking about what had happened then was too painful. And that was all Simon's fault. She typed quickly, rage moving her fingers across the letters.

You need to remember how this started, and who was to blame. You destroyed me once. I can't allow you to devastate my life for a second time. Any pain that poor child is suffering was brought about by you. It's down to you to help her.

Take better care of your daughter. Don't contact me again.

She pressed send then let fresh tears fall.

31

SIX MONTHS AGO

Meg

Meg had to take a break from filming. It was too hard, too draining. She stood at the foot of the stairs and strained to hear if Grace was still crying. There was no sound coming from her bedroom, but that didn't mean anything. She imagined Grace's dark waves spread across her pillow while silent tears rolled onto her cheeks. What a devastating mistake they'd made in lying to her for so long.

She went into the front room, where Simon was scrolling on his phone. He looked up when the door opened. In his eyes was the concern she'd become accustomed to. How she longed to see something else there. He'd once looked at her with desire in those big blue eyes, with humour, admiration even. Now his sandy eyebrows were always slightly raised in a question, as if on the verge of checking if she was in pain or needed him to do something for her.

When they'd moved to this house, when Grace was a year old and Simon was settled in a job nearby, she'd listened at the base of the stairs like she had just then. That time, when she heard Grace was quiet, she'd slipped into this room and found Simon sitting where he was now. The brown leather sofa was brand new then and she'd done a sexy striptease between the doorway and the sofa, Simon's eyes agape, taking in her curves until she reached him and sat astride him in her matching bra and thong.

Now the brown leather was creased and bore the marks of spilled tea and sticky fingers: the DNA of family life. Christening it while their baby slept upstairs seemed like a scene from another lifetime – one very different to the relentless parade of hospital visits and hard conversations they were living now.

'How are you doing?' asked Simon. He'd changed out of his school clothes into joggers and a fleece. He still had the little paunch he'd developed over the years, but his clothes were all baggier than they used to be. When she'd addressed his weight loss, he'd said it was because he needed to be healthier. He didn't add it was because he was all Grace would have left.

She rolled her shoulders. 'It's hard.'

Simon nodded. 'You don't have to—'

'I do,' she said.

'I could help? I could film with you.'

'Thanks, but I want to tell my story, how I saw it and why I did what I did,' said Meg. 'You can tell her yours afterwards, face to face.' The reality of what that meant hung in the air. 'Have you been up to see her?' Meg nodded in the direction of the stairs.

Simon scratched under his chin, like he did when he was uncomfortable. 'I tried. She won't talk to me.'

'Give her time,' Meg said. 'It's a lot for her to take in.'

'Yep,' said Simon. 'It's brought it all back. I'm struggling with the memories myself and I'm... I'm not sure you should be putting yourself through recording it now. Maybe you should—'

'Wait?' She dropped her head to one side and let the silence grow between them. He knew as well as she did the time for waiting was over.

Simon stood and gathered her in his arms. He held her gently these days, as if she was a bouquet of fresh flowers and he didn't want to crush the blooms. 'I love you.'

She drew back and took his face between her hands, kissing him gently on the lips. 'I love you too.' She was suddenly aware of her breath. Her mouth was permanently dry because of the medication, and her teeth had started to become loose in her withering gums. Her breath probably smelled like rotting meat. She lifted his arms from her and, keeping her face averted, she said, 'I'd better finish up in there.'

He let her go and she wished she'd looked away before seeing his eyes fill with tears. There was too much pain in their house; they were all drowning in it.

Back in the kitchen, she adjusted her headscarf, then pressed record on her phone.

'When I saw Cassie looking down at us from the window, I rushed back inside. Your dad met us at the top of the stairs, and I handed you straight to him. It felt wrong to walk into a room where Cassie was with you in my arms; kind of disrespectful. I can still remember how cold my arms felt without you in them. I don't know how to describe it.' She looked up to the left, trying to find the right words. 'Imagine you were starving, and someone gave you a delicious plate of food.' She smiled. 'And you had one bite and it was the most succulent, mouth-wateringly good thing you'd ever tasted. And as much as you loved that mouthful, you were still hungry and excited for the next taste, then all of a sudden, someone takes the plate away from you and you're left still ravenous, and with the taste of that delicious food still in your mouth.'

She closed her eyes and shook her head. 'That's probably a bonkers comparison, but I'm sticking with it. From my first taste of spending time with you, I was hungry for more. You were and still are the sweetest treat, my darling girl; the one thing I can't get enough of.' She leaned into the screen. 'And now I'm craving chocolate.

'Anyway.' She was trying to lighten the mood again. She still wasn't sure if that was the right thing to do. Perhaps it would make this easier for Grace to take in if Meg was just the same as she usually was. 'I handed you to your dad and then we all went through to where Cassie was waiting. It was a flat in a Victorian conversion, so the front room was huge with a high ceiling and great big bay window. She was standing by the window with her arms wrapped around herself like this.' Meg hugged her frame, feeling her ribs under her fingers. 'Your dad walked over to her and offered to hand you to her, but she kept her arms tight around her and shook her head. I was desperate to take you from him then, but I made myself sit. I had this tatty old sofa I'd covered in a batik throw and I remember wondering what she'd make of my studenty flat. She was only a few years older than me, but I still felt like an immature wannabe next to her.'

She glanced away from the screen. 'I suppose I was jealous of her. She was beautiful in a put-together sort of way that I couldn't even aspire to. I hadn't found my style by then and still felt like a bit of a try-hard, with my sharp bob and red lipstick. That confident look was a front, I can see that now.' She thought back to that Chanel China Berry lipstick in its gold casing. It was such an extravagance. When she applied it, she'd felt like it gave her some kind of sexy superpower. In truth, she was hiding behind it. She'd stopped using it as soon as she knew Simon really saw her for who she was under the makeup and thought she was enough without any kind of mask.

'I've always known you had Cassie's lovely thick, wavy hair. I know we pretended to think you were dark because of me, but those gorgeous waves and the reddish tint come from Cassie.' She stared directly into the screen. 'I'm so, so sorry we lied to you, Grace. If it's any consolation, I wanted what you believed to be true more than anything else in this world. You have always been my girl. You always will be.'

Her mind went back to sitting in that room with her hands clasped in her lap, rigid with embarrassment and fear. 'I was absolutely convinced Cassie was going to say she wasn't going to let us see you any more. I was shaking. I remember staring at you when he sat next to me, trying to commit everything about you to memory because I was so certain she would take you away and I wouldn't be allowed to see you again.

'When she turned away from the window and looked at us, I was taken aback by how empty her eyes were. It was like she wasn't really there. I'd first seen her on the day when she caught your dad and me... and it was like she was a different person, a ghost of herself.' Meg rubbed her forehead. 'I instantly felt an overwhelming guilt. The fact I'd been the cause of that change in her has haunted me ever since. I'm not saying I regret what happened. I could never regret being allowed to be your mum, but seeing Cassie that day... well, the guilt of what we'd done to her has stayed with me.'

She sipped at the water and cleared her throat. 'She sat in the armchair at the other side of the room, and it struck me that she hadn't looked at you, not properly. I couldn't keep my eyes off you, but it was like she was doing everything in her power to avert her gaze. Your dad asked why she wanted to see both of us, and I could tell she was trying not to cry. I was too, to be honest.

The guilt along with the fear she might take you away was making my bottom lip tremble. That made me feel like a stupid little girl. I wanted to reach for your dad's hand, but that would have been inappropriate too. I'd taken this woman's husband and all I wanted in the world was to have her baby too. What kind of woman did that make me?'

'"I need a clean break," she said, and I thought I was right, she was about to say she wouldn't continue to let us take care of you after what we'd done.' Meg remembered she'd started to shake then. It had only been three months, but she truly felt like a mother already. The thought of losing Grace was agony. 'But then Cassie said, "I've tried, I've tried so hard, but I don't feel like Grace's mother. I cry all the time, and that's clearly not good for her. She cries nearly as much as I do and nothing I do seems to soothe her." I was looking at her then, confused. With us, you were a dream baby, but then I wasn't suffering from depression.'

Meg looked into the screen, imagining she was being watched by her daughter. 'What happened then has absolutely no reflection on you, Grace. Cassie was ill. She was severely depressed, so depressed she couldn't see any other way out for herself. She'd resisted going to the doctors and had convinced herself starting over was the only thing that could help her.

'"I want you to take Grace," she said. I remember looking at your dad and seeing his mouth hanging open. "What do you mean?" he said. That's when she told us that she wanted me to adopt you. She'd looked into it. She'd need to consent to giving up her parental rights, meet with social workers so they could see she wasn't being coerced. She wanted to start divorce proceedings straight away, then when you'd lived with us full time for six months, I could apply to adopt you. All she wanted in return was for us to stay away from Bromley, to never contact her again. She wanted to start a new life as if she'd never met Simon, never had a baby. That was the only way she could envisage living a life she could bear.

'I'm not proud of the way my heart soared. I hope it didn't show on my face. Cassie was crying and your dad was dumbstruck for a minute, then he asked if she'd really thought it through. She said she had, and the way she spoke, I believed her. Obviously, your dad talked about her depression and going to the doctors. Don't get me wrong, he wasn't trying to dissuade her, he just wanted to make sure she knew what she was asking and was prepared for the repercussions.'

Meg took another drink. She wasn't used to speaking for this long and a headache was building behind her eyes. 'We talked for hours. You got hungry and I made up your bottle and your dad fed you. It still didn't feel right to hold you in front of her, but when it started to get dark and you were getting tired and fractious, your dad suggested I put you to bed. I looked at Cassie and she nodded. After your bath, I brought you into the room where they were still talking, and I asked if Cassie wanted to say goodnight to you.'

Tears welled in Meg's eyes. 'She came over to me. She bent her head to yours and I heard her take in a breath through her nose. She was breathing in your scent to store away in her mind, I'm sure of it. She kissed you gently on your forehead and whispered, "Goodbye, little one."' Meg swallowed. 'A tear fell onto your face, and I didn't wipe it away. It was still there, glinting on your cheek when I turned out the light in your room.'

32

PRESENT DAY

Cassie

Cassie tensed at the sound of Luke's key in the front door. Her bladder was full. She hadn't moved from the sofa for hours. Her limbs were too heavy to lift. She dragged herself to sit up straighter, holding the velvet cushion tight on her lap.

'Cassie?' he called. She supposed he'd be wondering why she was home from school. She'd usually stay to finish her marking when Alf had football practice. She heard his shoes thudding onto the floor.

'In here.' Her voice rasped. She cleared her throat.

'You're home early.' His head appeared around the door. He gave a brief, unconvincing smile. 'Cuppa before I pick Alf up from footie?' She could tell he was trying to be cheerful, but the usual light in his eyes was missing. She'd done that. She'd dimmed this lovely man's glow.

'Come in,' she said. She patted the sofa cushion next to her. 'Sit down. There's something I need to tell you.'

He took a step into the room. 'Sounds ominous.' His movements were tentative. He sat at the edge of the far side of the sofa, as if poised to make a quick getaway. Two short weeks ago, they'd snuggled together on this sofa, bowls of crisps on their laps, glasses of wine at their feet, no cares other than which film to choose. Two weeks seemed a lifetime ago. Luke checked his watch. 'I've got to go in fifteen minutes. Can it wait?'

Luke never wanted to wait to talk. He was all about expressing feelings, not bottling things up. But now he just wanted to get away, and she didn't blame him.

'I've been suspended from work.'

His eyes narrowed. 'Suspended?' The word came out in a disbelieving whisper.

'Well, when they add today to what happened the other time, I imagine that will be the outcome, or possibly worse.'

Luke ran his hand around the back of his neck. 'What did you do?'

The question stung. She'd expected him to ask what happened, so 'what did you do?' felt like a brutal judgement. But it was her. She had done it. 'I dragged a boy's shoulder to make him face me.'

Luke shook his head. 'Dragged? Why?'

Such a simple question. She tried to answer it simply. 'Because he was walking away from me, and I wanted to know what he'd said to his younger brother to make him taunt Alf.'

Luke's eyes opened wide at the mention of his son. 'I don't understand. Which boy? What's Alf got to do with it?'

Cassie's head was too heavy on her shoulders. She dropped it back onto the cushion. 'Oliver Simms. I found out this morning he has a brother at Alf's school called Perry, and he's the boy Alf had the altercation with when he grazed his head.'

'Fuck,' said Luke. He rubbed his neck again. 'Why do I

recognise the name?' His face went slack with understanding. 'Isn't Oliver Simms the boy you swore at?'

'Yep.' Cassie nodded. 'I think that's when it started. He got in trouble for keying the headmaster's car and then didn't want to get into more for accidentally splitting my lip, so he told his parents I'd dragged his clothes and sworn at him to get in a kind of pre-emptive strike. I played into his hands by not reporting it.'

'Which I still can't get my head around,' said Luke.

'I know. If I could turn back time, I would go straight to the office and write down every last detail. But I'd had a shit week, I knew I was in the wrong too, so I was hoping it would go away. It was stupid. I know.' If she did have a time machine, she would never have opened Simon's email. No, she would go further back than that. She would never have met Simon in the first place, or at least she wouldn't have fallen for him. She would have run in the opposite direction at the first twinkle of those stupid blue eyes.

Luke was watching her face, and she immediately felt guilty. If everything was different, then she might never have met Luke, or had Alf, and she would never wish to change that. She couldn't bring herself to wish Grace didn't exist either, not now. Not when she'd seen how beautiful she was, how full of life and fire. It all hurt too much. She had an ache in her chest. She pulled the cushion closer in.

'So you think he told his brother... what?' Luke's eyes were searching hers and she wanted to hide. There was too much he didn't know, and she was sure the guilt of it would be written all over her face. The weight of it pressed her into the sofa. She had the urge to splurge everything out to Luke. If she unburdened herself, maybe he could forgive her. His feelings about honesty slid into her head. He valued that above all else. He had categorically asked her to be honest with him and she had promised she would be. But a lie of that magnitude would end her marriage. She had to bear the weight on her own.

'I suspect he said something unpleasant about me, and Alf got upset and lashed out.'

'Okay, that makes sense.' He let out a long breath. 'But he's seven.'

Cassie's cheeks burned. 'I know, I know.' She covered her face with her hand. 'I'm ashamed of myself.'

'What the fuck were you thinking?' The frustration in his voice was rare, but even Luke had his limits.

She let her hand fall. 'I don't know. I wasn't thinking.' She massaged her temples. 'We need to work out what to do now.'

'But before that—'

A strangled sound escaped her throat. She couldn't do this. She didn't want to examine what caused her to march after Oliver Simms like a demented banshee. She already knew fourteen years of suppressed pain had come to the surface, and she was fighting to save her family and her sanity.

'Cassie, you can't go on like this. You've clearly been suffering since that email from Simon, and until you address what went on in your past, I'm worried you'll struggle to move forwards. I understand you don't want to talk to me about it, God knows, I've tried.' There was exasperation in his voice now. 'But let me make an appointment with Bella at the practice?'

'No.' Cassie threw the cushion on the floor. 'I don't want to see Bella. I don't want to talk about my past. I want to help Alf and get on with my life, that's all.'

Luke stood, holding his hands out in front of him. 'If you really want to help Alf, you need to help yourself. This situation is hard for him too. I know what it feels like to be a kid living in a house with an atmosphere. He's not stupid. He picks up on things, just like I did.'

He was right. She was ruining Alf's life. The certainty of that pounded into her like a wrecking ball. 'I'm sorry,' she said, 'I can't do this.' She walked past Luke's outstretched hands, up the stairs and into bed. She pulled the duvet over her head and let the emotional darkness in.

33

PRESENT DAY

Cassie

The brightness from the overhead light in the bedroom was blinding. Cassie shielded her eyes with her hands, then rolled onto her front, burying her face in her pillow. She could smell her own saliva on the fabric, but if she raised her head, she'd have to face Luke, and she was too exhausted to do that.

'I've got an early appointment,' said Luke gruffly. 'I need you to take Alf to school.'

She'd been in bed since their conversation last night and he'd slept in the spare room. Her sleep had been fitful, and the cold absence on his side of the bed hadn't helped matters. 'What time is it?' Her voice was muffled by the pillow.

'Seven.'

She'd been in bed for thirteen hours. Even with broken sleep, she should feel at least slightly refreshed, but her head pounded and her eyes felt like they'd been weighted down. She imagined her lids with coins on, like they used to do with the eyelids of corpses. 'I'm tired.'

'We're all tired. Alf is saying he doesn't want to go in again.'

Cassie rolled onto her back, squinting against the bulb on the ceiling above her head. 'Maybe he could have a—'

'No,' Luke snapped. 'You can't keep him off school because you don't feel like taking him in. And even if he is having a hard time at school, it's up to us to sort that out alongside him and his teacher. The last thing I want him to do is to think he can just avoid difficult thoughts and feelings and hope they'll go away, because they don't, do they?' That was pointed, and it hit the mark. She was getting sick of Luke's sanctimonious therapy-speak. He'd developed his strategies for dealing with his past, and she'd developed hers. Just because he'd become a counsellor didn't make him right all the time.

'I'm sorry I don't come up to your standards of behaviour.'

'That's not what...' He rubbed his neck. 'I can't make you see Bella, or anyone else, but let me make you an appointment at the doctor's. Maybe they can suggest something to help you through... whatever this is.'

Cassie had a flashback to Simon standing in the kitchen of the house they used to share, staring at the dirty plates left on the table and the pile of baby grows on the floor by the washing machine. She heard him begging her to go to the doctor. Grace's wails rang out in the background and Cassie covered her ears to block out the sound.

'Cassie. What are you doing?' Luke's face was a mixture of exasperation and worry.

She came back to the present and let her hands fall away. 'Okay, I'll see a doctor. I'll make an appointment.' She didn't need medication, though. How she was feeling was circumstantial, not that she could explain that to Luke.

Luke's shoulders relaxed. 'Thank you. I'll call the surgery, it's all right.'

She heard the code for *I don't believe you'll do it*. He stood in the doorway, his lips twitching as if he had more to say. Eventually, he looked down at his watch. She'd bought him that watch when they got engaged. It didn't seem right to her that she got a ring and he didn't get anything, so they'd chosen a watch on the shopping trip where they'd bought the solitaire diamond engagement ring she had worn every day since. She'd been so sure, back then. It had been the start of her new life. She wanted that life back so much it was agony.

'Can you get up, please? I need to know you're getting ready to take Alf to school.'

She heard his therapy-speak again; always saying *I need*, instead of *you have to*, to make sure she didn't feel the blame. She still did. Rightfully so. He didn't trust her to do anything she said, and he was probably right. She was so tired that if he walked away now, she could easily close her eyes and fall back to sleep with the light on. She wrenched herself off the pillow and rested her feet on the carpet. She looked at him and tried to smile. The sides of her mouth were too heavy to lift. 'I'm up. I'll get Alf to school. Don't worry.'

The way his eyelids partially raised told her that 'don't worry' was a stupid thing to say.

* * *

She could hardly hear the car radio over the sound of Alf's crying. Getting him onto his booster seat in the back had been a struggle, especially since he was adamant he was too big to need one. She'd considered letting him sit in the front with her, but when she imagined what Luke would say, she insisted he got in the back and closed her ears to his protestations. When they were halfway to school, he was still wailing about how it wasn't fair that he had to go to school when she didn't. She wanted to tell him the only reason she wasn't in work right now was because of Perry Simms' brother, but even she knew that wasn't true. She'd been suspended because of her inappropriate actions towards a pupil. And she'd reacted that way because her emotions were heightened due to Simon bloody Gately.

'Stop it, Alf,' she said when he started to kick the back of her seat. It was unlike him to be so difficult, and she didn't have anywhere near enough tolerance to cope with it this morning. She needed coffee. She needed sleep. She needed to be out of this metal box.

'I'm not getting out of the car,' said Alf, his red lips making an exaggerated upside-down smile. Surely if Luke could hear his son's pitiful cries, he wouldn't be making them both do this. Half of her wanted to turn around and defy Luke. But things were already so broken between them, letting Alf stay home might be the tipping point.

She juddered as Alf's kicks made the seat bang against her back. She was so tired. She didn't have the bandwidth to deal with his distress or his anger. 'You will get out of the car and you will go into school and be a good boy.' Her jaw clenched tight as he kicked the seat again.

'No, I won't.' She wasn't in the mood for his petulance. She tried to remember how Luke dealt with Alf when he was being a pain. He'd go down to his level and talk to him reasonably, face to face. The thought made goosebumps prickle on her skin. She'd thought they'd been a team, but when she looked back, all she could see was Luke being a brilliant parent and her basking in the delight of being part of a perfect family. None of it was her doing. She was a bystander, and an ineffectual one at that. She'd thought she was getting it right this time, but in reality, she was just as terrible a mother as she always had been.

She pulled up to the roundabout at the end of the ring road. She glanced at the car drawing up beside her. A woman with bright skin and a perfectly made-up face was smiling in the rearview mirror. Looking into the back seat, Cassie saw two equally healthy-looking children, laughing along with whatever the uber-mother had said. She turned her gaze to her own rearview mirror, seeing Alf's tear-stained face, cheeks red and snot dribbling from his nose. He caught her eye and scrunched his mouth, aiming another kick at the seat.

'Stop it.' He kicked again. She leaned around and swiped at his shoe but must've taken her foot off the brake and dragged the steering wheel because the car jerked left just as the perfect family's car sped up to take advantage of a gap in the traffic. There was a crunch of metal and the seatbelt snagged across her throat as the airbag detonated and Alf's screams ricocheted around the car.

34

PRESENT DAY

Cassie

Cassie sat on the blue bunk inside the ambulance next to Alf, trying not to think of how much worse things could have been. She imagined all the people before her who'd laid where she was currently sitting, oxygen masks on their faces, heart monitors beeping as the ambulance screamed through the streets. She was only here because of a stupid, reckless mistake. She didn't deserve the kind attention of the paramedic who'd introduced herself as Adeola and was now holding Cassie's chin and swabbing the blood from her nose.

'Hold this,' Adeola said, handing Cassie a wad of cotton wool. 'Press it tight and pinch the soft part of your nose, but don't put your head back.' She checked Cassie was following her instructions correctly then moved on to Alf, whose face was whiter than Cassie had ever seen it. 'How are you feeling?'

Alf looked up at Adeola, his eyes blinking fast as though he was trying not to cry. 'All right, I think.'

'Not feeling sick or dizzy?'

Alf shook his head. Cassie reached for his hand and squeezed it. His skin was cold. The fact she could have killed him tramped around her head in heavy boots.

Adeola smiled. 'You're very brave.' She stepped out of the back of the ambulance and surveyed the scene. From where she was sitting, Cassie could see another ambulance dealing with the perfect family from the other car. She strained her neck to see if they were okay, not quite sure how she'd cope if she'd injured someone else. The mother emerged from the back, looking pale and shaken. She turned to help her children down and Cassie let out a breath when she saw they appeared unharmed, physically at least.

'Back in a sec,' she said to Alf. 'Stay there.' She jumped down from the van and crossed to where the woman was standing, looking at her car. The front wing was a crumpled mess and Cassie's car was still wedged against it, not looking much better. Two police cars were parked at the side of the road and cones blocked off the roundabout.

She tapped the woman on the elbow. She turned, looking down her nose at Cassie. 'I'm so sorry,' Cassie said. 'Are you all okay?'

The woman scowled. She pulled both of her children close into her side. 'What were you thinking?'

'I'm so sorry.'

'Have you given your insurance details to the police?'

Cassie blinked, watching the police talk to a man who pulled up in a pick-up truck. 'Not yet. I will.' Blood trickled from her nose. She'd left the wad of cotton wool in the ambulance. She tried to wipe it away with the back of her hand but there was too much, and she felt it smear across her face.

The woman watched in horror. 'I think you need to...' She pointed a ruby red fingernail at the ambulance. A fleeting look of pity passed across her face before she dipped her head to check on her children. Cassie went back to where Alf was sitting, looking tiny and fragile amongst all the medical equipment. She didn't blame the woman for being angry with her. If anyone had put her child in danger, she'd have been livid.

She remembered herself. Someone *had* put Alf in danger: her.

* * *

'We need to take you to the Princess Royal Hospital to get checked over,' said Adeola. 'I don't think either of you have concussion, but there's no harm getting another opinion.'

Cassie shook her head. She wanted to refuse to go to hospital, but if there was anything wrong with Alf and she didn't get him checked by a doctor, she would never forgive herself, but she couldn't go to the Princess Royal. She just couldn't. 'Can we go to Queen Mary's?' she said. 'It's closer to home.'

'No can do, I'm afraid. We have to go where Control sends us so...' She shrugged as if it was no big deal. But it was a big deal. Massive. Cassie hadn't been anywhere near the PRUH since the day she was discharged with Grace. Even the thought of that hospital made her lightheaded. Luke had always been understanding about her refusal to go anywhere near their local hospital, even insisting she gave birth to Alf at Queen Mary's in Sidcup, due to believing her baby had died at the Princess Royal. In truth, it was because her baby had lived.

She gripped Alf's hand as the ambulance drew up to the Accident and Emergency department at the side of the chrome and red-clad building. When Adeola helped them both out of the ambulance, she said, 'You're shaking. Good job we brought you in. You must be in shock.'

Cassie wasn't in shock, or if she was, it was in response to the trauma of being back in the place that represented the very worst moments of her life. It was only the feel of her son's small hand in hers that made her take one step after another into the building.

* * *

The concern on Luke's face when he entered the hospital waiting room after they'd both had the all clear made Cassie want to bawl. Alf jumped off Cassie's lap and hugged his dad. Luke glanced at her, then leaned over to kiss Alf's head. When he straightened up, he said, 'Thank God you're both okay.'

Her tears started then. Not because of the throbbing in her sinuses, not because she'd caused an accident that had put so many people in danger, but because her husband's first response wasn't to blame her, or demand to know what had happened. He was just glad they were all right.

'I'm so sorry,' she said. She stood and wrapped her arms around him and their son. She needed to feel their warmth, even though she didn't deserve it. 'I don't know how I managed to do that.'

'We'll worry about that later.' Luke pulled back and examined her face. 'The airbag works then?'

He smiled and she laughed through her tears. 'Looks like it.' She could still smell the blood in her nose and feel the scratch of the dried remnants in her nostrils. 'Can we get out of here? I really hate this place.'

Luke nodded, sympathy in his eyes, and guilt coursed through her. She didn't deserve a second of his sympathy. 'Come on, then. Let's get you two home.' He rubbed Alf's head and they made their way past the miserable people still waiting to be seen. 'The lengths you'll go to for a day off school, eh?'

Alf started to whimper when they got out into the fresh air. 'It was my fault, Daddy. I was kicking Mummy's seat because I was cross about going to school and she turned around to try to make me stop and that's when the car crashed.'

Cassie stopped dead in front of the sliding doors. She leaned down to Alf's level, horrified to see the remorse in his watery eyes. 'It wasn't your fault, sweetheart. I shouldn't have turned around. I lost my temper and that was my fault. I'm the grown-up. I was driving. I was the one who crashed the car, not you.' She stared into his eyes, willing him to absorb her words. She knew what guilt could do to a person and she didn't want her sweet boy to suffer a moment of it. 'Seriously, Alf. None of what happened today was your fault. Do you understand that?'

Alf nodded and they made their way quietly to Luke's car. Even the car park sparked awful memories of following Simon as he carried the car seat with Grace tucked under blankets against the frigid December air. She closed her eyes as soon as she was in the passenger seat, but the image of Simon leaning over and buckling their newborn baby in, his eyes already full of adoration, wouldn't leave her.

Back at home, when Alf was settled in front of the TV, Luke followed Cassie into the kitchen. She went to switch the kettle on, hyper aware of him carefully taking a seat at the table. Her shoulders tensed. Questions were on their way. As she dropped teabags into two mugs, she tried to get the events that led up to the accident straight in her mind. She recalled feeling jealous of the woman in the next car, with her perfect face and perfect family. How ironic that only a couple of weeks ago, she'd followed her own small family into the party venue, thinking how perfect their life was. Pride before a fall, she thought. And what a fall it had been.

She scrabbled in her memory but couldn't recall the crash in detail. In her head it was a jumble of sharp metallic sounds and white-hot terror.

'I think what happened this morning is symptomatic of your state of mind, Cass,' said Luke.

She turned, surprised. He wasn't going to ask about the accident, then. He was going bigger. 'It was a mistake. It could have happened to anyone.' She got a teaspoon from the drawer. Any excuse not to face him.

'No,' he said. 'People who are acting rationally do not drive into other cars.'

After a breath, she turned to him and said, 'It was only because Alf—' She stopped. She'd promised she wouldn't blame Alf, and she didn't. It wouldn't be fair to use him as an excuse.

'Alf what? Alf was kicking your seat?' Luke lay his fingers flat on the table, as if reaching for control within himself. 'Do you know how many seven-year-olds kicked the back of their parents' seats on the way to school this morning? I bet it's in the thousands.'

'It was an accident.' The sound of the kettle boiling mimicked the bubbling panic inside her. 'It was just a stupid accident.'

Luke slammed his palms on the table. 'An avoidable one.' Those words smacked into her brain. He was right. She was to blame. She was a terrible mother, and Luke knew it. 'You're in chaos, Cassie. Look at yourself.' He flung out an arm. 'You've been suspended from your job, you're clearly in a depressive episode, you don't sleep, you don't want to get out of bed, and now you've put our son in danger.'

'I didn't mean to.' She had no defence. He was right.

'No, I don't suppose you did, but that doesn't change the fact it happened, and since you won't help yourself, it's my job to make sure it doesn't happen again.'

Panic tightened her throat. 'What do you mean?' The kettle clicked off and the room fell silent apart from the clock's slow tick.

Luke kept his eyes on his hands, which were clasped firmly in front of him, turning his knuckles white. 'I can't go on like this. I can't watch you self-destruct and do nothing... and I won't let you damage Alf.'

'I'm not...' She stopped mid-sentence. She couldn't pretend she wasn't hurting Alf because she knew she was. It was her fault Perry Simms was making school miserable for him. Her state of mind was impacting his home life, and now she had put his actual life in danger. Her husband was looking at her like she was a stranger. Everything was falling apart and there was only one thing she could think of doing to try to claw it back.

She had no choice. She had to tell Luke the truth.

35

PRESENT DAY

Cassie

When Luke returned from depositing Alf next door with Marie, Cassie couldn't stop her body from shaking. 'Is he okay?'

'Yeah. Marie's going to make biscuits with him, so we've got a while to talk.'

He sat opposite her at the kitchen table, his face hard. She couldn't blame him for putting up a shield. He knew she'd hidden things from him and that she was about to hurt him. 'Could you get me a drink, please?' She didn't trust herself not to drop the bottle if she tried to get it herself.

'Tea?'

The mugs still sat on the counter next to the kettle, but she needed something stronger. 'Gin, please.'

'It's only...' Luke stopped himself. 'All right.' He went to the tall cupboard in the corner where they kept the spirits. They'd bought the gin in duty free on the way back from a holiday in Gran Canaria and it had been in the cupboard ever since. It was a magical holiday. She could still hear Alf's exhilarated shrieks as he came down the water slides, his mouth open and eyes shining. Would they ever go on a family holiday again? The thought almost made her change her mind about what she was about to do. But it was too late. They couldn't carry on like this. The bottle's metal lid scraped open like a complaint at being awoken from a deep sleep. Cassie kept her eyes on the table as the fridge suctioned open. There was a fizz and slosh before she heard the fridge door close again. When he returned to the table, Luke was carrying two glasses. He put one down in front of each of them.

'Aren't you working this afternoon?' she said.

'Funnily enough, when you get a call to say your wife and son have been in a car crash and you need to get to the hospital, you tend to cancel the appointments for the rest of the day.' The sarcastic tone was new. She'd turned him into someone else, someone less kind. It was probably a defence mechanism. He had to defend himself against her. How terribly sad.

'Sorry.'

'So you said.' He took a slug of his drink and it seemed defiant, like he was saying, *Look, you've brought me down to your level. Happy now?*

Cassie sipped her gin. It was strong. She had a memory of Simon pulling a face when he'd first tried gin at university. 'Yuck,' he'd said. 'It's like drinking liquidised Christmas trees.' Simon. That was where she needed to start. She took another drink. 'I haven't told you everything that happened back then, with Simon and Meg, I mean.'

'I'm listening.'

She turned her glass, probing her brain for the right words. 'When I had the baby...' Her mind went back to waking up from the anaesthetic. Her mouth immediately went dry. She could still feel the scratch of her throat and the aching in her gut.

More harrowing still, the relief that it was all over came back to her, the hope she could walk away from the tragedy of the last nine months and start again. 'I wasn't well.'

'I know that. No one would be after going through what you did. I know you blame yourself because you almost had a termination, but that's not why your baby died. I wish I could make you understand that.' His voice was softer now and she wished she could curl up and pull the cover of his kind words over her.

Instead, she had to tell him the truth. She tensed every muscle in her body. In a quiet voice, she said, 'The baby didn't die.'

'What?' He leaned forwards, top teeth bared in incomprehension. 'I'm sorry, what did you say?'

'The baby... mine and Simon's baby, she wasn't stillborn.'

'So... what, she lived for a while after she was born, then? God, it must've been so awful to have that hope and then—'

'No. She's still alive.' Cassie gripped the glass so hard she expected it to shatter; wanted it to. She wanted to feel the shards of glass pierce her skin and see her blood leak onto the table. Anything but the silence in the room only broken by the ticking of the clock.

Luke took in a breath, then stood, his chair scraping along the tiles. He walked to the patio doors, his hand combing through his hair. He turned to her. 'Make this make sense, Cassie, because I'm struggling here. You told me she was stillborn.'

Cassie shook her head. 'I never said that.'

He marched to the table and lay his palms flat on the wood. 'You led me to believe the baby was born dead.' He lifted his hands and let them hover in the air. 'God, what an idiot I am.' His eyes looked wildly around the room. 'You always said things like "lost" and "gone" and I thought it was like when people say someone has passed because they can't bring themselves to say "dead". But that wasn't it, was it? You were using words to cover up the truth. You used semantics to lie and deceive me for ten fucking years... Christ, Cassie.' He turned away again, pushing his hair back from his forehead before snapping back around. 'Where is she now, this living, breathing child of yours?'

Cassie could hardly speak for the tears blocking her throat. 'With Simon.'

Luke leaned in, as if trying to hear. 'With Simon?'

Cassie nodded, unable to raise her eyes to his.

'So for the entire time I've known you, you've had a daughter who is living with your ex-husband?'

'She's called Grace.' Saying her name brought back the picture of Grace standing in the school car park watching Cassie, tentative, nervous, but brave and oh so beautiful.

'Have you been in contact with her all that time?'

'No. I gave up parental rights soon after she was born, as soon as the authorities were satisfied that was what I really wanted, then Meg formally adopted her. It took about a year for all the paperwork to go through.' There was so much he didn't know. This was agony.

'Alf has a sister.' Luke paced the room, his words coming fast. 'And you didn't ever think we might want to know that?'

'I wasn't well.' It was all Cassie could think to say.

Luke stopped pacing. 'I understand you were depressed. I've been very sympathetic about that, but you led me to believe it was because of the guilt you felt about almost aborting a baby who then went on to die. That would mess with anyone's head.' His eyes bored into her. 'Is any of that even true? Did you even go to the clinic or was that your attempt to add more pathos?'

She crumpled. 'Don't be cruel.'

'Me, cruel?' His voice was high pitched with incredulity. 'I'm not the one who's lied and denied their own flesh and blood for fourteen years.'

'I didn't see her because Meg adopted Grace.'

He nodded, taking in the information. 'Right. But why did she adopt her? Why did Meg bring up your daughter and why didn't you tell me she existed? I've treated women who've given babies up, I've worked with women who've had their children taken into care, and I don't judge them. You know that.'

'I do know that,' said Cassie. 'But it was never about you judging me.' She wondered if that was true. Men walked away from their children every day and society didn't blink. But a mother voluntarily giving up her child had the kind of stigma that made it shameful, monstrous, even. 'I was denying it to myself. I thought pretending those nine months had never happened was the only way I could move on and be happy again.'

'And how's that working out for you?' He spat the words, then appeared to regret them. He sat heavily. He sighed. 'What else have you lied about?' he said quietly.

Cassie wiped tears from her face. 'The email from Simon telling me Meg had died.' She rolled her lips over her teeth, not wanting to carry on, but knowing she had to. 'That was Simon asking me to help with Grace.'

'Help?' Luke took a gulp from his drink.

'She's struggled since Meg died.'

Luke nodded. 'And what did you say?'

Cassie took a sip of gin. She wanted to gulp it down, then pour a neat one and swallow that. She wanted oblivion. 'I said I couldn't.'

'You couldn't?' His raised eyebrow made it clear what he thought. She disgusted him. She always knew she would if she told him the truth.

'I'm not her mother. I never have been.'

Luke sat back and crossed his arms. 'Did she always know about you, that you were her biological mother?'

Cassie shook her head. 'Not until just before Meg died.'

'Poor kid.' Luke closed his eyes and breathed in through his nose. 'So, she's fourteen and the only mother she's ever known dies, then she's told her mum wasn't her birth mum, but her natural mother gave her up, and then that mother rejects her again when her dad reaches out.'

A spark of anger ignited in Cassie. 'You make it all sound so black and white, like it's all my fault. So much for not judging. Everything else I told you is true. I did go for an abortion when I saw Simon and Meg together, because my life had been completely destroyed. But Simon begged me to go through with the pregnancy. I agreed, thinking I could move past what he'd done, but I was already depressed by then, I was in this thick black fog, and I couldn't find my way out. Seven months later, I fell after I found out Simon was leaving me for Meg and my placenta ruptured. That's why I ended up having the emergency Caesarean, and when I came around, I believed the baby had died, and...' Her sobs were coming fast, but she had to say the worst of it, then it would all be out there and Luke could hate her as much as she hated herself. But she couldn't find the words. It was too awful. She laid her head on the table and let the tears flow.

A second later, a warm hand touched her back. 'That's a lot to cope with, Cassie,' Luke said. He moved until his arm rested around her back and his mouth was close to her ear. 'You've been through an awful ordeal.'

But he still didn't know everything. She lifted her head when his arm left her back. He was standing above her, holding out a tissue. She took it and gave a weak smile of thanks. 'Grace came to find me.'

Luke sat down with a sigh. His cheeks sagged, like the last fifteen minutes had physically aged him.

'She came to work. She'd found the email Simon sent to my school email address and worked it out from there.'

'When was this?'

Cassie calculated the days. Everything had been a blur since Simon's first email. Time had warped, with one hideous episode merging into the next. 'The day I was home late. That's why I was at the station. I took her straight there.'

Pain filled Luke's eyes. 'God. The poor girl. That's...' He shook his head. 'I'm trying to understand, I really am, but you sent her away and she's only a kid. I'm struggling to get my head around all this. The way you've reacted, the lies. That's not you, Cass. That's not the woman I know.'

'I didn't feel like I had any other choice.'

'I remember asking you to tell me what was wrong. I knew you were hurting and that hurt me, too.' His eyes filled with tears.

'I was trying not to hurt you.' The words sounded empty, even to her, and she wasn't surprised when he shook his head again and dropped his gaze to the table.

'How was she, Grace?' He added her name as if trying it out in his mouth, this person who he hadn't known existed half an hour ago, but who was now inextricably linked to his family.

'Sad.' Cassie didn't know what else to say, other than that she was even more beautiful than Cassie had allowed herself to imagine, and more courageous, and strong and... She swallowed. 'Very sad.'

'You could have brought her here. Taking her back to the

station was...' He lifted his arms instead of saying whatever brutal thing was at the tip of his tongue.

Cassie took a drink. 'It didn't feel like an option, and anyway... she wasn't exactly impressed with what she found.'

'What do you mean?'

Cassie remembered Grace's face when Cassie said she should go home to her family. 'Just that I don't think she'll be in a hurry to see me again.' She took a shuddering breath. 'So, now you know everything, and it's over, I suppose.'

'Over?'

'I pretended none of it had happened as a way of surviving. Simon had been everything to me. Finding out about his affair on the same day I discovered I was pregnant sort of connected the two things in my head. I couldn't bond with Grace and that compounded my self-loathing, and I truly couldn't see any other way out than walking away completely. I've thought about her every day of her life, of course I have, but I can't regret making the decision to let Meg adopt her just because Meg died. Up until that point, Grace had a wonderful mother. She told me that herself.' She glanced at his face, then away, not able to read his expression. 'You've seen the state I've been in since Simon got in touch. The dark feelings have been swallowing me up.' Her tears dripped onto the table. 'I can't go back there. More than anything else in this world I want to forget any of this happened and get back to normal.'

A small laugh escaped from Luke's mouth. 'Get back to normal?'

She wanted to plead with him, beg him to see she'd only lied because she loved him and Alf so very much. 'I mean, you, me and Alf—'

'Cassie, can you hear yourself speak? You think something like this can be brushed under the table and ignored? Seriously? That's why you've never fully recovered, because you've never really dealt with what happened.' He paused. 'I think you need to talk to Simon—'

'No.' Cassie shook her head. This had to be the end of it. Giving up Grace again would be too much to bear if it didn't end here, with her family intact. 'No. I don't want anything to do with him ever again.'

'But Grace—'

'Grace is better off without me.' Cassie blew her nose and tried to slow her breathing. 'Please, can you forgive me for lying to you now you know the whole story? Can you try to see that I did what I did to survive the pain?'

There was sympathy in Luke's eyes, and a flicker of hope sparked at the base of her throat. 'You lied to me for ten years, Cassie.' The flicker went out.

She swallowed. Her hands began to tremble uncontrollably, so she clasped them together in her lap. She'd known this would happen from the start, that the truth would destroy them. That was why she'd hid her past. Why couldn't he understand that?

'As long as you've known me, you've been aware of how important honesty is to me.'

'I know, but...' She stopped. He was crying now and every tear that fell onto his cheek was a spear in her heart. 'I'm so, so sorry.'

Luke stood and she felt the gap between them widen. 'I need to... erm...' He pulled in air through his teeth, then went to take a tissue from the box. The room was quiet while he dried his face. Finally, he turned to her. 'If it's okay with you, I'll take Alf to my mum's for a couple of days. That will give us both time to think.'

If it's okay with you. He was even considerate when he

suggested splitting their family in two. He was a good man. She loved him so very much. And she had destroyed everything.

36

SIX MONTHS AGO

Meg

'Even before Cassie asked me to adopt you, I felt like your mother.' Meg looked away from the screen, searching for the right sentiment. Her gaze landed on the red and white striped blinds at the window. Simon had thought they were too bold, but Grace said they were cheerful and Meg agreed. She tried not to think of all the bigger, life-changing decisions her daughter would have to make in future without her guidance. 'Not your mother, exactly, that sounds too formal. I was your mum, your mummy, even though I know you think that sounds too childish now. I was the one who blew raspberries on your tummy to make you giggle. I knew how to distract you when I was about to rinse the shampoo off your hair in the bath so you didn't cry when the water got in your eyes. Not that I let it get in your eyes if I could help it. I did everything I could to keep you safe and happy.'

She made a pinched lipped smile. 'You're going to think this is silly, but I was a little bit obsessed with making things smell nice for you. I washed your bedding far more than I needed to and changed your bib whenever it got damp with dribble.' She laughed. 'You were a shocking dribbler.'

What she wouldn't give to be able to go back and touch those plump baby cheeks again. At least she had appreciated it properly the first time around. Grace had been her miracle baby, and she cherished every minute. She sighed. 'What I want you to understand is that, even though I didn't give birth to you, you have always been my girl.' She adjusted her headscarf where it started to itch above her ear. 'That's probably the main reason we never told you about Cassie. As I said before, it never seemed to be the right time, but if I'm brutally honest, if this hadn't happened' – she gestured to her hairless face and scarf – 'I'm not sure I would have ever told you. I was too selfish. I wanted you to be mine in every way possible. I suppose I was afraid you might be curious about your birth mum, and I would be side-lined.' She dropped her gaze. 'A pathetic, needy excuse, I know.

'Your dad and I have talked about it a lot; why we made the decision we did. For the longest time we told ourselves we were just doing what Cassie wanted. We felt righteous, I suppose, stepping up and being the best parents we could be.' She looked away from the camera. 'But I can see now that we told ourselves the story we wanted to hear. It suited us to believe that we'd done the right thing. Now I'm not so sure. We could have stopped what's happening now – the impact it's having on you. If you'd always known about Cassie, then it wouldn't be such a shock now, and you'd have had the option to find her whenever you wanted.' She rubbed her forehead. 'We could have reached out to Cassie over the years and given her the chance to have a relationship with you. It didn't need to be so black and white. I can see that now.

'I suppose what I'm trying to say is that I think we were selfish. But the time to greedily keep you to ourselves is up. I'm convinced telling you about Cassie is the right thing to do and I wanted to do it whilst... I didn't want your dad to have to do it on his own, since it was something we'd both decided together. I wanted you to know why we did what we did, and I wanted at least a little time to try to comfort and support you through it, if you can bear to let me now you know the truth.'

She closed her eyes and raised her head. 'I had such plans for us, my darling girl. When you were older, we were going to be ladies who lunched. We would go for afternoon tea in London hotels, then to the theatre, like when we saw *Mean Girls* then walked along the South Bank in the sunshine, but with added cocktails. When you went to university, your dad and I would visit you and stay in bed and breakfasts and try not to intrude too much on your life but find it hard because we would miss you so much.' She laughed. 'I would have been a nightmare, trying to be the cool mum, wouldn't I? I'd get it all wrong.' Tears ambushed her. 'I wish I had the chance to get it all wrong, then try to put it right.'

She wiped her eyes and composed herself. 'But since I'm not going to be there' – her bottom lip wobbled – 'then at least I want you to have the opportunity to have another woman in your life who you can turn to if you need her. We will leave it up to you whether you want to get in touch with Cassie. You might not want to now, but you could change your mind when you're older. At least now you know the truth and you have choices.' She swallowed and looked down at her hands. 'I have looked Cassie up now and again, over the years. I don't know why. Curiosity, I suppose. She doesn't do a lot on social media. What sane teacher does?' She glanced at the screen. 'But I've seen pictures on her school website. Is that a bit stalkery? Even though I told myself we'd done the right thing, I've always carried a lot of guilt about what your dad and I did to her. It's reassuring to see she seems... well, she looks fine. I hope she is.

'And if you do get in touch with her, I hope she appreciates how lucky she is to have someone as wonderful as you back in her life.' Meg looked intently at the screen. 'I will always be grateful to her for allowing me to be your mum.' Her voice wavered. 'I always wished I could say thank you to her properly. I doubt she has any idea what an incredible gift she gave to me, when I probably deserved it the least. If you ever speak to her, maybe you could tell her that.' More tears fell. 'And can you please tell her I'm sorry.'

37

PRESENT DAY

Cassie

The plate of freshly made biscuits Alf had brought back from Marie's sat on the kitchen table. Cassie broke a piece off, then flung it back on the plate. She couldn't eat; not when she could hear Luke issuing instructions on what Alf needed to pack for a few days at Nanna's house.

Luke's mum only lived three miles away, but the emotional distance was a thousand times further. Cassie's husband couldn't stay in the same house as her, now he knew the truth. He didn't trust her to take care of their son. She wondered if he would tell his mother about Grace. Was her relationship with her about to be fractured too when she discovered her daughter-in-law was no different from her ex-husband? She briefly considered asking him not to mention what had happened, but that would be another lie of omission; exactly the reason Luke couldn't bear to be near her. Would she ever learn that covering things up was like painting over mould? It didn't solve the problem. It was still festering underneath, black and poisonous, forever creeping closer to the surface.

She stood and rifled in the cupboard for a Tupperware box with a lid that fit. Eventually she found one and slid the biscuits inside. She sat numbly watching condensation fog the lid. They must still be warm, she thought. She was about to open the box to let the air out, so Alf wasn't disappointed they'd gone soggy, when she heard Luke and Alf come downstairs. On wobbly legs, she took it through to the hall and held them out for Alf with a dredged-up smile. 'Give these to Nanna.' She touched the end of his nose. 'And don't eat them all yourself.'

'Why aren't you coming?' Alf looked up at her, his little nose creased, and she wanted to hold him to her.

'Mummy's got lots of marking to do, mate,' said Luke, not looking at her. 'So it's a boy's trip this time.'

She wanted to say, *Who's lying now?* But she didn't want Alf to know the real reason her husband was taking her son away from her, so she just nodded. 'I'll miss you, though. I'll see you soon, okay?' She bent and hugged him, kissing the top of his head. His dark waves reminded her of Grace. She hoped Simon gave her the hugs she needed. She hoped she was surrounded by love.

'I'll miss you. Is your nose all right after our crash?' Alf pulled back and examined Cassie's face.

'It's not too bad.' Cassie put her hand to her nose, glad of the excuse to cover her face. The effort of not crying was becoming too much. 'Be a good boy for Daddy.'

'Come on then, pal,' said Luke, turning the door latch. Cassie longed for him to drop his bag and hug her. He held the door open to the grey day and Alf walked under his arm and out of their house onto the wet driveway. 'I'll call you,' Luke said over his shoulder, his voice thick with emotion. Then he closed the door, leaving her standing in the hall all alone.

* * *

Cassie was on the sofa staring into space, wrapped in a blanket that smelled of her son, when the doorbell rang. She glanced at her phone screen. It was 4 p.m., so unlikely to be the postman. She was in no mood to talk to Jehovah's Witnesses, so she closed her eyes and ignored it. When it rang again, she pulled the blanket over her head, dragging it down in exasperation when the ringing started up again at the same time a message lit up her phone screen. It was from Becca, saying:

> Open the bloody door xxx

She heaved her heavy limbs to the front door and opened it. Becca stood on the doorstep holding a red box of Celebrations, her mouth downturned. 'Luke messaged. He said you could do with a visit.'

Cassie's knees weakened. Even when Luke couldn't be with her, he made sure she wasn't alone. How had she allowed herself to turn that lovely man against her?

'Come on, Mrs.' Before she knew it, Becca was by her side, ushering her through to the front room, as Cassie cried so hard she couldn't speak. Becca buzzed around, finding tissues and making them cups of tea as if Cassie was an invalid who needed extra special care instead of a liar who deserved everything she got. Soon, Becca ran out of things to do and sat in the armchair next to the sofa, letting out a long breath. 'Want to tell me what happened, or shall we watch *Love Is Blind* and eat chocolates till we're sick?'

'I can't eat,' said Cassie, taking another tissue from the box on her knee.

'Shit, it really is bad,' said Becca, making her eyes comically wide. 'I take it this isn't just about you being suspended?'

Cassie's stomach lurched. With everything that had happened since, she hadn't even thought about the fact she might be about to lose her job. 'Just a sec.' She opened her phone and clicked onto her work emails. There it was, the formally worded email from Keith Finnegan. It asked her to stay off the school premises until the governors' meeting on Monday. After that, they'd decide what action to take and inform her in due course. She handed the phone to Becca, then tugged the blanket up to her shoulders.

Becca scanned the email. 'Bollocks. If you're going down for it, you could've at least kicked the little scrote in the balls to make it worthwhile.'

'That's a lot of testicles in one sentence,' said Cassie, immensely grateful to feel the first inkling of a smile that day, even though it disappeared as soon as it arrived. 'I think that would make it a police matter, not just a school one, and I've already had one run-in with the police today. That's more than enough for me.'

Becca's jaw dropped. 'What happened? Luke just suggested I might want to pop around. He didn't say why.'

'I had a crash this morning, with Alf in the back,' said Cassie. 'I went straight into another car with two little kids in the back. Thankfully no one was badly hurt, but they could've been. And it was entirely my fault.' Shame washed through her and it was all she could do not to lift the blanket over her head and try to hide.

'Oh, love, that's awful. At least no one was badly hurt. I did think your nose looked a bit swollen but didn't like to mention it. You can't just turn up and tell someone their nose looks shit, can you?' Becca's voice became serious. 'That's a lot to handle, after all the school stuff. I'm not surprised you're on the sofa with a blanket. Have you got a bottle of gin tucked under there? I would have.'

If only it was just getting suspended and crashing the car. On any other day that would be bad enough. 'Luke's taken Alf to his parents,' she said, fresh tears falling.

'Because Alf was in the car? That's... I mean, you would never intentionally hurt him. Surely Luke knows that? It's a bit harsh to—'

'It's not because of the accident. Well, not just because of that. It's because of my other child. The one I've never told you about.' For once, Becca seemed speechless, and so Cassie took a deep breath and continued. 'I had a baby with my first husband, and she lives with him and his wife.' She paused. 'At least she did, until his wife died and he got in touch with me... Anyway, Grace, their daughter... my daughter, turned up at school last week and things have been pretty messy since then.'

'I'm sorry, what now?' Becca scrunched her eyes tight then opened them and stared at Cassie in disbelief. 'Say that again, and this time make it make sense.'

As fresh tears fell, Cassie told her best friend the whole sorry tale.

38

PRESENT DAY

Cassie

In the following days, Cassie lay in bed, unable to gather the energy to shower or dress. For the second time in her life, there was a gaping chasm where her family should be, and this time the blame lay with her.

Becca messaged occasionally, but Cassie read judgement under the caring tone. After *Be kind to yourself* and *Stop beating yourself up*, Cassie read the invisible words that Becca didn't type but she was sure she thought: *...despite the awful things you've done.* Now Becca knew that Cassie had walked away from her own baby, of course she would judge her. Anyone would.

She tried hard to lift her voice when she spoke to Alf in the evenings, but the effort left her drained and tearful. All conversations with Luke were perfunctory and she longed for the connection they'd had before she ruined everything.

When a call came through from Alf's school at lunchtime three days after Luke and Alf left, Cassie jumped at the sound of the ringtone. She was still in bed with the curtains closed and the screen lit the room with an eerie glow.

'Hello.'

'Mrs Monroe? It's Mrs Miah here.'

'Hi.' Cassie's pulse began to race.

'Don't worry, Alf is fine. But I was hoping you'd be able to come in and have a little chat with us this afternoon. Alf said you're not working today.'

Cassie sat up, her stomach lurching at the thought of what else Alf might have shared. 'He hasn't been in another fight, has he?' If he'd been hurt because of her she would never forgive herself.

'No, no, nothing like that.' There was a pause and Cassie could hear Mrs Miah's breathing. 'But Alf tried to leave the school premises at the start of lunch.'

'Leave? What do you mean?' Cassie got to her feet, running her fingers through her greasy hair. The fog in her brain lifted as she imagined her little boy alone on busy streets, dodging fast cars and dangerous strangers.

'I think it would be better to discuss this face to face, if that's possible? I have a student teacher working with me at the moment so could meet with you in an hour, if that's convenient?'

'Yes, of course. I'll see you then.' Cassie clicked off the call and switched on the overhead light, surveying the messy sheets and undrunk cups of tea with filmy tops. She cursed herself for malingering, then assessed how much time it would take her to shower, dress and get to school. She'd have to order a taxi because her car was in the garage after the crash. The adrenaline spike made her dizzy after days of inactivity and she had to flop back on the bed for a moment to gather herself.

After a quick shower, she scraped her hair up into a tight

ponytail to disguise the fact she hadn't had time to wash it. She looked at her reflection in the mirror. A gaunt, ghostly figure stared back. She applied some blusher and mascara to try to mask the fact she felt like the ghoul she saw, unsubstantial, not really present in the world. She tried a brighter lipstick than usual, then felt like a pantomime dame, but had no time to wipe it off because the taxi horn sounded outside. When she stepped outside her house, the world seemed too bright and busy. The taxi driver had all the windows down and the roar of car engines, the smell of petrol fumes and the feel of the wind on her face overwhelmed her senses.

Her pulse thumped in her neck when she paid the driver and walked towards the reception at Hillside Primary. Sweat sprang up on her skin. Since she'd been spending her days in a darkened room, she'd underestimated how warm the weather had become, and her long-sleeved T-shirt stuck to her back. She pressed the intercom. 'Mrs Monroe here to see Mrs Miah.'

The door clicked open. Mrs Miah was standing in front of the reception desk, wearing a floaty green dress. A sympathetic expression appeared on her face when she turned to see Cassie. Pity meant Mrs Miah knew something about her situation. She braced herself and held out her hand. 'Hello.' Mrs Miah's hand was warm and soft. It was the first human contact Cassie had experienced since Becca hugged her three days ago, and it brought a lump to Cassie's throat.

'Thank you for coming in.'

'Is Alf...?' Cassie glanced around the reception, hoping to see her son. The pictures mounted on sugar paper and stuck on every wall were too bright. She didn't want to see other children's paintings, she wanted to set eyes on her boy. She wanted to wrap her arms around him and squeeze him close.

The Daughter She Gave Away

'He's in class at the moment. I wanted a quick chat, one-to-one, first, if that's okay?' Mrs Miah waited for Cassie to sign in and then led her once again to the store cupboard that doubled up as a meeting room. She gestured for Cassie to sit, then closed the door and took a seat next to the wall of exercise books. 'There are two reasons I wanted to speak to you in person. I'm afraid the first is a little delicate.' She rubbed the material of her dress between her thumb and forefinger, and her obvious nerves made Cassie's even worse.

Cassie swallowed. 'Go on.'

'As I said on the phone, Alf was caught trying to leave school at the beginning of lunchtime. Thankfully one of the staff on duty noticed him walking along the road outside the fence, and—'

'He was actually outside the grounds?' Sweat sprang up on Cassie's top lip as the image of him negotiating traffic on his own returned. The smell of dusty paper was too strong. She had the urge to stand and march out of the room and tour the corridors looking for her son.

'Not for long. The staff member chased after him and escorted him back here. I'm just glad he saw him in time.'

Cassie pictured her sweet boy being frog-marched through the gate like an escaped prisoner. 'Did he say where he was going?'

Mrs Miah looked down at the material between her fingers. 'He said he was on his way home to check on you.'

Bile burned the back of Cassie's throat. 'Right.'

'He said he'd being staying at his grandmother's house with his father and he planned to get the bus home to see you because he was worried about you.'

Cassie nodded. Tears pricked in the corners of her eyes and

shame burned inside her for putting him in that position. No seven-year-old child should ever have to worry about their parent.

'He had his dad's Oyster card, so he'd clearly done some planning. I tried to call your husband as well as you, but I couldn't get through.'

'He's a counsellor. He can't have his phone on if he's in a session,' said Cassie, glad she was the one in this meeting. Her own judgement was enough, without having to suffer his too. That could come later. 'We've had some differences recently, which is why Alf is staying with him at his nanna's.'

Mrs Miah smiled softly. 'I don't want to pry into your personal business. But since it's come to our attention like this, I had to let you know how Alf is being affected. They pick up on more than we give them credit for.'

Cassie was floored by self-loathing. 'He's a sensitive boy. We should have been more mindful of that. I'll speak to him. We both will. I'm sorry you've had to deal with this.'

'Oh, that's no problem. I just want to make sure Alf is all right. He's a good boy at heart.'

'When he's not in scuffles with older kids,' said Cassie, the memory of the last time they were in that room coming back to her.

'No one's perfect. And on that point,' said Mrs Miah, her face brightening, 'that was the second reason I wanted to speak to you. I had a very illuminating conversation with two girls in Year Five this morning. They're in Perry Simms' class and I trust them. You know the kind of girls, on course to be head girl somewhere, full of moral compass and righteous indignation.' She lifted her eyebrows and smiled.

Cassie knew exactly the kind of girls Mrs Miah meant. They

were the ones she always left in charge if she had to leave the room for a moment. She nodded.

'Well, they came to me and said they'd overheard Perry tormenting Alf.'

Cassie sat up straighter. 'Tormenting him how?'

Mrs Miah shifted in her chair. 'Again, I'm afraid this is a little sensitive, but apparently Perry was saying something about you.'

'Me?' The sweat on her back chilled.

'He said some unpleasant things about' – she rubbed at the material – 'about your teaching. More accurately, his brother had said some things to Perry and Perry was using them to get a reaction from Alf.'

Her cheeks burned. 'That's what I suspected.' Now she wanted to march through the school until she found Perry Simms and throttle the little fucker. But she'd made a mistake like that before. Instead, she calmly said, 'Would the girls be willing to put what they heard in writing?'

Mrs Miah shifted in her seat. 'We have done some investigations of our own, and it seems there's truth in what they said. Rest assured, we're dealing with the situation. The head teacher and I have an appointment with Perry's parents at the end of the school day.'

'They're not exactly fans of mine,' said Cassie. 'I was involved in an incident with their elder son, and they seem to believe everything he says.' She looked Mrs Miah in the eye. 'I suspect, like me, you've been teaching long enough to know any account a student gives of a misdemeanour is likely to have… should we say, a specific agenda.'

'Mainly to keep said student out of hot water.' Mrs Miah pursed her lips, and Cassie knew she understood completely.

'Exactly.' Cassie wondered how honest to be with her son's teacher, then decided she had very little to gain by being guarded. 'I'm afraid it's looking likely that I'm about to be suspended for yelling at Oliver Simms. I grabbed his blazer to make him look at me when I asked him what he'd said to his brother to make him pick on Alf. I'd sworn at him on a previous occasion, but that was in response to him accidentally splitting my lip when I was trying to break up a fight.'

'Goodness,' said Mrs Miah, her eyes narrowed. 'I see.'

'And I know I haven't exactly covered myself in glory, but their belief that I have some kind of vendetta against their son is…' She shook her head. 'Well, it's preposterous. I'm no fan of the kid, but if he wasn't actively trying to make Alf's life a misery, I wouldn't be giving him a second thought.'

'I've come across plenty of parents who think their child is an angel being picked on by a teacher with a grudge.'

'Yep, it comes with the job, I suppose. But now my career's on the line because of it. Even though, until I had the misfortune to come across Oliver Simms, I've never had so much as a verbal warning, in almost twenty years.'

Mrs Miah released the material of her dress and slapped her hands on her knees. 'In my extensive experience, nice parents have nice kids. Your son is a lovely little boy, which suggests to me that you and your husband are good people. I'm very sorry that this situation is causing so much upset.'

Cassie smiled for the first time in days. 'Thank you.'

'Call me an optimist,' Mrs Miah continued, 'but I believe that things tend to work out in the end, especially if they are given a nudge in the right direction.' She stood and before Cassie could ask her what she meant, she said, 'Do you want to see Alf before you go? I suspect it might do you both good.'

Five minutes later, Alf was sitting on Cassie's knee, his arms wrapped tightly around her. As she buried her head in her son's sweet-smelling neck, Cassie realised she had been open and honest with Mrs Miah, and instead of finding judgement, she'd been faced with compassion, understanding and the offer of help.

39

PRESENT DAY

Cassie

Cassie left a voicemail for Luke, briefly explaining what had happened and telling him she would be taking Alf home on the bus and he could meet the two of them there. She was nervous about his reaction. He'd taken Alf to his mum's to protect him, and Cassie hadn't argued, because she didn't feel like she had a right to protest. But Alf had tried to leave school because he was worried about her. That was enough to tell her that however dreadful she felt, she owed it to him to try to heave herself out of the darkness and be the best mum she could be from now on.

On the bus, they sat at the front of the top deck and Alf bounced in his seat. 'You can see everything from up here,' he said. He waved at an old man on a bus passing in the opposite direction, delighted when the man grinned and waved back. 'I love the bus, Mummy,' he said.

'And I love you.' Cassie gave him a squeeze.

'Love you more.' He hugged her then went back to seeing

how many people he could wave at and make smile. This was the Alf she knew, and she would do everything in her power to make sure he got back to his cheery, carefree self.

Back home, she made him a drink and a snack, then set about clearing all the mess she'd let fester while her family weren't there. A message arrived from Luke saying he'd be with them by 6 p.m., which gave her an hour and a half to make the house presentable. The deadline put fire underneath her, and soon she had the dishwasher running and her sheets in the washing machine. She paused after wrestling the clean fitted sheet over the mattress. The *Horrible Histories* theme tune wafted up from the TV downstairs, then she heard Alf's laughter, and it was the perfect pitch to penetrate her heart and lift her a little further out of the gloom. This was what she wanted, the sound of her son's laughter, the smell of fresh laundry. And she wanted Luke. She wanted their life together back and she would do whatever it took to make that happen. Grace's face appeared in her mind's eye. The pull on her heart told her she wanted her daughter too, but that was too much to ask for. Far too much, and far too late.

When Luke arrived, Cassie waited in the kitchen for him to come through. She and Alf were setting the table for a dinner from the freezer of fish fingers, chips and beans, since she hadn't been food shopping. She hoped Luke wouldn't look in the fridge and see how bare it was. On second thoughts, let him look. She would tell him the truth about how the last few days had been. She wouldn't hide anything else from him.

'Hello,' he said, walking into the kitchen. 'What's going on here?'

'I'm helping Mummy make dinner,' said Alf. 'I might want to be a cooker when I'm older, so I'm practising.'

'You might want to be an electric oven, or a gas one?' said Luke, kissing Alf on the head.

'No, silly. A cookerer.' He paused, his lips scrunched to the side. 'That's not right.'

'A cook or a chef,' said Cassie. She crossed to Luke and kissed him on the cheek. He smiled, but it was a sad smile. She noticed Alf watching them, so she brightened her voice. 'Dinner will be ready in ten minutes. Want a drink? Glass of wine?'

'Thanks, but I'm driving.'

Luke planned to drive back to his parents' then. 'I'll put the kettle on.'

'I'll do it.' He moved at the same time she did and they ended up in an awkward dance. A couple of weeks ago, Luke would have taken her by the waist and waltzed her around the room. Now he shuffled to the side and said, 'Sorry.'

She felt like crying, but that wouldn't help. She had to try to make things right, so she made cheerful conversation over dinner and forced food down her throat even when she thought it might choke her.

'Can I watch another *Horrible Histories*?' said Alf, scraping up ketchup with his last chip and shoving it into his mouth.

Luke looked at his watch. 'I'm not sure—'

'Maybe one episode?' Cassie put her hand on Luke's arm. 'We could clear up in here and have a chat.' She smiled at him, hoping he could read that she was putting on a show for Alf. She wasn't feeling light and cheerful. But they did need to talk.

Luke nodded. 'Okay,' he said. 'Just one episode.'

Alf scurried off and Cassie was glad he didn't ask if they were going back to Nanna's that evening. She could tell that was Luke's intention, but Alf seemed so happy to be home. She began to clear the plates and Luke ran water in the sink to wash the air fryer drawers. When she could hear the TV, she closed the door to the kitchen and went over to the sink. 'I hoped we could talk.'

Luke pulled a yellow rubber glove on as the sink filled with frothy bubbles. 'Okay.'

'Can we sit?'

Luke turned off the tap. The glove made a suction sound as he dragged it off and laid it over the tap. He came and sat opposite her at the table.

'I want to resolve this,' said Cassie. 'I hate being here without you two, and clearly Alf does too.'

'It's not what I want either, but...' He sighed. 'I can't get over the lies. It's thrown me. I'm really struggling.'

'I know, and I get it. I'm so sorry. If I'd known we'd end up married with a child of our own, I would have started off very differently. I'd have told you everything, honestly.'

Luke shook his head. 'I'm sorry, Cass, but when you say "honestly" it doesn't mean anything to me right now.' His eyes were bloodshot and Cassie imagined him awake in his childhood bedroom, wondering how he had ended up married to a liar. 'I feel betrayed on a deep level. You know everything about me. I opened myself up completely and I thought you had too. I thought our marriage was the one thing I could have absolute faith in. I spend all day long with people who are suffering. Most of them have dysfunctional relationships, and I feel like such a fool for believing we were doing marriage right, that we knew and trusted each other implicitly.'

He was getting further away from her. Desperation bloomed in her chest. 'I'm so, so sorry. I wanted to tell you. I promise you, I did. I made a mistake at the start, an enormous one, but I want to make it better. I want to be honest and for you to know every last thing about me.'

'You have a fourteen-year-old daughter, Cass. Do you know

how hard it is for me to get my head around that? I've been thinking about all the ways you kept her a secret. The fact you preferred to go into your maternity checks on your own, things like that. I stayed in the waiting room, thinking I was supporting you because you couldn't handle talking about your last pregnancy in front of me, when really it was to protect your lies.'

Cassie hung her head. Maybe she couldn't make this better. Perhaps she'd broken it so utterly there was no way back. 'I'm so sorry. I made so many terrible decisions. I thought I was protecting what we had, but that's no excuse, I know.'

'You've admitted now that you thought about the daughter you gave up every single day. And while I understand that, and I'm not saying it's a bad thing at all, it makes me feel like you lied to me every single day too, even if it was a lie of omission.'

She couldn't argue with that. Grace was always in her head. Now she'd seen her again, she knew she'd always been in her heart too. But now Grace thought Cassie was a monster and didn't want anything to do with her, so trying to save her relationship with Alf and Luke still felt like her only option.

He rubbed at the back of his head. 'And you've refused to get help. It feels crappy, frankly, like you don't believe what I do for a living is worthwhile. I mean, you're clearly suffering with your mental health, but you won't see a therapist or a doctor.'

'I will,' she said. 'I'll do that. I'll see Bella. I'll see anyone you want.' Her voice was high, almost hysterical.

Luke closed his eyes and shook his head. 'It shouldn't be about what I want, Cassie. You can't just have therapy because you think that's what will make things right between us. We've all been impacted by this, all of us, including Grace.'

'I know,' she said, resisting gripping his arm to show him how much she meant it. 'I want to change, and I want you and

Alf to come home. I want everything to go back to how it was before.'

Luke's shoulders slumped. 'That's the problem. Things can never go back to how they were.'

Cassie's stomach turned to liquid.

Luke looked directly into her eyes. 'We need to talk about Grace.'

40

PRESENT DAY

Cassie

'I'll tell you anything you want to know,' said Cassie. 'But I don't know much about her now, and that's the truth. She doesn't want anything to do with me.'

'What makes you say that?' said Luke.

'I'll show you.' The kitchen was suddenly too warm. Cassie opened the patio door and let the breeze cool her face before fetching her phone from where it was charging on the worktop. 'She sent this.' She opened the email from Simon's account and handed it to Luke. It was another thing she'd kept from him and even though she feared the repercussions, she knew the time for lies was gone.

She watched Luke's hazel eyes scan the text, digging her nails into her palms as she remembered how Grace had said she hoped she'd never had kids. She heard Alf laugh again from the other room and swore to herself she would never let him down the way she had Grace.

'Reading that must've hurt.' Luke handed the phone back to

her. How like him to acknowledge her pain before anything else.

Cassie's lip wobbled. 'It's no worse than I deserve.'

'You've said that a lot recently.'

'What do you mean?'

Luke's face softened. 'You seem to think you deserve to suffer.'

'That's because I do.' It came out before she thought about it.

'Why?'

Cassie let the tears fall. It was time to tell him about the darkest moment of her life; the one thing she could never forget or forgive herself for. 'You know when I told you I thought the baby had died after my placenta ruptured?'

Luke nodded.

'What I didn't say was... I hoped she had.' Saying it out loud made it real and the horror of it tightened her scalp. 'I hoped my baby had died, that's how much of a monster I am. That's why I didn't deserve to be in touch with her or watch her grow into the beautiful young woman she is.' She stopped to wipe the tears flowing down her cheeks, then continued, her voice catching on her sobs. 'That's why I resisted having children with you at first. I don't deserve to have Alf, and I don't deserve to have you. I'm broken. I'm not fit to be a mother. The guilt of wishing Grace hadn't survived the birth almost killed me, and to see it written there, to know she sees me for what I really am.' She covered her face with her hands. 'I'm sorry.'

'You're not a monster, Cassie,' Luke said gently. He took her hands away from her face and looked into her eyes. 'You were ill. If I'm honest, I think Simon had a responsibility to you and he reneged on that. Even if you wouldn't let him help you, he could have tried harder to ensure you had a relationship with your daughter.'

'I was pretty explicit about what I wanted.'

'Then, yes. But fourteen years have passed since. He could have reached out at any point if he'd had Grace's best interests at heart.'

Cassie shook her head. 'I made it clear that wasn't what I wanted.'

'You did what you thought was best at the time, and you said yourself, Grace has been loved and cherished her whole life.'

'She has. Thank God.' Cassie got up and tore off a piece of kitchen roll to wipe her face. 'I hope Simon is looking after her now.' It was a relief to speak the thoughts that had been swirling around her head out loud. 'I've been so worried about her. I hate to think of her suffering.'

'Then tell her that.'

'What?' Cassie almost laughed. 'You read the email. She doesn't ever want to hear from me again.'

Luke shook his head. 'I don't agree. I hear the words of a hurt child.'

'But I'm the one who hurt her.' Cassie would have to live with that for the rest of her life.

'She was hurting before she knew about you. Her mother had just died. She needed someone to lash out at, and you fit the bill.'

Cassie fell back into the chair. 'See, I am a monster. I turned away a grieving child. What kind of person does that?' Grace's sorrowful face came back to her and more tears fell.

'Why did you turn her away?'

'Because I was frightened of all the feelings Simon's email brought back, I suppose. I thought I didn't deserve a relationship with her, and because I was terrified I would lose you and Alf if I didn't.'

'And have you?'

Cassie examined his face for the answer, and she only found kindness there. 'I don't know. I hope not.'

Luke reached for her hand. 'Now I know more about what's going on in that head of yours, I feel like I can at least make sense of why you did what you did. And I don't think you're the only one to blame here. They could have done more.'

The muscles in her shoulders loosened. 'But can you forgive me?'

'I think the bigger question is, can you forgive yourself?'

41

PRESENT DAY

Cassie

When Alf was tucked up in bed that night, Cassie and Luke sat together on the sofa in the front room. The light from the lamp made one side of Luke's face shine, as though the goodness in him had come to the surface. Cassie almost drowned in gratitude that he'd agreed to stay and talk more.

'I really think it would help you to reach out to Grace,' he said, putting his glass of red wine down on the floor. 'I think you need to deal with your past before you can move forwards.'

Cassie bit her bottom lip. 'What she said in that email seemed pretty clear to me. I feel like I should respect her wishes. The main thing stopping me trying again is that I don't want to hurt her any more than I already have.' She realised that was true. She wanted Grace to find happiness again after what she'd been through, and she certainly didn't want to be the reason her misery was prolonged.

'Simon, then? You could scope out how Grace is really feeling by speaking to him.'

Cassie shuddered. 'I don't want to talk to that man.'

Luke pursed his lips. He breathed in through his nose like he did when he was thinking hard. 'How long were you two together?'

Cassie thought back to meeting Simon at university. 'From when I was eighteen. I had Grace when I was twenty-five.'

'You were very young.'

Cassie thought about that. 'I suppose we were.'

'Those are important and formative years.' He stroked a finger along the back of Cassie's hand. 'You know the human brain doesn't fully mature until the age of twenty-five. You were essentially big kids making huge decisions. I'm not trying to minimise what happened back then, but... do you think those seven years together should have the power to affect the rest of your life? All of it, I mean. You're not even forty yet, and you will hopefully have at least another forty years left. Should what happened, specifically in the last year you were together, blight all the other years of your life?'

They were quiet while Cassie considered the question. The depression had lasted a few years after the split, but Luke was right, she had allowed what happened with Simon to colour everything. It still had the power to bring the darkness back, even now. 'I don't know how to stop it.'

Luke nodded thoughtfully. 'The key might be to meet with Simon. I'm not going to pretend I think he handled things well, or that his motives in keeping things from Grace were entirely selfless, but he's become a huge demon in your head and that's not helping you. I bet if you saw him now, you'd see he was just an ordinary bloke who messed up big time when he was in his twenties.'

'An ordinary bastard.'

Luke exhaled through his nose. 'All right, an ordinary

bastard. There's a lot of them around. I do think he'd take up less space in your head if he became real to you again though, rather than solely existing in the negative memories of who he was and what he did. While he squats like this ogre in your mind, he still has power, and I think you'd be able to move forward better if you took that power back.'

He moved towards her, and the warmth of his arm around her shoulders, pulling her close, made her breath catch. 'I'm scared,' she said. 'I'm scared I'll get ill again, if I have to face him.'

'I doubt very much that Simon will have the effect on you that you expect. Would you have left Grace with him if you thought he was a bad man?'

Cassie shook her head. 'He was brilliant with her, and all the kids at his school adored him. I don't suppose he is what you'd call a bad man.'

'And you loved him once.' Luke pulled her closer. 'It's the bad thing he did to you that affected you so deeply, and I get that. But he can't betray you again. You're not his to betray.'

Cassie let those words sink in. It was true. He couldn't destroy her again like that. 'But what about Grace? I'm frightened of hurting her again.'

'You could take it at her pace, let her decide what she can handle.'

'What if I can't cope?'

'I'll be there for you. I'll have your back.'

Her eyes brimmed. 'Will you?' He had no idea how much those words meant. He nodded and pulled her tighter into his arms. Knowing he would be there for her made the idea of facing up to her past seem possible. 'I'll think about it over the weekend, if that's okay?' She had the meeting with the governors on Monday, but she didn't want to mention that while she was nestled against Luke's warm body. She took a breath as she realised not mentioning things had got her into enough trouble. 'I've got the disciplinary meeting on Monday. Can we talk about it after that?'

42

PRESENT DAY

Cassie

Cassie was surprised to be facing Keith Finnegan alone on Monday morning. Her palms grew wet when she entered his office and found him sitting behind his enormous desk, long fingers knitted together in front of him. She presumed the governors had already met and left the head teacher to deliver the damning verdict on his own.

'Ah, Cassie, take a seat.' He sat back, appearing considerably more convivial than she'd expected. There was even a smile under his bushy moustache. 'How are you?'

'Nervous,' she said. 'I feel like I'm facing a firing squad.' She sat opposite him, imagining him lifting a rifle from under the desk and aiming it at her head. Her pulse rate couldn't have been any higher if he did.

'Hmm.' He tapped his forefingers together. 'Well, you can relax. You live to fight another day.'

'Fight another day?' What on earth did that mean?

'Continue the battle to instil knowledge in the younger

generation.' His tone was inexplicably jovial. 'And an increasingly bloody battle it is. Despite that, if you could try not to swear at the students or chase them down corridors and grab them, it would be much appreciated. Lovely as it is to see you one to one, I'd really rather not have another of these meetings.'

She didn't dare hope she'd understood him correctly. 'What about the governors' meeting?'

'Cancelled,' said Finnegan. He pulled an open laptop towards him and tapped on the keys. 'I forwarded the email I got from Mrs Simms late on Friday night and they all agreed no further action should be taken.' He looked at her over the top of his glasses. 'Ordinarily I check my work emails at the weekend, in case anything urgent crops up, but we were visiting our youngest at university and my dear lady wife insisted I was "present".' He made speech marks with his fingers on the last word. 'Unfortunately, that led to you experiencing an unnecessary weekend of worry. I'll tell Angela that next time she wants me to be mindful and live in the moment.' He turned the laptop to face Cassie. 'Take a look.'

Still baffled, Cassie focused on the screen, then began to read the email.

Dear Mr Finnegan

I have just returned from a very difficult meeting with teachers at my younger son's school. I learned some things about my offspring which both shocked and saddened me. I have since had a very frank discussion with both boys and feel it only right to contact you immediately to prevent any further miscarriages of justice.

Cassie's mouth hung open as she read the detailed apology

and the explanation about how Oliver and Perry had been affected by their parents' recent split. The email ended with:

> In conclusion, I request that no further action is taken against Mrs Monroe. She and her little boy have gone through enough at the hands of my family.
>
> I hope Oliver's future school career will be less eventful, but please feel free to contact me immediately with any ensuing concerns.
>
> Kind regards
>
> Jennifer Simms.

'Bloody hell,' said Cassie, flopping back in her seat.

'What have I told you about swearing?' said Finnegan, winking. 'Rare, though, isn't it, a parent accepting their child is in the wrong?'

Cassie was tingling with relief. 'Poor woman,' she said. 'Imagine having to write that email.'

'I know,' said Finnegan. 'I have a lot of respect for her. She's a lawyer, which is lucky because if Oliver carries on the way he's heading, he's going to need one.'

'Puts it in perspective, though, doesn't it?' Cassie thought back to Oliver's permanently furrowed brow. Behind that was a child whose life was changing in a way that probably frightened him and he didn't know how to manage those difficult feelings. 'And I know what she means about how being angry or sad can affect people's behaviour.' She thought about Grace's email. Perhaps Luke was right. Maybe she was just lashing out.

'Yes, I'll cut the kid some slack,' said Finnegan, 'Unless he messes with my favourite English teacher again.'

Cassie smiled. 'You old smoothie. Don't say that in Becca's hearing, though. She'd resign on the spot.'

'I wouldn't dare,' he said. 'And you're all my favourites, just in different ways.'

'You've ruined it now.' She laughed. 'I did not expect to finish this meeting with a smile on my face.' She looked at her watch. 'So, I suppose I should get to next period? I haven't got my stuff with me.' She grimaced.

'Because you thought you were going to get shot?'

'Yep.'

'Then it's only right you take the rest of the day off. I'd already booked cover for today, since I also thought...' He bared his teeth. 'Anyway, I'm glad it's been resolved positively, so on you go.'

'Sure?'

Finnegan flapped his hand. 'Go on, before I change my mind.'

Cassie jumped from the chair, glad to have a little spare time. She had an email of her own to compose.

43

PRESENT DAY

Cassie

At the end of the school day, instead of waiting outside Hillside Primary for Alf, Cassie pressed the buzzer to be let into the building. The reception thronged with children and staff, and Cassie stood next to the desk, searching the faces for Mrs Miah. At last, she saw her standing with a younger woman at the head of a line of children making their way to the exit.

'Mrs Miah,' Cassie said as she drew close. 'Could I have a quick word?'

Alf was halfway down the line and Cassie could see the conflict in his face; did he run to his mum, or stay in line until he was out in the playground as he was supposed to? Cassie waved at him and gestured that she'd meet him in the playground. He nodded and straightened up as Mrs Miah asked the student teacher next to her to see the children outside.

She came to Cassie's side. 'Mrs Monroe. How lovely to see you looking so well.'

Cassie grinned. 'Thanks to you.' She dipped out of the way as a red-cheeked child hurtled past.

'Harvey, slow down,' Mrs Miah said. The child slowed to an urgent walk. She turned back to Cassie. 'Not at all. The truth will out. I'm just glad Mrs Simms was open to discussing the situation candidly.'

'Yes, it can't have been easy for her,' said Cassie, her eyebrows raised. 'I'm very grateful for how you handled it. You saved my skin.'

Mrs Miah watched the children flowing past her, her eyes catching on one or two of their faces. 'I've found that contented children rarely cause trouble for others. If you can get to the root of why a child is unhappy, then you can forgive them most things and, hopefully, make changes.' A small girl wandered past, singing loudly. 'Inside voice, Cecilia,' said Mrs Miah. The girl dropped a couple of decibels and went merrily on her way. She turned back to Cassie. 'And I've reviewed my thoughts about nice parents having nice kids. Turns out only one of the parents needs to be... how should I put it... right-minded. And in that case, there's still hope if that particular parent has some sway, which sadly too often, they don't.'

Cassie nodded. 'I hear you.'

'And I'm pleased to report Alf seems to be back to his cheerful self.' She waved at a tiny girl with corkscrew pigtails who was waving enthusiastically in her direction. 'See you tomorrow, Lois.'

Cassie's heart swooped. 'Thank you, Mrs Miah.'

Mrs Miah returned her warm gaze to Cassie. 'No thanks needed. It's my job.'

'Well, you're very good at it.' She decided Alf's teacher was due an extra special end-of-term gift this year. Cassie smiled and made her way into the sunshine to collect her happy little boy.

* * *

When Alf was in bed, Cassie showed Luke the email she'd drafted to Simon. Her pulse rate picked up again and she wondered if she'd ever be able to think about her first husband without her nerves jangling like an alarm bell. At least now Luke knew everything, she didn't have to make the hard decisions on her own.

He balanced the laptop on a cushion. 'Do you mind if I read it out loud?' he said. 'I find it's easier to get a sense of what's really being said when you hear how it might sound to someone else.'

'Go ahead.' Cassie didn't really want him to. It felt cringy, but he had more experience at this sort of thing than her, and she was still immensely glad he was back home and willing to sort things out between the two of them.

'Hi, Simon.' It was strange to hear her ex-husband's name coming out of her current husband's mouth. 'I've had time to think since our last email exchange, and I've decided...' He stopped reading and turned to her. 'Is decided the right word?'

'What do you mean?'

'Well, it implies you've come to a decision.'

'It doesn't imply it. It says it.' The English teacher in her was a little irritated.

'Okay, but I think you need to imply more flexibility. It's not just down to you to decide things, is it?'

'Why don't you get to the end, and we'll argue about the semantics after you've read the sentiment.'

'All right.' He lowered his gaze to the screen, and she

watched his eyes scan the words. 'I've decided that I may have acted rashly.' He looked up. 'Do you—'

'Read to the end.'

'...I may have acted rashly when I said I wouldn't have contact with Grace. Since she came to see me, she's been very much on my mind. I think, up until I saw her in person, she only really existed to me in my memory and imagination in an indistinct kind of way, a bit like a dream. I suspect that may have been my way of protecting myself from all the hurt back then. Your first contact reminded me of how I felt during that period, and I found it intensely difficult, but I'm deeply sorry I caused Grace pain, in reaction to those memories. I regret that enormously and would like the chance to put it right, if she is willing.

'I've spoken to my husband, Luke – who is an experienced and qualified counsellor – and we both agree that trying to help Grace navigate this difficult time could be a good thing. Hopefully for both her and me. Since I didn't handle it well when Grace and I met, I think the wisest course of action would be for you, me and Luke to meet in order to discuss how best to move forwards. Let me know if this is something you're open to. Cassie.'

Luke turned to Cassie, his eyes filled with compassion. 'I don't think you need to change a thing.'

'You sure?' Her stomach fluttered.

'I'm sure.' Luke passed the laptop to her. 'You ready to send?'

She bit her bottom lip and looked up at him. 'Should I?' He just smiled. She moved the arrow to the blue send icon and pressed.

44

PRESENT DAY

Cassie

Cassie felt sick. She looked around the pizza restaurant near the Royal Festival Hall on the South Bank, where they'd arranged to meet Simon, scouting for the face of the man who'd caused her so much pain.

'How are you feeling?' said Luke, pouring water into both their glasses. He'd held her hand all the way on the train and she suspected if he wasn't there to support her, she might well have turned around and gone home.

'Like I might throw up all over the table. What about you?' Luke had expressed more than once that he thought Simon could have handled things very differently over the years, and Cassie had begun to see that it must've suited Simon and Meg to allow her to walk away.

'I'm here to support you. Don't worry about me.'

'You're not going to punch him for everything he did to me?' Cassie nudged his foot under the table.

'Tempting as that is, I don't think it would help the

situation.'

'It would help me,' she said petulantly. He smiled and shook his head. The bell above the door jangled and she jumped. A blonde woman entered with a miserable-looking teenage boy skulking along behind her. Cassie turned away from the door to examine the lower level of the restaurant. 'He could already be here. He might be sitting down there.'

'There were only two tables of people down there when I went to the loo,' said Luke.

'Did either of them have a man with devil's horns sitting at them?' said Cassie. 'And a fiery trident.'

Luke shook his head. 'Stop it. He's just a man. Breathe like I showed you. This will all be fine.' He laid a hand on her knee and breathed in through his nose and out through his mouth along with her, keeping his eyes on hers.

A waiter in a black apron brought the bottle of wine they'd ordered and showed them the label. Cassie nodded, willing him to open it quickly so she could take a slug. It took a year and a half for him to go through the performance of uncorking it. When he was halfway through, her bladder told her she urgently needed the toilet. 'Back in a sec.' She scurried down to the lower level, then into the ladies' cubicle at the back.

The hand dryer did a poor job, and she was wiping her palms on her jeans when she arrived back at the lower level. When she looked up, two people were sitting at their table. Her heart leaped to the base of her throat. She wanted to turn and run back to the toilets and hide in a cubicle until Simon gave up and left. She swallowed and forced her foot onto the first step. She'd forgotten how to walk. Was it toe, heel, or heel, toe? Her pulse hammered in her ears and jumbled with the noise of the chattering diners. She paused, taking in deep breaths.

Luke turned and saw her. He smiled. Simon must've

followed his gaze because he turned, and Cassie met those blue eyes that had once been as familiar to her as her own. She took another step, and another. Simon stood. A paunch protruded through his jacket, and his forehead was larger, now his hair was receding. The lines on his face were even more pronounced than they were before, and his eyelids drooped as if sadness was his most common expression. She looked for horns. There were none. Her shoulders relaxed. Luke was right, he was just a man. And he looked beaten down by life.

She moved her eyes to her husband, who was still sitting, smiling reassuringly at her. His eyes were warm and full of love. She felt the support he was transmitting and it gave her the strength the take the final steps to the table.

'Hi, Simon.' She sat straight away in case he felt he should hug her or politely kiss her on the cheek. He might not be bearing a fiery trident, but she still thought his touch might burn her.

'Hi.' His voice crackled. He cleared his throat. 'How are you?'

'All right. You've met Luke?'

He nodded. 'Yes, I was brought straight to the table, so...'

He went quiet and Cassie couldn't think of anything to say. Luke lifted the bottle. 'Wine?'

'Just a small one, thanks,' said Simon. His words were stuttered and Cassie noticed sweat on his top lip. The Simon she had known was confident and self-assured. Perhaps losing his wife had changed him. He waited for Luke to pour, took a sip, then turned back to Cassie. 'Thank you for seeing me. I know I don't deserve... But I'm so worried about Grace. That's why I got in touch.'

'She's been through a lot in the last year.' Luke's voice was gentle and Cassie wondered if she would find it in herself to be so kind to someone who had once broken his heart.

Simon nodded and looked down at the table. 'It's been hard.' When he raised his head there were tears in his eyes. 'It was so quick. I mean, Meg had a few symptoms, but nothing... We couldn't believe it when the diagnosis came. And after that... it was so fast. We were shell-shocked, I suppose.'

'That sounds very difficult,' Luke said. 'I'm sorry for your loss.'

Cassie thought she should probably say the same, but it felt too strange. Looking at Simon, she was surprised to feel pity. She hadn't expected that.

'And Meg wanted to tell Grace about you.' He looked at Cassie, his eyes still brimming. 'And I couldn't deny her that, not when she was...' He swallowed. 'She always felt guilty about what we did to you. We both did, but Meg felt like you'd given her this gift, you know? She and Grace had such a bond right from the start.'

Cassie remembered seeing Meg with Grace in the garden that day and bit down on the inside of her lip. She was already battling with too many emotions.

'How has Grace coped?' Luke said. Cassie was so glad he was there. She was afraid she'd cry if she tried to speak.

'She's been quiet. She didn't used to be. She was always a bubbly kid, you know?' He smiled and Cassie imagined all the memories he was replaying in his head. She probably had similar ones of Alf. The thought of her little boy warmed her. 'But since Meg died, she spends all her time in her room. I know she's a teenager so that's not exactly unusual, but it's like the light's gone out in her. She's given up all her extra-curricular stuff. She was learning piano and had singing lessons. She's got a beautiful voice. She was in the local musical theatre group, and they put on really professional productions. Meg and I used to help out, but Grace wouldn't let us get too involved. You know what kids are like.' He looked between them and Cassie saw pride in his eyes. 'But she won't do any of the stuff she used to enjoy. She's listless all the time. She doesn't even want to see her friends.'

He took another sip from his wine. 'Meg did these videos for her, after she told her about you being her biological mother. Grace watches them all the time. I'm not sure it's healthy for her. I pass by her room, and I hear Meg's voice.' He swallowed hard. 'But Meg made them to let Grace know what happened back then.' He glanced at Cassie, then down at the table. 'She wanted to tell Grace the truth, but mainly she wanted Grace to have the opportunity to meet you and to have someone else in the world to support her.'

Cassie nodded slowly. 'Well, I made a poor job of that.' The image of Grace striding towards the station, with her chin held high, replayed once again in Cassie's mind.

'After she came back from seeing you that time,' Simon said, 'she told me she thought she was depressed and that you must've passed it down to her.'

'What?' Cassie tensed. 'No, that's not...' She looked at Luke for help.

'Cassie thinks her depression at that time was probably a reaction to the specific circumstances,' said Luke, and Cassie loved him for his diplomacy.

'And it's no surprise Grace is going through something similar now,' said Cassie. 'Has she seen anyone since Meg died, like a therapist or a doctor?'

'She refuses,' said Simon. 'I don't know how to get her there when she won't engage. She says if it's genetic, there's no point, this is just the way her life is now.'

Cassie felt Luke's eyes on her and could imagine him thinking he knew where that stubbornness came from. 'I honestly don't think it is genetic. I can't think of anyone else in my family who's suffered with their mental health, not more than the average person, anyway.'

'How are your parents?' said Simon, as if he thought he should ask.

'Same,' said Cassie. 'We don't really see them.' She was in no hurry to engage about anything other than Grace. 'I don't want Grace to suffer for as long as I did. Do you think she'd listen to me, if I suggest she gets some support?'

'I honestly don't know.' Simon scratched under his chin in a way that was so familiar it stopped Cassie in her tracks. She looked at Luke in an attempt to ground herself in the present. He smiled at her and reached for her hand. 'But we could try.'

'Should we arrange a meeting?' said Cassie.

Simon shifted in his seat. 'She's actually here, at the BFI. We agreed she'd watch a film while I talked to you. I watched the first half with her, then came here.' He picked his phone out of his pocket and looked at the screen. 'It finishes in about ten minutes. Shall I tell her I'll collect her and bring her here?'

45

PRESENT DAY

Cassie

Cassie poured the last of her wine into her mouth. It was sharp on her tongue, and she could already feel the acid gurgling in her stomach. Simon had been gone almost fifteen minutes and the muscle fibres at the base of her neck clenched more with every second she waited.

Luke stabbed an olive with a toothpick from the bowl of nibbles they'd ordered. He put it in his mouth and chewed, then took out the stone and set it in the little white saucer. She didn't know how he could eat. But then he wasn't waiting for judgement day. 'Top up?' He gestured to the wine.

'No, thanks. I should probably be sober for this, shouldn't I?'

He nodded. 'Ordinarily I'd say yes, but if you clamp your jaw any tighter, I think your teeth might shatter, so...' He lifted the bottle and poured them each half a glass.

Cassie let her jaw relax. Her teeth ached from being clenched and her shoulders and neck felt the same. 'I feel like

I'm on death row and it's got to execution day,' she said. 'I'm bloody terrified.'

'You'd have chosen a better last meal than olives and roasted almonds, surely?' He stabbed at another olive, chasing it around the bowl with the pick when it slid away. 'What would your last meal be?'

She smiled. 'Laudable effort to distract me, Mr Monroe, but the way my blood is currently pumping, this might well be the last thing I ever taste before my arteries burst.' She lifted her glass to her lips and sipped.

The doorbell jangled and she turned to see Simon. He stopped and waited. A second later, Grace followed him, her steps slow, her gaze lowered. Cassie couldn't breathe.

Luke's hand squeezed her knee. He whispered, 'It's okay. This is hard, but we can do hard things.' He often quoted the title of Glennon Doyle's podcast to Alf when he was struggling with something. It was the perfect phrase for now. This was going to be intense. But with him by her side she could do it.

Cassie smiled as they approached the table, but Grace didn't look up. She was wearing khaki combat trousers hung low on her narrow hips and a denim jacket over a white vest. She looked like one of the cool kids at Cassie's school, and Cassie wondered what her friendship group was like. She wanted to know. She realised she wanted to know everything about this beautiful, unhappy girl.

Simon pulled out a chair and Grace perched on the edge, keeping her hands in the pockets of her denim jacket. 'This is Luke, Cassie's husband,' said Simon.

Grace glanced up. 'Hi.'

'Good to meet you, Grace. I was sorry to hear about your mum.'

Grace bowed her head, then began to shake it. 'No,' she said. 'I can't do this.'

Simon put his arm around her. 'It's all right, lovely. It's okay.'

Grace's shoulders shook. 'No. It's not okay. Nothing is okay. I don't want to be here. I just want my mum.' She shook Simon's arm away and stood.

'Grace, I...' Cassie stood, instinctively reaching out her hand.

'No,' said Grace. Tears dribbled onto her cheeks. She turned to Simon. 'Sorry, Dad. I thought I could do this, but I can't.' She turned to Cassie and looked her in the eye for the first time. 'I just want my mum back.'

'I understand,' said Cassie, her heart breaking for the child she'd given to another mother.

'Can we go?' Grace took a step towards the door.

'Sorry,' said Simon. He gave them a sad smile, then followed his daughter outside.

* * *

When the restaurant door closed behind Simon and Grace, Luke took Cassie's hand. 'You okay?'

'I don't know.' She watched them walk past the window towards Waterloo station, Simon's arm protectively around Grace's shoulders. Cassie tried to put words to her feelings. 'She looked devastated, didn't she?'

'She did.'

'But even though she didn't want to stay, I don't feel like this is the end. I can't imagine going back to pretending she doesn't exist, because she does, and I'm glad she does.' That was the first time she'd even admitted it to herself.

'She very much does.'

'She's beautiful, isn't she?'

Luke smiled and nodded.

'I want to help her, if she'll let me.' If she'd imagined this situation, she would have been sure she'd breakdown and cry, but her eyes were dry. She felt intensely sad, but calm and strong too. It wasn't her place to be upset. A child was suffering and it was her job, and her greatest desire, to take positive action to make things better. 'I think it was too soon for us to meet again. We need to take it more slowly.'

'Okay.' Luke nodded.

A plan was formulating in Cassie's mind. 'Let's get the bill, and I'll tell you my idea on the train.'

46

PRESENT DAY

Cassie

The following morning, Luke collected Alf from a sleepover at his nanna's. Cassie waited in the kitchen, her nerves making her wipe down clean surfaces and refold the tea towels into perfect squares in the drawer. Despite the jitters, she couldn't help but grin when Alf bounded in. His curls had been tamed into a neat side parting and slicked down with some kind of gelatinous hair product. 'Has Nanna been at your hair again?' she said, smiling as her gorgeous boy grimaced.

'Yeah, and she put this slimy stuff in it.' He lifted a stiff strand. 'Gross.'

'She used to do the same with mine when I was your age,' said Luke, coming into the kitchen to join them. 'But as she's always telling me, yours is so much thicker and more lustrous than mine ever was.' Luke rolled his eyes and smiled.

'You can always ask her not to, if you don't like it,' said Cassie, who also always reminded Alf he didn't have to kiss and cuddle people he didn't want to. She didn't want him to be a people pleaser like her. Though she also dreaded the day when he told her he didn't want to be hugged as often as she had the urge. 'As long as you do it politely.'

'It's okay,' said Alf. 'It makes her happy.' He shrugged his narrow shoulders, and Cassie didn't think she could love him more.

'Sit at the table and I'll get you a smoothie,' said Luke. 'We want to talk to you about something.'

Alf climbed onto a chair. 'If I'm allowed a smoothie before lunch, this must be serious.'

Cassie laughed despite her nerves. Her little boy was growing up so fast. When the pink drink was in front of him, Luke joined them and Cassie took a deep breath. 'You know how Billy in your class is adopted?'

Alf's chin puckered. 'Am I adopted?'

'No. God, no,' said Cassie, taking his hand. 'Not that that would be a bad thing.' She was already messing this up. 'But you definitely came out of Mummy's tummy and you are our little boy.' His reaction made what Grace had recently experienced all the more real. She must've been through hell in the last few months. 'I just wanted to make sure you knew what adopted meant.'

'Billy's real mummy and daddy couldn't look after him, so he got a new mummy and daddy.' Alf's mouth was still turned down at the corners.

'Exactly, although it might be better to call Billy's first parents his birth parents, because real suggests the mummy and daddy he has now aren't his real parents.' Alf's eyebrows creased and Cassie wondered if she was going into too much detail. She looked to Luke.

'If you're adopted, the parents who love you and look after

you are your parents, whether they were the ones who made you or not,' said Luke.

Alf nodded and opened his mouth. The way he narrowed his eyes made Cassie think he was about to ask exactly how parents made children, and although she was willing to be open about that, this was not the time. 'The thing we wanted to talk to you about is that before I met Daddy,' she said, 'I was married to somebody else.'

Alf looked between the two of them, eyes like saucers. 'You had another husband?'

Cassie nodded. 'We were very young.'

'Like twelve?' said Alf.

Cassie smiled. 'Not that young. We met at university – which is like a big school, for when you're almost grown-ups – when we were eighteen and...' This was hard. But she could do hard things. She looked at Luke, who gave her a small nod. 'And we had a baby.'

Alf's eyebrows knitted in a frown. 'You had another baby before you had me?' There was a wobble in his voice as the news appeared to sink in.

Cassie nodded. 'Yes, but it doesn't change anything about how I feel about you. I love you, you're still my precious boy, okay?'

'I don't really understand.' He looked from Cassie to Luke, blinking fast.

Luke held Alf's hand. 'This is a lot for you to get your head around. You can ask us anything you think of. We will be honest with you.'

'I'm sorry I kept her a secret,' said Cassie. 'It was wrong of me, and I don't want to keep any more secrets from you.'

'She? It was a baby girl?'

Cassie nodded. 'She's called Grace. But she's not a baby any more. She's fourteen now.'

'Fourteen?' His jaw dropped.

Cassie knew that to Alf that would sound ancient. 'That's right. She's in Year Nine at senior school.'

'Where does she live?'

'She lives in Essex, about an hour and a half away from here.'

Alf took a drink of his smoothie. When he raised his head, he had a pink moustache. 'Who does she live with?'

'She lives with her dad. He's called Simon.'

'Did you used to be married to that Simon?'

'That's right.' This was more complicated than Cassie thought. Alf was doing well to keep up. The next part was going to be the trickiest. 'And after Simon and I split up, he married someone called Meg. Meg adopted Grace.'

'But why?' said Alf. 'My friend Maisie, her mum and dad got divorced and she didn't get adopted.' His gaze flitted between his parents. 'Did she? Is that what happens when people who get divorced marry other people? Does that mean their mummies aren't allowed to be their mummies any more?' His chin puckered. This was clearly hard for him to digest.

'No, sweetheart, that's not what happens. What happened in our case is very unusual.'

'Mummy wasn't well at the time,' said Luke carefully. 'Because she was poorly, Simon, Meg and Mummy all decided it was best for Simon and Meg to take care of Grace on their own.'

'But you got better?' Alf's eyes searched hers as if looking for signs she might be about to give him away.

'I'm absolutely fine. Don't worry. But I imagine this is a lot for you to take in, so please ask me anything you want to know.'

'So is she my sister? If she was adopted?' His voice wobbled.

'She's your half-sister, because she has a different daddy, but yes, she's still your sister.'

'Why don't I know her?'

'Because we all agreed Simon and Meg would bring her up on their own, so I wasn't in touch with her either. That's why I didn't tell you about her, because she wasn't part of our lives, even though I thought about her every day.' She didn't want Alf to think any child was dispensable.

He took a drink, then looked up again, his hazel eyes full of questions. 'But...' He stopped and took another drink. 'Can I meet her, now she's not a secret any more?' Cassie shuddered. What a fool she'd been to keep Grace from her family. No person should be kept a secret. 'Do you think she'll like having a little brother?'

Who couldn't love having a brother like Alf? But Cassie knew she couldn't make any promises. 'Grace has had a very sad time recently. Her mummy, Meg, got very poorly and unfortunately, she died.'

'Poor Grace.' Alf's eyes filled with tears.

'And so what I thought we could all do is make some videos for Grace, telling her a little bit about ourselves. Then, one day, if she wants to, she could come and meet us. But I can't promise that will happen.' She didn't want to lie to him. She never wanted to lie to anyone ever again.

Alf turned to Luke. 'Are you going to make a video for Grace?'

'I am,' said Luke. 'When someone is unhappy it's nice to do something to let them know there are people out there who want the best for them, isn't it? I'm going to tell Grace about myself and about Mummy. Because I think you and me know Mummy best in the world, don't we?' Alf nodded enthusiastically. 'So there's nobody better to tell Grace all about her, is there?'

Cassie looked between her husband and her son. At last, they did know everything about her, but now she wanted Grace to know her too. She didn't want anything in return. Grace might never be ready to meet again in person, but if Cassie could add a little stability to her life from afar, then she would do her very best to make that happen.

'Can I go on the trampoline first?' said Alf, climbing down from the chair.

'Course you can,' said Cassie, opening the patio doors, incredibly grateful for her resilient little boy and for the man they both had the good fortune to have as his father.

47

PRESENT DAY

Cassie

'So, you'll do it?' said Cassie, tugging her bottom lip with her teeth as she waited for Becca's reply.

'Of course I'll do it,' said Becca, gripping Cassie's hands. The two of them were the only ones left in the staffroom at the end of the school day and Cassie had outlined her plan to make videos to send to Grace before she decided whether she'd like to meet again in person. She thought that if Grace heard from the most important people in Cassie's life, as well as from her, she'd get a more rounded picture. 'Do I have to be nice about you?'

Cassie laughed. 'I want you to be honest, so clearly not.' She squeezed Becca's hand then let go. 'I can't believe I thought it might be the end of our friendship after I told you about Grace.'

Becca screwed up her nose. 'What are you on about?'

Cassie lifted her shoulders and let them drop. 'I thought you'd judge me. They're not exactly the actions of a kind and loving person, giving up a baby then lying about it for fourteen years.'

Becca shifted along the sofa and pulled Cassie into a hug. 'Mate, that was your messy head talking. I know you. You did what you did for good reasons. The only person judging you was yourself.'

Cassie took a moment to feel the softness of her best friend's body and breathe in her familiar lime and basil perfume before pulling away. 'Bloody love you, mate, but I'm about to suffocate in your ample bosom.'

'Bloody love you too.' Becca patted her chest. 'It's a very comforting bosom, even if I do say so myself.'

'True.'

'When are we doing this video then?'

'Now, if you're up for it?'

Becca's lips moved to the side. 'I don't know what to say. The only thing that springs to mind is that you're not always a massive twat.'

Cassie huffed. 'Praise indeed.'

'You said Luke and Alf have already filmed one?'

'Yes. They're doing a few, but they've done their introductions.'

'Can I see them to get an idea of tone?'

'It's not a novel. You don't have to think about genre and narrative style.'

Becca raised her eyebrows. 'Shall I go with "Your mum's not always a massive twat" then?'

Cassie tensed. 'It's best not to mention the M word. Meg was her mum. I'm trying to be her friend, if she'll let me.'

Becca put her hand on her arm. 'Sorry, mate. Completely get that.' She nodded to Cassie's phone, which was on the low table in front of them. 'Go on, show me Luke's and Alf's.'

Cassie picked up her phone and tapped the screen.

Luke's face appeared. He was sitting at their kitchen table

with a cup in front of him, steam rising from the top. 'Hi, Grace. As you know, I'm Luke, Cassie's husband. We've been together for ten years and I thought I knew everything about her. I suppose you and I were both surprised to find out we didn't know as much as we thought we did about the people we lived with. I admit, I was shocked to find out about you at first, but the more Cassie has explained what happened when you were a baby, the more I understand why she did what she did; why they all did.

'The fact is, the more we talk honestly, the more we understand each other. I suppose I would say that. I'm a counsellor, you see, so talking is my thing. I hope you have someone to talk to, Grace. You've been through a hell of a lot in a short space of time, and I can only imagine how painful this experience has been for you.

'I also know your first contact with Cassie was difficult to say the least. In an effort to repair the damage already done, we thought it might help if people who know her and care about her filled you in on what she's really like.' He leaned forwards and grinned. 'The good and the bad.' He sat back. 'Seriously, though, if you're watching this, I hope having a little insight into Cassie's life will allow you to see her as someone real, because we can all be guilty of building other people into something that might not be entirely accurate, especially if we feel we've been wronged by them. Doing that makes us feel safe, it allows us to settle into our beliefs and avoid change. Change is hard. I understand all of this must be incredibly hard for you. But we can do hard things. I'm going to make a series of short videos for you, and in each one, I'll tell you a story about Cassie. I hope by the end you'll see her a little more clearly, because she really is an extraordinary woman, and I love her very, very much.'

The screen went blank, and Becca turned to Cassie with tears in her eyes. 'Mate!'

'I know,' said Cassie, wiping her own eyes. 'Remind me of this next time I complain he hasn't put the bins out.'

'You never get to complain again,' said Becca.

'Wait until you've seen Alf's,' said Cassie. 'The cuteness is off the scale.'

'How's he taking having a bonus sister?'

'Bonus? I like that. He's okay. He comes up with new questions every day, like if she's going to live with us and will he have to share his Lego.'

'Bless him.' She nudged Cassie with her elbow. 'Show us then.'

Cassie flicked to the video on her camera roll. Alf's face appeared, making her heart swell. 'Hello, Grace. Mummy and Daddy say you're my half-sister, which was weird at first but now I think it might be all right because all my friends have got brothers and sisters and sometimes they're really annoying but sometimes they aren't. I hope you aren't annoying. Jake in my class says I'm annoying but that's because he's the goalie in my football team and I'm a striker and I get loads of goals. Do you like football? I support Bromley FC. Who do you support?' He glanced away from the screen, eyebrows furrowed, as if listening to someone. 'Oh, yeah, I'm seven and I won't be eight for ages and I'm in Year Two. Mrs Miah is my teacher and she's nice. Who's your teacher?' He put his finger on his chin and hummed. 'I like going on my trampoline. If you come to my house, you can go on my trampoline.' He looked off screen. 'Is that enough stuff about me? I don't know what else to say.' He listened then turned back to the screen. 'If I think of anything else I'll come back and say it. Bye.'

'Too cute!' said Becca. 'Makes my atrophied womb twang. How do I follow that?'

'You don't have to offer her a go on your trampoline if you don't want to.' Cassie grinned.

'Trampolining, with my bladder?' said Becca. 'That wouldn't be pretty.'

'Perhaps you don't mention your atrophied womb, incontinence, or your enthusiastic sex life.'

'Then what's left?' said Becca, pouting.

'Fair point. Maybe I'll ask Finnegan to do a video instead of you.'

'Don't you dare,' said Becca, snatching the phone from Cassie's hand. 'I'll talk about you, and despite the fact you're very dull in comparison to me, I'll think of something to say.'

Cassie grinned. 'All right then. And no swearing.'

'Christ,' said Becca, 'You don't ask for much, do you? Go on then.' She flapped her hand at Cassie.

'What?'

'I can't be nice about you to your face. Sod off and come back in ten minutes.'

'You're going to talk for ten minutes?'

Becca shook her head. 'Nah, I'll probably have to do twenty thousand re-takes when I accidentally say bollocks or something.'

'How are you still a teacher?'

'Fuck knows. Off you trot. See you in a bit.'

Becca wouldn't let Cassie see what she'd filmed while she was still in the room, so Cassie didn't watch it until she was sitting in her car in the car park.

'Hello, Grace.' Becca's eyes crinkled when she smiled. 'My name's Becca and I teach with Cassie. She's my best friend and, since you don't really know her yet, I thought I'd tell you a little bit about her. It feels weird to be nice about Cassie, because we bicker a lot. I mean, a lot. But you only banter with people you know well, and people who are funny, don't you? And Cassie is funny. But she's also kind and calm and she's loyal, the kind of person who always has your back. I've had a rough few years.' She paused. 'Nothing like what you've been through, but I got divorced and being on my own for the first time in decades was tough. My daughters were teenagers then, and I had to put on a brave face for them, and I don't know what I would have done without Cassie. Luke too. They're the kind of people who always have the spare bed made up in case someone might need it. Luke's the listener, I suppose it comes with the job, but Cassie will do anything she can to make life better for other people. She's a brilliant teacher. The kids love her, and she goes above and beyond, you know what I mean?

'Anyway, I just wanted to say that if you did decide to be in contact with Cassie now, or in the future, then you'll find out for yourself that she's one of the good ones. The best, in fact. I love her. I love the whole family, and I've heard Alf said he'd give you a go on his trampoline.' She raised her eyebrows. 'He's never offered me a go and I turn up with sweets for the little sod.' She covered her mouth. 'Whoops, I said I wouldn't swear. Sod's only a baby swear word, so I might squeak that one through. And he's not really a sod. He's actually the most adorable little boy I've ever met. Since you two have some biology in common, I suspect you're pretty adorable yourself. If I ever get to find out in person, I guarantee to welcome you with open arms. In the meantime, you take care, Grace. I hope you know Cassie's friends and family are thinking of you and wish nothing but good things for you. Sending lots and lots of love your way.'

48

PRESENT DAY

Cassie

When all the videos were filmed, Cassie's confidence in the idea stalled. Meg had made short films for Grace and now it looked like Cassie was just jumping on the bandwagon. At the weekend, she emailed Simon to see whether he thought the videos were appropriate, and was surprised by the reply, which arrived on Saturday evening.

> I'll try anything at the moment, to be honest. Grace seems to be falling further into her grief, and I'm getting really worried about her. We've spoken about you a lot and in response to that, I'm attaching the videos that Meg filmed for Grace. It was Grace's idea to share them with you. I get that they might be a hard watch for you, but Grace thought this might be a good way for you to understand her loss and why she's struggling to come to terms with what she's learned about her background.
>
> Obviously, you don't have to watch them, but if you do, I

hope they give you a sense of the family we were; the family you allowed us to be. I know Grace isn't in a place where she can be grateful for that, yet, but I am and always will be.

Cassie swallowed hard. She could hear Luke singing along to the radio in the kitchen as he cleared up their dinner things. She lifted her finger and clicked on the first link, then almost closed it down when a gaunt face filled the screen. Forcing herself to press play, she watched as Meg, older and considerably thinner than in Cassie's memory, began to speak. 'To make you understand why we did what we did, I think I need to start with how your dad and I met.'

'No.' Cassie pressed the cross in the top righthand corner. She couldn't do it. The memories were less excruciating now they were no longer a dark secret, but she still wasn't sure she could watch Meg tell her about falling in love with the man who had been her husband.

'All done.' Luke's head appeared around the sitting room door. 'I'm craving hot chocolate. Fancy one?' His eyes stayed on Cassie's ashen face. 'You all right?'

'I'm not sure,' she said. 'Simon's sent through the videos Meg made for Grace, telling her about what happened... back then.'

Luke came into the room. 'Why has he sent those?'

'He said that Grace thought it was a good way for me to get to know more about her, and what she's lost.'

Luke sat beside her and took her hand. 'Right. God.' He blew out his cheeks. 'Do you want to watch them?'

'I don't know.' She gazed at him, hoping he might tell her what to do. He just stared back with kindness in his eyes. 'I suppose I'd get to understand more about what made Grace who she is, and that would be a good thing, wouldn't it?'

'It could be.'

Cassie bit her bottom lip. 'I'm scared.'

'What scares you?'

'That it will bring it all back again.' She thought about that. She'd had to face all those emotions again in the last weeks and she'd survived. 'And that maybe Grace wants me to see them to punish me.'

Luke squeezed her hand. 'That's possible, but it's also possible that she wants you to understand why this is all so painful for her. She could be trying to connect.' He exhaled. 'I don't know what her motives are, but whatever you decide, I'm here.'

She looked inside herself and for the first time in a very long time, she knew that she was strong enough to handle the past, the present and the future. Grace was the one who needed protecting. 'I'm going to watch them.'

'Do you want me to sit with you?'

She nodded, her heart beating against her ribs. 'I think I'll have a wine instead of a hot chocolate, though.'

'Coming right up,' said Luke, getting to his feet. 'And I think I'll join you.'

* * *

Half an hour later, both their faces were wet with tears. Cassie turned off the last of the videos and lay her head back on the sofa cushion. 'I spent so many years hating her,' she said. 'And all that time she was just a normal woman who once did a bad thing.'

'Try not to beat yourself up any more,' said Luke.

'There was no real malice in what she did to me, what they did to me.' Cassie took a tissue from her sleeve and dabbed her eyes. 'Not like I imagined. I wish I'd known that. There are so many things I wish I'd known.' She blew her nose. 'And she was such a good mum. You could see that, couldn't you? They were a happy family.' She looked up at her husband. 'Just like we've been a happy family. We all ended up with the right people, the people we were supposed to spend our lives with.'

Luke wrapped his arm around her shoulders and kissed the top of her head.

'It's so sad that she's gone. Poor Grace,' she said. 'How unbelievably sad for all of them.' More tears fell. 'I'm going to email Simon back tomorrow and tell him I've watched them, and see what I can do to try to make this easier for Grace in any way I can.'

Luke kissed her again, and when they went to bed that night, she felt peaceful at last, with a new sense of purpose.

But on Sunday morning, when she was about to open up her computer, her phone rang. It was Simon, and his voice was full of panic. 'Is Grace with you?' he said.

'With me? No? Why would she be?'

'She's gone.'

'Gone where?' said Cassie, panic filling her own chest.

'I don't know.' Simon's voice caught. 'But she left me a note saying she wanted to be with her mum.'

49

PRESENT DAY

Cassie

Cassie's mouth went dry. 'What did she mean, she wanted to be with her mum?' She couldn't stop her brain from adding, *Her mum's dead.*

'I don't know.' Simon's voice was high through the phone's speaker. 'That's why I was hoping she might have come to see you. I've been trying to work it out since I discovered the note this morning. Her phone's off, so I can't track her. I went to the crematorium's memorial garden where there's a plaque for Meg first, thinking that might have been what she meant, but she wasn't there. I've rung all her friends, but no one's seen her and she hasn't said anything to them. I've been driving around the streets, but I can't find her.' He was spluttering through tears now. 'I don't know what to do, Cass. I can't lose Grace. I can't lose her too.'

'Okay,' she soothed, despite the dread flooding through her. 'We'll find her. It's okay. Think, Simon,' she said with urgency. 'Where does she associate with her mum? Let's start there.'

'I don't know,' he said. 'Everywhere, everything.'

Cassie thought of the videos and understood what he meant. The two of them were so close. Everywhere Grace looked she would see reminders of the woman who was her world. 'Did they go to a specific café, or... I don't know, swimming, or something?'

'I can't think,' he said. 'Do you think I should call the police?'

'Maybe.' Something tapped at the back of her mind. 'What about the theatre? In the videos, Meg said they liked to go to the theatre, didn't she? Was there a show they saw more than once, or a restaurant or café they went to a lot?'

'*Mean Girls*,' said Simon. 'They saw a matinee at the Savoy Theatre just before Meg's diagnosis. They loved it so much that Meg got returns a week later and they went again.' Hope rose in his voice. 'Both times they went down to the South Bank afterwards and walked along the river.' His voice cracked. 'I can't believe I arranged to meet you with her on the South Bank that time. That was fucking insensitive of me. I'm so stupid.'

Cassie's mind raced. 'I remember Meg talking about that. Do you think she might have gone to the theatre, or to South Bank?'

'I don't know. Maybe.'

Cassie rushed into the kitchen where Luke was waiting for the kettle to boil, two mugs with teabags in front of him. He turned, a look of concern on his face as she spoke quickly into her phone. 'I can get a train into Waterloo. Why don't I try looking for her along the river, and you get the Tube and go to the Savoy to see if she's at the theatre? Call the police now and report her missing, and keep in touch, okay?'

Simon sounded calmer as they agreed the plan. It was only when Cassie clicked off the call that she allowed the tears to come. 'Grace has gone missing,' she said to Luke as she dragged on her denim jacket. She tried to compose herself as she filled him in on what she knew and rushed to leave, but the horror of the situation gripped her throat, and she was still crying when she left for the train.

50

PRESENT DAY

Cassie

When the train stopped at a signal just outside Waterloo East Station, Cassie thought she might explode with exasperation. She checked her phone again. Nothing from Simon. At last, the train creaked into motion and slid the last few metres towards the platform. By the time the light appeared around the exit button, Cassie's finger was poised ready to press, and she leaped out as soon as the door swooshed open. She wound around the casual weekend day-trippers, pushed through the barriers and ran down the escalator into the main station. She rushed through the concourse, down the steps and across the road towards the river, all the time her eyes scanning left and right, desperate to see a dark-haired girl with big blue eyes.

When she reached the steps by the Royal Festival Hall, her heart swooped to see a girl with familiar dark waves ahead of her. Panting with the effort, she took the steps two at a time, ignoring the looks from the irritated people shifting out of her way. She lost sight of the girl, so she shouted, 'Grace, stop.

Grace!' At the top of the steps, she stood with her hands on her hips, trying to catch her breath. She searched for the dark head and let out a cry of relief when she saw her nearing the barrier overlooking the river. Cassie rushed forwards, then halted suddenly when Grace turned to greet someone coming in the opposite direction. Only, it wasn't Grace. It wasn't even a girl. It was a woman of around twenty-five and she was now kissing a man with a beard.

Cassie let out a moan. She'd been so sure it was Grace. The day was hot and sweat ran down her back as she looked around, disappointment and indecision paralysing her. Should she go right towards the National Theatre, or left towards the London Eye? She rang Simon for advice, but his phone went to voicemail. He was probably on the Underground. She clicked off the call and walked towards the river, leaning against the black rails, looking out over the grey-brown water. A Thames river boat full of tourists sailed slowly past and a busker with red hair played Ed Sheeran songs to the delight of the masses of people parading along the South Bank, enjoying the rare cloud-free day. The breeze lifted her hair and cooled the back of her neck. She imagined she must look carefree, taking in the view on a beautiful day, when really her mind raced and her heart thundered in her chest.

She took a breath, then turned left in the direction of the London Eye, walking with the river to her right. She forced her feet to slow down so she could scan the crowds of people who seemed to be multiplying just to taunt her. The Ed Sheeran tunes faded, replaced by the shouts of a street magician trying to gather a crowd. Cassie swivelled her head, desperately examining the face of every dark-haired person in the vicinity. She passed a merry-go-round, then a bright orange food stall. The smell of fried onions made her mouth water. She hadn't eaten a thing this morning and she was suddenly desperately thirsty. Cursing herself for not bringing her water bottle on such a sweltering day, she queued up behind a family who were bickering in French. She saw the irritation on the mother's face as her teenage daughter called her 'Maman' and whined about something Cassie didn't understand. She wanted to tell the woman to give the child whatever she wanted; to tell her life was short and children were precious. She wanted the woman to gaze around her at the magnificent view, feel the sun on her face and the joy of having her daughter by her side. Tears welled in Cassie's eyes at the thought of what Grace had been through over the last few months, what she was still suffering now. If she found her, she would do everything in her power to give her the life she deserved.

She gulped down the cold water as she continued her search, half wishing she'd bought another bottle to pour over her wrists to cool her down. The big wheel of the London Eye loomed ahead, a long queue snaking all the way back to Jubilee Gardens, where people were sitting and lying on the browning grass, faces turned up to the sun.

One figure wasn't enjoying the warmth, or taking in the bustle of the crowds by the river, though. A lone girl sat, arms wrapped around her shins, dark head resting on her knees. Cassie's breath faltered. She moved tentatively forwards, hardly daring to hope. Moments later, her shadow fell over the shoulders, and she could see now that they were shaking. 'Grace?'

The girl squinted up, her cheeks wet. It was Grace. Cassie had found her, and it was all she could do not to fall onto her knees and take her in her arms. 'Grace, it's me, Cassie.'

'I know who you are.' She rubbed her hand across her eyes, her chin jutting out in defiance. 'What are you doing here?'

'Your dad rang. He was worried about you. He said you'd

turned your phone off and he didn't know where you were. We've both been looking for you.' Cassie kept her voice gentle. She didn't want Grace to think she was in trouble.

'I forgot to charge my phone last night,' said Grace. 'It's dead.'

Cassie took her phone from her pocket and held it out. 'Want to call him now and let him know you're okay?' Grace nodded. 'All right if I sit?' Grace nodded again.

She turned away when she made the call, but Cassie heard the tearful apology. Grace turned and handed the phone back to Cassie. 'He wants to talk to you.'

Cassie took the handset and held it to her ear. 'Hi.'

'Oh, thank God.' Relief rang out in his voice. 'Thank you, thank you, thank you. Is she okay?'

Cassie looked at Grace, who was tugging at a strand of dry grass. 'I think so.'

'I'll come now,' he said. 'I'm on The Strand. Where are you?'

'Jubilee Gardens, just by the London Eye.'

His breath became ragged and she imagined him marching in their direction. 'I should be there in about fifteen minutes. Can you stay with her until I get there?'

'Of course.' Of course she would stay. There was nothing that could tear her away from this beautiful, sad girl now that she had found her.

After she ended the call, they sat for a minute, silent, watching the people go by. Eventually, Grace turned her dewy eyes to Cassie. 'How did you know where I'd be?'

'The videos your dad sent. I watched them last night, and when your dad told me about your note, we remembered Meg... your mum, saying how much you both loved the theatre and then coming down here.'

Tears spilled onto Grace's cheeks. 'I miss her.' Her shoulders rounded and she buried her face in her knees. Cassie hesitated, then placed a hand gently on Grace's back, feeling the rise and fall of her ribs as she cried for the mother she had lost. 'She said she'd never leave me.' Sobs juddered through her. 'She promised. I thought she'd gone once when I was little. I ran around the house looking for her.' The pain in her voice went straight to Cassie's heart. 'And now I feel like I'm doing that all the time, just looking for her with this kind of... desperation. And I know I'll never find her and it's... And there's all this anger. I'm angry with her for leaving me, and I feel guilty about that because I saw how sick she was. But she promised and mums are meant to keep their promises.'

Every word touched Cassie deeply. 'She wanted to stay with you, Grace. She wanted that more than anything in the world. She loved you so, so much.'

'But she promised. She promised she'd never go away. I don't know what to do without her. It hurts too much. I want my mum. I just want my mum.'

Cassie wrapped her arm around Grace and pulled her close, her heart splitting in two for her. Her own tears dropped into Grace's hair and melted into the soft dark waves this precious girl had inherited from her. 'I'm so sorry. I'm so sorry that this happened to both of you.' Grace stayed tucked into Cassie's side until her breath steadied, then she gently pulled away.

Cassie dug in her bag for a packet of tissues, handed one to Grace, then wiped her own eyes. 'She was a wonderful mum, wasn't she?' Static buzzed in her head. She was so desperate to get this right. 'I'm glad you asked me to watch the videos. The bond between you two was... well, it was a once-in-a-lifetime thing.'

Grace raised her head, her eyes fixed straight ahead.

Cassie kept her gaze forward too. 'I'm sorry for everything

you've been through, Grace. We made mistakes... I made mistakes, and I am truly sorry.'

Grace's fingers tugged at another strand of grass. After a moment she said, 'Mum said you weren't well, back then, I mean.'

Cassie's throat constricted. 'I wasn't. I wasn't myself for a long time. To be honest, even when I think back to that time, it's kind of fuzzy.' She watched the water froth behind a boat further up the river, trying to keep her breathing level. 'It was never about not wanting you, Grace. I promise. I honestly thought you'd be better off with your dad and Meg. Truly.' She stole a glance at Grace. She was watching a seagull swooping above them. Her pupils were tiny black circles in brilliant pools of blue. 'I remember I went to their flat one time and when I arrived, your mum was in the garden with you in her arms. She was looking at you with such adoration.' The memory replayed in Cassie's mind and she had to work hard to keep more tears at bay. 'She was pointing out the flowers, even though you were so tiny, you wouldn't have understood a word she was saying. Seeing the way she was with you, the love in her eyes, the way she held you as if you were the most precious thing in the whole universe, that's when I knew she was your mum, not me.'

She couldn't stop the tears from falling then, and when she looked at Grace, tears were streaming down her face too. 'I'm sorry, Grace, I didn't want to upset you even more. That's the last thing I want. I wanted you to know I get that Meg was your mother in every way except biology, and even though I'm really hoping, when you're ready, that you and I can have some kind of relationship, I'll never try to take her place. I know you only had one mum, but I would love it if I could be your friend.'

Grace wiped her arm across her face and Cassie was surprised to see she was smiling. 'Mum told me about that time in the garden,' she said. 'In the video, she said it was spring and she was showing me the daffodils.'

Cassie nodded. 'That's right.'

'And in the videos' – Grace turned to Cassie, her beautiful eyes bright – 'she told me to tell you she was sorry.' She hiccupped out a sob, then carried on. 'And she asked me to thank you for allowing her to be my mum.' They were both crying hard now. 'So, thank you, from both of us. I'm glad I had fourteen years with the best mum in the world. And now she's gone, I think maybe I wouldn't mind you being my friend.'

Her heart full of love and admiration for this brave, wonderful girl, Cassie held out her arms and, after a moment's hesitation, Grace melted into them.

51

PRESENT DAY

Cassie

'What if nobody comes?' said Cassie, staring around the function room. The DJ they'd hired was setting up behind the decks and Alf was playing hopscotch on the black and white squares of the dance floor. A banner with *Happy 40th* in huge pink letters was stuck onto the wall behind two enormous speakers.

Luke opened his mouth to speak but was interrupted by the door opening and Becca marching in, followed by a tall man with grey-brown hair. 'Happy birthday,' she yelled and ran over to Cassie, enveloping her in a Jo Malone-scented hug. 'This is Graham.' She flapped her hand for the man to come over, making her impressive chest wobble above the tight belt of her bright orange wrap dress. After introductions, they all turned to see Finnegan arrive, along with his wife and several other teachers. Soon the place was thrumming with conversation over the beat of the music. A few of the baby group who Cassie and Luke had met when Alf was born had also brought their seven-year-olds along and the kids danced with the kind of abandon only children possessed, while intermittently stopping to skid across the floor on their knees, before their parents noticed and stopped them.

Luke arrived at Cassie's side with a glass of champagne. He followed her gaze to the door. 'You nervous?'

'Yeah,' she said. 'I hope this isn't too much for her.'

'You gave her the option,' said Luke. 'She said she wanted to come.'

Grace and Simon had been to their house on the day of Cassie's actual birthday the week before. Both Grace and Alf had been reticent at first, quietly sipping smoothies and watching the adults' polite conversation. Cassie eventually suggested Alf show Grace his trampoline. She opened the patio doors and the two of them went into the garden. Cassie had tried hard not to watch, afraid they would continue to be stiff and stilted with each other. She needn't have worried. Within minutes, the sounds of laughter rang out and when she watched through the glass, she saw they were taking it in turns to do seat drops, their matching dark curls bouncing around their heads.

The venue was almost full when Simon and Grace arrived. Cassie rushed over to greet them, thrilled when Grace gave her a quick hug hello. She pulled them over to meet Becca and soon Simon and Graham were deep in conversation about a play they'd both recently seen in the West End. Becca started to ask Grace questions about school, but was interrupted by Alf, who appeared by Grace's side with a little girl in a sequined dress. 'Hi, Grace,' he said, out of breath from his exertions on the dance floor. He turned to the little girl. 'See, she's here.'

'Hello, Alf,' said Grace.

'Lilly didn't believe I had a big sister,' said Alf.

'I've never seen you before,' said Lilly, her head on one side, eyes narrowed.

Cassie froze, watching for Grace's response.

'That's because I was his secret sister, and now I'm not,' said Grace, simply.

'Oh,' said Lilly. She tugged at one of her blonde ringlets. 'I'm going to ask my mummy if I can have a secret sister.'

Alf reached for Grace's hand and Cassie had to swallow hard when Grace took it. 'Not everybody gets one,' he said, proprietorially.

'Only the very best children,' said Grace in a hushed voice, winking at Alf, who grinned as widely as Cassie had ever seen.

'Come on,' said Alf, leading Grace by the hand to the dance floor.

Cassie sipped her champagne, hardly able to believe what she was watching. Luke came to one side of her and Becca appeared at the other as Taylor Swift's 'Shake it Off' came on and all the young children crowded around Grace, following every move she made as she danced and laughed along with her new groupies.

'She's a superstar,' said Becca. 'What a girl.'

'Look at the pride on Alf's face,' said Luke, grinning as Alf tried to follow Grace's steps.

Simon joined them. 'I haven't seen her laugh like that in months,' he said, watching as Grace shimmied her shoulders and the children surrounding her did the same. His eyes shone with love and pride.

'You've done a great job,' said Cassie.

'Thank you,' said Simon. 'And thank you so much for bringing her smile back.' He hesitated, then addressed all three of them. 'I'm so grateful to all of you for allowing us into your lives like this. I know I don't deserve—'

'Let's not look backwards,' said Cassie. She nodded towards the dance floor, her heart lifting as Grace took Alf's hand and swirled him around as he giggled. 'Let's concentrate on the future, because from where I'm standing, it's looking pretty bright.'

52

SIX MONTHS AGO

Meg

Meg leaned forwards and pressed the red record button. She smiled at the screen, seeing herself and her gorgeous daughter reflected back at her. Grace was heavy on her knee, pressing her bony thighs hard against the seat, but she was so pleased Grace had agreed to sit on her lap to film the last video. She squeezed her daughter around the middle, noting how her waist was narrowing now she was growing into a young woman. 'Stop squirming.'

'I'm not squirming. I'm trying to get comfortable.'

'Anybody would think you didn't like sitting on Mummy's knee.' Meg used the voice she used to use when Grace was tiny, and they both laughed. 'You used to follow me everywhere,' she said. 'You'd toddle after me with your arms like this.' She lifted her arms and stuck out her bottom lip.

'Yeah, well, I was, like, two or something,' said Grace. Her eyes were red-rimmed, but she'd eventually left her room and agreed to do this last film with Meg. It had been an exhausting evening, but Meg was satisfied she'd recorded everything she needed to say.

'You'll always be my baby girl,' said Meg. 'Always.'

The smile fell from Grace's face, and she turned and buried her head in her mother's shoulder.

'Hey, hey, come on.' Meg lifted Grace's dark hair and kissed her cheek. 'Let me film this last bit of wisdom with you here, so I can be sure you're listening to what I'm saying. I want to be able to see your lovely face.' She put a hand under Grace's chin. 'Will you let me?'

Grace lifted her head and nodded. She turned to the screen, her head next to Meg's.

'What I wanted to say was, you're at a pivotal time in your life, my lovely girl. Up until now, me and your dad have been the main people in your life. Obviously, there's the extended family and your friends, but until now we've been your home. But things don't stay the same, and neither should they. Even if all this wasn't going on with me, your life will soon grow beyond these four walls. Teenage friendships are intense, and there will be boyfriends, or girlfriends.'

She grinned at Grace, who rolled her eyes. Meg became serious again. 'I regret not telling you about Cassie. I see now that it's possible you could have had a relationship with her before now, and that might have made what's happening to me more bearable.'

Grace shook her head and pouted.

Meg smiled at her stubborn girl. 'There is so much love waiting for you out there, Grace; don't resist it. Being your mum has been the greatest joy and privilege of my life. And you'll always have your dad and the rest of the family. But the world is big and wonderful, and you are at the start of a magical adventure in it. Embrace the love that is waiting for you. Open your heart, my darling girl, and let the love in.'

'I just want you,' said Grace, her eyes brimming with tears. 'I want you to stay.'

'I will,' said Meg. 'In here.' She put her hand on Grace's chest. 'I'll be one of the many people who will always live inside your heart. But I want to be in good company, so promise me you won't close down. Let people who are worthy in. Promise me.'

Grace turned to her mother. 'I promise.'

'Thank you. I love you Grace, and I always will.'

'I love you too.'

Meg pressed the button to end the recording and turned to hold her precious child.

ACKNOWLEDGEMENTS

My first thanks go to my brilliant editor, Isobel Akenhead, for her enthusiasm, insight and much-appreciated collaborative approach. This is my first book with the powerhouse that is Boldwood Books and I already feel like part of something special. Their commitment to supporting their authors and building a sustainable career for us is refreshing and incredibly welcome. Publishing a book is a team effort, and my thanks go to the whole Boldwood gang.

I owe a huge debt of gratitude to my fantastic agent, Laura Williams, who asked me what I wanted to achieve in this rollercoaster industry and has done her utmost to help me attain it. Having an agent who always has your back is a beautiful thing and I don't take that for granted.

To my lovely early readers, Emma Warburton, Sam Salisbury, Hannah Maynard-Slade and Ruth Rutter, thank you for your time and your honesty. I don't know what I'd do without you.

My thanks also go to the fabulous online reading community, especially the following Facebook book groups, whose support has been invaluable to me and instrumental in helping new readers find my books: The Bookload, Fiction Addicts Book Club and The Fiction Café Book Club. If you are looking for a place to share your love of books, I recommend these groups wholeheartedly.

The writing community is the most positive and supportive

bunch of people you could hope to find. Both online and IRL, I've found my tribe, my strength and inspiration in the friends I have made since I began my writing life. There are too many to name individually, and I would hate to leave anyone out, but if I've met you through writing, I'm talking about you.

Finally, my thanks go to my family. I am incredibly fortunate to live with people who make me laugh every day, ensure my feet are always firmly on the ground, and fill my life with love... and endless new material for family dramas.

If you enjoyed *The Daughter She Gave Away*, I would be very grateful if you could leave a brief review wherever you buy your books. Even a few words can make an author's day, and help new readers discover our books. Thank you!

ABOUT THE AUTHOR

Lisa Timoney is the author of emotional family dramas filled with devastating secrets and explosive revelations. Originally from Yorkshire, Lisa started her career teaching English and Drama. She now lives in London with her husband and two teenage daughters.

Sign up to Lisa Timoney's mailing list for news, competitions and updates on future books.

Visit Lisa's website: www.lisatimoneywrites.com

Follow Lisa on social media here:

- X x.com/LTimoneyWrites
- instagram.com/lisatimoneywrites
- facebook.com/LisaTimoneyAuthor
- BB bookbub.com/authors/lisa-timoney
- tiktok.com/@lisatimoneywrites

BECOME A MEMBER OF
THE SHELF CARE CLUB

The home of Boldwood's book club reads.

Find uplifting reads, sunny escapes, cosy romances, family dramas and more!

Sign up to the newsletter
https://bit.ly/theshelfcareclub

Boldwood

Boldwood Books is an award-winning fiction publishing company seeking out the best stories from around the world.

Find out more at www.boldwoodbooks.com

Join our reader community for brilliant books, competitions and offers!

Follow us

@BoldwoodBooks

@TheBoldBookClub

Sign up to our weekly deals newsletter

https://bit.ly/BoldwoodBNewsletter

Printed in Dunstable, United Kingdom